BATTLESONG

BATTLESONG

LIAN TANNER

Feiwel and Friends
New York

A FEIWEL AND FRIENDS BOOK
An imprint of Macmillan Publishing Group, LLC
175 Fifth Avenue, New York, NY 10010

Our books may be purchased in bulk for promotional, educational,
or business use. Please contact your local bookseller or the Macmillan Corporate
and Premium Sales Department at (800) 221-7945 ext. 5442 or by e-mail at
MacmillanSpecialMarkets@macmillan.com.

Originally published as *Fetcher's Song* in 2016 in Australia by Allen & Unwin.

First published in the United States by Feiwel and Friends.

Library of Congress Cataloging-in-Publication Data is available.

ISBN 978-1-250-05218-6 (hardcover) / ISBN 978-1-250-12888-1 (ebook)

Feiwel and Friends logo designed by Filomena Tuosto

First US edition—2017

1 3 5 7 9 10 8 6 4 2

mackids.com

For my beloved nieces,
Annie, Sal, Meg and Gwyn

PROLOGUE

It was the last time they would ever meet, though neither Ariel Fetch nor Professor Serran Coe knew it. Within a week, one of them would be a fugitive, hunted across the country by the Anti-Machinists. The other would be dead.

But for tonight at least, they were safe. They huddled, deep in the bowels of the ruined university, and finalized their plans. Between them burned a single candle.

"Have you heard from Lin Lin and Admiral Cray?" whispered Ariel Fetch.

"No," replied Serran Coe. He was thinner than when they had last met, and his stiff white collar was frayed at the edges. "But I did not expect to. They will be deep beneath the sea by now, beyond the reach of the Anti-Machinists."

"Such a hard life they have chosen."

"We have all chosen hardship in one form or another."

"Not me." Ariel Fetch shook her head so that the beads in her hair clacked together. "All I have to do is sing and tell stories."

They both knew it was far more than that. If anything, she and her family had chosen the most dangerous path of all.

"Have you worked out what to do with the code?" asked Serran Coe.

"Yes. Do you want to—"

The professor raised his hands, as if to ward off danger. "No! The fewer people who know about it the better. Just tell me—is it subtle enough? Will it remain hidden until it is needed? Is it strong enough?"

"It is as subtle and strong as I can make it," said Ariel Fetch.

A gust of wind whistled through the broken building and the candle guttered in its jar. There was no more electricity—the Anti-Machinists had destroyed the power stations weeks ago, in this and many other countries. There were no more automobiles or omnibuses, no telephones or wireless stations. The world was being dragged into chaos, and no one seemed able to stop it.

"What will you do now?" asked Ariel Fetch.

"I had thought of going home to the mountains before the city becomes unliveable." Serran Coe sighed. "Apparently, the Anti-Machinists are forcing people into the countryside, people who have never farmed in their lives. Anyone who refuses to go is killed. It will not be long before the great cities of the world are nothing but ghost towns."

A flicker of uncertainty crossed Ariel Fetch's face. "It *is* worth it, isn't it—what we are doing? I know that the science must be saved, and everything else that you and Lin Lin have set out to preserve. But what my family and I are doing—"

Again Serran Coe held up a hand. "There is history—true history, not the curdled sort the Anti-Machinists want us to teach—and there is science and medicine and the making of machines. But there is another sort of knowledge too, just as valuable. Lin Lin and I are trying to save the mind of the world. You will save its heart."

On a sudden impulse, he reached into his pocket and drew out a watch in a silver case. "Please," he said, "take this. I made it myself; perhaps it will be useful to you in some small way. . . ."

As he handed it over, another gust of wind blew the candle out. The conspirators made no move to relight it. Instead, they sat in the darkness and talked quietly, for the last time, about family and friends. Neither of them said anything more about the greater darkness that was coming.

They had done what they could. Now it was up to those unknown people of the future.

CHAPTER I

THREE HUNDRED YEARS LATER

GWIN STOOD IN THE MUDDY FIELD OUTSIDE THE VILLAGE OF Swettle, counting the beats. *One, two, three—*

"Hup!" she cried, which was the cue for her twin brother, Nat, to vault onto the shoulders of their ox, Spindle. And, "Hup hup!" which sent Spindle lumbering in a circle with Nat on his back.

Like all the villages in this part of West Norn, Swettle was dank and miserable. Spring was struggling to gain a foothold, and mud covered everything, including Gwin's bare feet. She curled her toes in the slush and glanced at Papa, who stood to one side with his fiddle tucked under his chin and his eyes half-closed as he played "The Chase of Madden."

It was supposed to be a dance tune, and there was a time when the villagers would've been stamping their feet and hallooing at the tops of their voices, no matter how tired and hungry they were. Nat would've worn a grin a mile wide, and Papa would've laughed as he sawed at his fiddle.

And Mama?

Gwin swallowed the dreadful lump in her throat. Mama would've rattled out the beat on her tambour and danced as if the world was as bright and beautiful as anyone could wish.

Even now, Papa didn't play badly; he was too much of a Fetcher for that. But his heart wasn't in it, and no one in the audience so much as tapped their feet.

They gaped, though. Everyone gaped when they saw Nat performing. They knew he was blind, knew that what he did would be hard even for someone who could see. But there he was, leaping off Spindle's sturdy shoulders and back on again, as quick and fierce as a wildcat, while the fiddle music wove around him.

The old ox lumbered round to the front of the circle again, and Gwin went up on her toes. *If I do this next bit perfectly*, she thought, *everything will be all right. Papa will be happy again. Nat will stop being so angry. Nothing bad will happen to either of them if I do this perfectly.*

On exactly the right beat, she dashed forward with her beaded plaits flying. "Hiii!" she cried.

Despite his anger, Nat never got his timing wrong. He reached out in the direction of his sister's voice, and she grabbed his hand and bounced off the ground onto Spindle's broad back.

Her leap *wasn't* perfect, of course. She and Nat might be twins; they might have the same strong limbs and the same red hair; they might both wear ragged knee pants and rabbit-fur bands on their upper arms, but Gwin had none of her brother's natural brilliance. When she jumped, one of her legs always seemed to lag a little way behind. When she somersaulted, she felt more like a bundle of sticks than like a wildcat.

All the same, she sat behind Nat for a count of seven, with a determined smile on her face. Then she leaned forward. "Eight, nine, ten," she whispered, and as Nat raised his hands in the air, she jumped from a sitting position to standing, gripped his hands and leapt onto his shoulders.

The audience gasped, and a group of ragged children in the front row opened their mouths and cried, "Oooooh!"

Gwin smiled again, a wide Fetcher smile that covered up everything she was feeling. She smiled at the buds that were just starting to open on an apple tree. She smiled at Nat's dog, Wretched, sitting in the audience with his head on a little boy's lap and his tail thumping gently. She smiled at the men and women whose children had died of hunger or been stolen by the Devouts and who couldn't take their eyes off Nat and Gwin.

And all the time she was smiling, she watched for signs of danger.

She saw nothing out of the ordinary. Swettle was just like every other village they visited. Dismal, hungry, and muddy.

With a whoop, Gwin dropped onto Spindle's back. And as the old ox skidded to a halt, she and Nat jumped off, landing with their knees bent and their arms wide.

If things were working the way they were supposed to, Nat would've reached for his clarinetto then, and Papa would've pushed the wooden box into the circle, then raised his bow, ready to play.

But hardly anything worked the way it was supposed to these days. Gwin handed the clarinetto to her scowling brother, then grabbed the box and dragged it forward.

"Papa," she whispered. "It's the Hope song."

Her father started, as if he'd been miles away, and touched bow to fiddle.

When Gwin was small, Mama used to say, "Anyone can sing when they are happy, my darling, and the sun is shining. But to sing in the middle of a storm, when the winds are howling and it feels like the sun will never shine again, that's different. That's our job, as Fetchers. We help keep the heart of the world beating."

Gwin still found it hard to think about Mama without weeping, especially when she wove the beads into her plaits in the exact same pattern Mama had always used or stepped onto the box and began to sing, as she did now.

"How tall the tree,
The first to fall . . ."

Her voice wasn't anywhere near as beautiful as Mama's, just as her leaps weren't as astonishing as Nat's. But she didn't even think of stopping. For the last couple of months she had been the only one holding the little family of Fetchers together. If she stopped, everything she knew would come to an end.

"How wise to flee
The worst of all . . ."

The rat appeared halfway through the first verse. Gwin

had no idea where it had come from, but it crouched in the shelter of Spindle's cart, peering up at her.

She slipped her hand into her pocket, took out a stone and threw it.

No one in the audience so much as blinked. There were rats everywhere in West Norn, spoiling what little grain the villagers managed to hide from the Devouts, gnawing holes in the thatch so the rain came in, burrowing into cellars and taking bites out of the last few stored apples. Throwing stones at rats in the middle of a conversation (or a song) was as ordinary as scratching a fleabite.

This rat, however, ducked so that the stone flew over its head. Then, instead of running away as any normal rat would have done, it sat up on its haunches, crossed its front paws like an old man and made a *tsk–tsk–tsk* sound.

It was so unexpected and so ridiculous that for the first time in weeks Gwin almost smiled. A proper smile. A *real* one, like a tiny spot of warmth in her overburdened heart.

"But hear the song," she sang,
"The singer gives.
The trunk is gone,
The root still lives."

All the way through that first verse, the rat seemed to listen attentively. *Except it's not really listening*, thought Gwin. *Someone's trained it, that's all. But who'd train a rat? And why?*

And then, because she was being as cautious as possible, to keep what was left of her family safe, she thought, *Could it be dangerous? It doesn't look dangerous, but it's not ordinary either, not with those silver eyes. How can a rat have silver eyes?*

She was so busy puzzling over it that she didn't see the *real* danger signs until it was almost too late.

Gwin and her family had always lived on a perilous edge, fetching trouble just as surely as they fetched songs and stories out of the distant past. But until two months ago, Gwin had believed that nothing could really touch them.

Now she knew better; Papa or Nat could be snatched away from her in an instant, just like Mama. And so, wherever she was, she kept her eyes peeled for any sign of approaching disaster—

Like the woman leaning against the apple tree, her fair hair pulled tight against her head, her face worn almost to the bone by grief and hard work. She was one of those who had been watching Gwin and Nat so hungrily, but she wasn't watching them now. She was staring at her neighbor, who kept glancing over his shoulder toward the village, as if he was expecting someone.

The woman took a couple of steps toward him so she could see the Northern Road. Her body stiffened. She turned back, her face a picture of dismay, and mouthed at Gwin, *The Masters! Go! Run!*

But Gwin couldn't move. "Masters" was what the villagers called the Devouts, who were the enemies of every Fetcher ever born. Last time Gwin's family had run from them, Mama had fallen. . . .

Gwin tried to catch her breath and couldn't.

Mama had fallen and hit her head. Gwin and Papa had managed to drag her up onto the oxcart in time to escape, but Mama never woke up from that fall. A week later, she passed away.

And now the same thing was happening again! Only this time it might be Papa who fell. Or Nat. Or the Devouts might catch them and hang them—

Gwin wrenched her thoughts out of that awful spiral and did a quick dance step on the box—*thump thumpety thump-thump-thump.*

It was a Fetcher signal, almost as familiar as the hills that surrounded Swettle. As the music cut off, the villagers struggled to their feet, dragging their children up with them and scattering in all directions.

The rat ran too, though Gwin didn't see where it went. She grabbed the box with one hand and Nat's arm with the other and dashed toward the oxcart, with Papa only a step behind them. Spindle, who knew the signal as well as any of them, was already backing between the shafts.

While Nat scrambled into the cart and Gwin's fingers flew over the straps and buckles of Spindle's harness, Papa jumped into the driver's seat and grabbed the whip. Wretched was tearing toward them, his ears flat, his tail tucked between his legs. Behind him, the woman who had warned them was struggling to get away from her neighbor, who held her by both wrists.

Wretched flung himself up onto the cart beside Nat, and Gwin jumped up next to Papa. Spindle threw his massive shoulders against the harness.

The woman broke free. She looked around frantically, then picked up her skirts and bolted for the cart. Behind her, three men in dark brown robes came out from between the huts, leading a mule.

The neighbor shouted and pointed to the cart and the running woman. Two of the robed men broke into a sprint.

If Mama had been there, either she or Papa would have hauled the woman up onto the cart beside them. If there was one thing Gwin's parents had always loved almost as much as they loved music and laughter, it was snatching someone from the clutches of the Devouts.

But Mama was gone forever, and Papa was not himself. So it was Gwin who grabbed the woman's outstretched hand and hauled her up onto the seat in a breathless, frantic bundle.

Papa cracked the whip. Spindle broke into a rocking gallop. And with a strange woman on board and the Devouts hot on their tail, the Fetchers ran for their lives.

CHAPTER 2

HILDE

Somewhere along the Northern Road, twelve-year-old Petrel crouched on the lee side of a barn. The stone wall at her back was crumbling and worn, but it kept her out of the wind and away from prying eyes while she waited for her friend Fin.

Every now and again, she squinted around the corner of the barn in the direction of the village.

"Wish he'd get a move on," she muttered to herself. "I don't like these villages one bit. What wouldn't I give to see a nice bit of ice instead! Proper ice, so deep and thick that even the *Oyster* couldn't bully its way through."

She fell silent, thinking of the life she'd left behind at the far end of the world. Parts of it had been beautiful, but it had been cold and miserable much of the time, and desperately lonely too, for someone who the rest of the *Oyster*'s crew had known only as Nothing Girl.

Petrel hadn't been Nothing Girl for months now; she had

true friends and was a valued member of the ancient icebreaker's crew. But the loneliness was a part of her life that she'd never forget, just as she'd never forget the ice.

She heard the scuff of footsteps, and Fin rounded the corner, dressed in the light brown robes of an Initiate of the Devouts.

Petrel leapt to her feet. "Did they talk to you? What'd they say?"

"Wait till I get this horrible . . ." Fin's voice grew muffled as he dragged the Initiate robe over his head.

There was a time when he'd worn a similar robe with pride, when he'd been a real Initiate, a coldhearted boy who loathed machines and the people who used them. But that was before he met Petrel and discovered that everything the Devouts had ever taught him was a lie.

Now he dropped the robe with a shudder and stood in his ship clothes of sealskin coat, trousers and boots. "Where are Sharkey and Rain?"

"Gone looking for something to eat," said Petrel. "Sharkey reckons he's had enough ship's biscuits to last him a lifetime, and Rain agreed. They'll meet us up the lane a bit. What'd the villagers say?"

Fin ran his fingers through his pale hair. "Nothing much. They were angrier than I remember."

"Have they seen Brother Poosk? Was he here?"

"Yes. Two days ago."

Petrel still found it hard to believe that the Devouts had sent Brother Poosk to do their dirty work. She had only ever seen the man once, in circumstances so confusing that she had no real memory of him. Rain, who was his niece, was afraid of him. So was Sharkey, though he pretended he wasn't. They had all thought that the other Devouts would've hanged Poosk by now, or imprisoned him at the very least, for tricking and humiliating them.

But just ten days ago, Missus Slink, a mechanical rat of considerable age and wisdom, had returned to the *Oyster* with the news that Brother Poosk had somehow talked his way out of the noose and persuaded the Devouts to send him north and then west, with two guards to help him.

His task? To find Fin's mam and bring her back to the Citadel for execution.

Petrel, Fin, Rain and Sharkey had immediately set out after Brother Poosk and his men, leaving behind them a ship abustle with preparations for an attack on the Citadel.

But the farther they'd come, the quieter Fin had grown. And so, as they set off along the lane to meet up with Rain and Sharkey, Petrel said, "What's the matter, Fin?"

"Nothing."

Petrel snorted. "Course it's not nothing! You might as well tell me."

Fin looked away. "I have been . . . wondering."

"Wondering what?"

"Nothing important."

"Sometimes," said Petrel, "you're as hard to get answers out of as an albatross. Wondering *what*?"

"About Mama. What if—" Fin stopped. Ahead of them, a small bird with a crimson chest dived into the hedge.

"Keep going or I'll pinch you."

The boy half smiled, then grew serious again. "I was only three when she gave me away, too young to remember her name or where she came from. What if she does not want me?"

"Not want you?" cried Petrel. "Of course she'll want you. She's your mam!"

"But she gave me to the Devouts."

"That was to save your life, and you know it. All those villages we've been through, with all those little graves, and the bratlings that *do* survive are bandy-legged from hunger— that's what your mam was thinking of when she gave you away. Don't you dare doubt her!"

That seemed to cheer Fin up, though Petrel suspected it wouldn't last. And she could hardly blame him. Because if they kept to their current pace, they'd soon catch up with Brother Poosk and his men.

And there was an important question to which Petrel hadn't yet found an answer.

What the blizzards do we do then?

SPINDLE TORE ALONG THE MUDDY ROAD WITH THE CART swaying and rattling so violently behind him that Gwin had to cling to her seat to keep from being thrown off. Beside her the village woman was trembling with shock, and Gwin wasn't much better.

They'll be after us, she thought. *We won't be safe till we're off the road.*

She scanned the hedgerows, trying to work out how many

bends they'd passed and how far behind them the Devouts might be. And all the while her memory replayed Mama's terrible fall, over and over.

Beside her, Papa's face was white and set, and although he said nothing, Gwin knew that he was thinking about Mama too and reliving the events of two months ago.

We have to get off the road!

Except they couldn't, not with a stranger in the cart. If Papa had been in his right mind he would have set the village woman down already, to hide in the hedgerow until the Devouts were gone.

Now Gwin must do it, before it was too late.

"Lady—" she began.

"Hilde. My name's Hilde." The woman raised her voice over the rattling of the cart, and words poured out of her. "That was Piddock who tried to hold me. Piddock, of all people! I cared for his wife when she was dying, and he said at the time he'd be grateful for ever after. Well 'ever after' didn't last long, did it? He would've handed me over to the Masters just because I warned you. Nasty sod he is."

Gwin glanced over her shoulder at Nat, who would've helped her once. But not anymore.

She turned back to the woman. "Hilde, you'll have to—"

"You want to be rid of me, I suppose, and I don't blame you. But I daren't go home. Piddock'll turn me in, I know he will. If he doesn't do it today, he'll do it tomorrow or next week, and then the Masters'll hang me. Can't I go with you, just for a little while?"

"No!" said Gwin, horrified at the thought. No one traveled with Fetchers except other Fetchers.

But before she could say so, Spindle galloped around the next bend, and the road turned from mud to stone. The wheels rumbled over the hard surface like a warning.

Dismayed, Gwin realized she'd miscalculated. *This is the last bend. If we set her down now, she'll see where we go!*

There was no time to turn back, not with the Devouts on their heels. Gwin could think of only one way of averting disaster. She ripped the rabbit-fur band from her right arm and held it out to Hilde. "Tie that across your eyes. Quick! And don't take it off until I say so."

Hilde stared uncertainly at the strip of fur.

"Do you want to come with us or not?" demanded Gwin.

Hilde nodded and tied the band over her eyes. Mere seconds later, Papa cried, "Brooms!"

Without a word, Nat reached under his seat and brought out four bundles of heather, each fastened to a stout pole. He strapped them to the back of the cart, and they *rat-tat-tat*ed along the road, brushing away the marks of hoof and wheel.

Gwin watched the hedgerow. "Papa, there!"

Her father flicked the whip in the pattern that meant "stop." As the old ox wheezed to a halt, Gwin leapt from the cart, ran up the bank on the right-hand side of the road and began to unweave the branches of the graythorn hedge.

Hilde sat very still. "What's happening? Where are we going?"

No one answered her. Fetchers didn't share their secrets with anyone, and besides, they had to get off the road and out of sight before the Devouts came chasing around that last bend.

Papa clicked his tongue, and Spindle began to turn. The bank was steep, so Gwin got behind the cart and pushed, and Papa climbed down and put his shoulder next to hers. The cart rolled up the bank and through the gap in the hedgerow, with Hilde crouched on the narrow seat like a flustered bird.

While Gwin wove the branches back together, and Papa swept away the last of the wheel marks, Nat felt his way into the driver's seat and flicked the whip over Spindle's head.

"Wait for us at the quarry," said Papa.

Nat drove off. Gwin checked to make sure that road and bank were completely clear of giveaway marks, then she and Papa scrambled through the hedge, fastened the last few branches back into place and raced after the cart, which had stopped in a disused quarry a few hundred yards off the road.

And there they sat in breathless silence, hoping they had covered their tracks as well as they thought they had.

CHAPTER 3

ARIEL'S WAY

GWIN COULDN'T HEAR A THING, WHICH MADE THE WAITING extra hard. In her imagination, the Devouts spotted something she'd missed—a clumsily woven branch, half a footprint. She pictured them crashing through the graythorn hedge and running toward the quarry. Her fingernails dug into the palms of her hands—

"They're gone," muttered Nat.

Papa heaved a sigh of relief, and the energy that had carried him away from Swettle seemed to seep out of him.

With an effort, Gwin loosened her fists. She made sure that Hilde's blindfold was secure and that they hadn't dropped anything in the quarry. Then, very slowly, they set off again.

But this time they took Ariel's Way.

Three hundred years ago, the very first Fetcher established a network of secret pathways across West Norn. These narrow tracks—wide enough for an oxcart, with not an inch to spare— teetered along cliff faces and over rocky moors; they crawled under waterfalls, into limestone caves and out the other end; they crossed bogs that could have swallowed a hundred pursuers, where the only solid path was marked with a few specks of white clay.

Gwin and her family knew every one of those tracks. They knew the difference between the slightly dangerous spots and the hair-raising ones; they knew where a sure-footed ox like Spindle could trot and where he must inch along while the Fetchers crept behind him, holding their breath for fear of tumbling to their deaths.

When Gwin was very small, there had been other Fetcher families traveling the secret ways, with their carts and oxen and beaded hair. Occasionally they'd all meet up for a night of songs and stories, far from villages and Devouts. But that hadn't happened for a long time. West Norn was a dangerous place for Fetchers, and not many of them reached middle age.

By the time night fell, however, they were far enough from Swettle to feel more or less safe. "Whoa, Spindle," said Gwin.

The old ox snorted and stopped. Wretched trotted over to the nearest tree and cocked his leg.

"Where are we?" asked Hilde.

Once it would have been Nat who answered her. He would've said something like, "No idea. Unless that water I can hear in the distance is Grump Gurgle. And the way the wind is whistling—sounds like we're near those old iron trees on the moor. In which case we're ten and a half miles east of Upper Meech."

Then Papa would have thrown back his head and guffawed, and Mama would've . . .

"We're east of Upper Meech," Gwin said quietly.

"But that's the Forbidden Lands," whispered Hilde. She turned her face from side to side, as if trying to see through the blindfold. "You've brought us to the *haunted* lands."

Because, of course, that was the other place Ariel's Way took them—through the old abandoned cities, where huge rusty structures loomed out of the ground like giant trees and where ancient buildings rotted in silence.

If you were going to believe in haunts, this was the place to find them. And because no one else ever dared go there, it was also the place to find wild mangels, thistles, cankerwort roots, rabbits and squabs. If things were working the way they were supposed to, the Fetchers would have stopped there for several days, replenishing their supplies.

But for all Gwin's efforts, nothing was the way it was supposed to be. What's more, they had a blindfolded stranger with them, and the sooner they got rid of her, the better. And so at daybreak they set off again.

Their journey was slow. Hilde sat on the front seat, occasionally licking her dry lips or fumbling for the water pot. Nat walked on one side of Spindle with his face closed against the world and everyone in it, and Gwin cast back and forth on the other, pulling up wild mangels and tossing them into the cart. Wretched disappeared for a bit and came back with a dead rabbit.

Papa sagged along behind them, looking as if his thoughts

were miles away. Midafternoon, he climbed into the back of the cart, wrapped himself in a couple of old sacks and fell asleep next to the rabbit. It wasn't long before Nat followed him. Neither of them had said anything to Gwin about her miscalculation or commented on the fact that she had brought a stranger onto Ariel's Way.

Gwin sighed.

Hilde turned toward the sound and said, "You're still there, Fetcher girl?"

"Yes."

"You're not afraid of haunts?"

"No."

"Don't suppose you can be, traveling all over the way you do. I've heard there are haunts everywhere in West Norn, not just here. Too many dead, that's the trouble."

Gwin scratched Spindle's neck with the handle of the whip. She wanted Mama back so badly that she could hardly breathe. She wanted Nat and Papa back too, instead of spinning away from her into their own little worlds of anger and sadness. She wanted—

"You still there?" called Hilde.

"Yes," said Gwin. And she smiled a wide Fetcher smile, even though the woman couldn't see her.

Evening found them in the bottom of a shallow ravine, with Wretched leading the way, and just enough of a moon for Gwin to see where they were going.

Sometimes, on nights like this, she felt as if she could walk right back into the distant past. She'd turn a corner, and there would be Ariel striding toward her, tall and beautiful. She'd take Gwin's hand, and something in her touch would transform Gwin, would make her strong enough and clever enough to hold what was left of her family together—

"When can I take this off?" asked Hilde, rubbing at the rabbit fur.

"What? Oh, soon," said Gwin.

"How soon?"

Gwin was in no mood for talking. "We'll be back on the common road in another quarter mile or so. We'll leave you at the bottom of the lane that goes to Lumming."

"Lumming?" Hilde looked startled. "That's no good. I don't know anyone in Lumming."

"Well, you have to go *somewhere*. You said you just wanted to come with us for a little way—"

"Not that little! I thought you might be heading for the coast; I've got cousins there. But I've got no one in Lumming, and I can't just walk into a village full of strangers and expect them to take me in. Can't I stay with you? I could make myself useful if I had this blindfold off. I can cook, and I know the best cure for eye blight, and how to get rid of fleas and bed bugs—"

"No!" said Gwin. "And be quiet—here's where we join the road."

There was no hedgerow here, just a narrow path that didn't look like a path. As Spindle jolted down one final slope onto the Northern Road, Gwin walked behind the cart, sweeping away their tracks. Then she swung herself into the driver's seat next to Hilde, and Wretched leapt up beside her, smelly and comforting. Behind them, in the body of the cart, Papa and Nat snored in unison.

There were four miles of the Northern Road before the lane that led to Lumming, and another two miles after that before the secret ways started up again. Gwin said, "You can take that blindfold off now. And tell me if you hear anyone coming." Then she bent over the dog and whispered, "You too, Wretched. Keep your ears pricked."

Hilde untied the rabbit-fur band and blinked at the moonlight. "No offense to your brother, but I wouldn't like to be blind, not one bit. I like to see where I'm going, don't you?"

Gwin nibbled the worn leather of the whip handle. She was always nervous when they had to take one of the common roads. The Devouts had a nasty habit of turning up where they weren't expected.

Maybe I should have stayed on Ariel's Way till moonset—

But that would've meant they had no light at all, which was a danger in itself. And besides, it was too late to go back. They were already descending into one of the hollow ways, where centuries of feet, wheels and weather had beaten the road down so deep and narrow between its banks that it'd take ten minutes of maneuvring to turn the cart around, and in that time they'd be completely helpless.

Gwin flicked the whip over Spindle's head. "Gee-up, beastie," she whispered, and the ox broke into a slow, rocking trot.

The cart swayed from side to side, but neither Papa nor Nat woke. Fetchers caught sleep wherever they could, and a noisy, swaying cart was as good a bed as any. The high banks on either side slid past. The moon flickered from light to dark and back again.

They were only a couple of miles from the Lumming turnoff when Wretched suddenly pricked up his ears, stared back the way they'd come and whimpered.

Gwin's heart skipped a beat. She couldn't hear a thing over the rattling of the cart, but the dog's ears were even sharper than Nat's. "There's someone behind us," she said.

She forgot all about letting Hilde off. "Gee-up, Spindle!"

They were coming up out of the hollow way now, into clear moonlight, and ahead of them was the turnoff to the mountains. No one ever took that rough track if they could help it, not even Fetchers. No one lived in the mountains except a few wild men, but stories drifted out all the same—stories of cannibalism and cruelty and of strangers who got lost and were never seen again.

Hilde peered over her shoulder. "What if it's the Masters coming after us?"

Gwin gritted her teeth. "Gee-up, Spindle!"

But instead of going faster, the ox began to slow down.

"What's the matter?" hissed Gwin. "Gee-*up*—"

"There's something on his head," cried Hilde. "Look!"

It was the rat with the silver eyes. It had appeared out of nowhere, just like last time, and was perched between Spindle's ears.

Gwin grabbed one of the mangels from the bottom of the cart and threw it. "Go *away*, stupid rat."

The rat ducked, and the mangel flew past it. Wretched whimpered again and tried to crawl under Gwin's arm. Spindle slowed a little more.

"I think I can hear hoofbeats," said Hilde, her face ashen. "Behind us. It must be the Masters!"

"They didn't have horses."

"They had a mule—I'm sure I can hear them. Listen!"

An owl swooped across their path, and Gwin flinched so violently that she nearly fell off the cart. They were right on top of the mountain turnoff now, and instead of continuing straight ahead, Spindle began to veer left.

"No! What are you doing?" Gwin leapt down and ran alongside the old ox, dragging on his halter with all her strength. The rat skipped out of reach. Spindle kept going.

"Spindle, no!" cried Gwin, but it made no difference.

Papa sat up, rubbing his eyes. "What is it? Why are you shouting?"

Gwin, still clinging to Spindle's harness, gasped, "Hilde thinks someone's after us, Papa, and—and Spindle wants to take the mountain track!"

"Stop him!"

"He won't listen to me. I think it's the rat."

"What rat?"

Gwin pointed, but by then Spindle had set his hooves firmly on the mountain track and was beginning to pick up speed again.

Just in time, Gwin let go of the halter and scrambled back onto her seat. The rat resumed its position between Spindle's ears. Papa, Gwin and Hilde stared at each other in helpless disbelief.

Whether they liked it or not, they were on their way to the mountains.

CHAPTER 4

LISTEN AND OBEY!

As the new day dawned, Petrel, Fin, Sharkey and Rain found themselves on the outskirts of a village called Bale, a mile or so off the Northern Road. It was a grimy sort of morning, with clouds scudding low across the sky and not much sign of the sun.

The four bratlings tucked themselves behind some trees, along with their sacks of food and the waterproof lantern, and Fin reluctantly donned the Initiate's robe. But just as he was about to leave them, Rain whispered, "Wait! Look!"

They crowded around her, staring between the tree trunks. A big, rough-looking man in the dark brown robes of a Devout was tiptoeing past one of Bale's chicken coops.

"That's not Poosk, is it?" whispered Petrel.

Rain shook her head. "It could be one of his guards. But we should not have caught up with them yet. They were two days ahead of us."

"They must've backtracked," said Sharkey. "Why would they do that?"

Petrel nibbled her thumbnail. "D'you think your mam's in there somewhere, Fin? D'you think they're trying to trap her?"

"This is—" Fin stopped, as he often did when his memories of being an Initiate overwhelmed him. "This is what the Devouts do when they are taking boys for Initiates, or girls for servants. They put men outside the village, and when the children"—he swallowed—"when they try to hide, they are caught. It might be nothing to do with Mama."

Rain patted his hand. Sharkey said, "It's a trap of some sort, that's clear." He rubbed his forehead, just above his eye patch, and glanced at Petrel. "We could spoil it if we wanted."

"Then they'd know we're here," said Petrel. "Best wait, I reckon."

She wished she could quiz Fin more closely. *Could this be your old village? D'you remember the houses? D'you remember those mountains to the north?*

But she knew how much he hated such questions. So she kept quiet.

Once again, it was Rain who saw the bratlings first. She put her finger to her lips, then pointed.

A boy was creeping out from behind one of the sagging hovels. After him came a younger boy, then three little girls. They were all horribly thin, and they looked scared half to death, as if they knew they were heading into a trap and couldn't do a thing about it. Their heads twitched this way and that; their bodies were stiff with fright.

"Why don't they run?" whispered Petrel.

Fin's voice was flat. "They never run."

He was right. When the rough-looking Devout loomed up in front of the village bratlings, the two smallest ones began to cry, but they all stood where they were, shaking so violently that they looked as if they might topple over.

Rain was shaking too, and Sharkey's face was bleak and angry.

The Devout took a cord from inside his robes and looped it around the bratlings' necks so that they were joined together like an anchor chain. Then he shouted, "I have them, Brother!"

Almost immediately, two more Devouts came hurrying out of the village, leading a heavily laden mule. A man and three women trailed after them.

"That's Poosk," whispered Sharkey, pointing to the smaller of the two Devouts.

Petrel was surprised by how ordinary Brother Poosk looked. His robes were old, his expression was cheerful, and his thinning hair curled around his ears.

Rain was singing under her breath, the way she always did when she was frightened. *"Hobgoblins tiptoe through the night . . ."*

When the villagers saw the captive bratlings, they began to weep. Poosk spoke gently to them—or so it seemed. Petrel wished she could hear what he was saying.

"I'm gunna try and get closer," she whispered to her friends.

The ground around the village was mostly churned-up

mud, but there were a few ragged shrubs here and there, and Petrel slipped from one to another until she was close enough to hear the occasional word. The mule rolled a curious eye at her, but the Devouts didn't even glance in her direction.

Brother Poosk's eyes were darting from villager to villager. ". . . have my promise," he said. "As soon as you . . . *mumble mumble*. We do not want . . . *mumble mumble mumble*, now do we?"

The villagers said nothing. They were still weeping, but it seemed to Petrel that there was something else underneath it. Anger. A slow-burning hatred, so well hidden that she almost missed it.

Poosk didn't seem to notice. He pointed this way and that. He patted the cheek of the smaller boy and chuckled. He gestured and cajoled.

He didn't make nearly this much fuss in the other villages, thought Petrel, *or we would've heard about it. Maybe he's really close to finding Fin's mam. Which means we must be close too!*

She felt a burst of excitement, which lasted no more than a second or two. Because in its wake came the realization . . .

Once Fin gets his mam back, he won't need me anymore.

Petrel was surprised that she hadn't seen it before. Of course Fin wouldn't need her once he had his mam! The two of them'd be so happy to see each other that no one from the *Oyster* would matter. There'd be all those lost years to catch up on, and cousins to meet, and maybe even brothers or sisters—

Petrel chewed her thumbnail and tried to be happy about it. *I'll still have Sharkey and Rain. And Krill and Squid and Dolph and Missus Slink. And if Mister Smoke and the cap'n ever come back, I'll have them too.*

It wasn't enough. Fin was the first human friend she'd ever had. He was special, and the thought of losing him brought all the old loneliness rushing back, all those old Nothing Girl feelings that she'd thought were gone forever.

We shouldn't've come, she thought.

Except that was just plain wrong. Just as it was wrong to hope, even for the briefest of moments, that they wouldn't find Fin's mam after all and that he and Petrel would go on being best friends forever, with no one coming between them.

She scrubbed the tears from her eyes. "We're gunna find her," she whispered. "And I'm gunna be *glad* about it!"

A sudden change in tone dragged her attention back to the scene before her. Poosk's cheerful expression had vanished, and he had drawn himself up to his meager height. "Listen and obey!" he cried. "For the vile machines shall be struck down and trampled beneath the feet of beasts, and the beasts shall be subject to mankind, and all mankind shall be subject to the Devouts!"

Then he swiveled on his heel, picked up the rope that bound the village bratlings together and marched away with them in tow.

Petrel's mouth hung open. That little speech of Poosk's was the silliest thing she'd ever heard. Except no one was laughing. The bratlings were weeping harder than ever, while their mams and das scrambled along behind, begging for mercy.

They might not have been there for all the notice Poosk

took. He marched through the mud, with his face set and his two guards bringing up the rear with the mule.

But even as Petrel watched, one of the villagers, a blunt-headed fellow with a withered arm, ran forward. He was weeping almost as hard as the bratlings, and when he stopped in front of Brother Poosk, he gulped several times, then nodded violently.

Poosk's cheerful expression was back in an instant. He let go of the rope and rubbed his hands together. "Excellent! I knew you could do it if you put your minds to it."

The man said, "*mumble mumble* . . . only send word out, gracious sir. Can't promise it'll reach . . . *mumble mumble mumble*."

"Of course it will," cried Poosk. "Off you go!"

With a last desperate look at the bratlings, the man set off away from the village, heading toward the Northern Road. As soon as he was out of sight, the Devouts tied their captives to a tree stump and began to unload the mule.

Looks like they're settling in, thought Petrel. *Waiting for that man to send out word. Wish I knew where he was sending it. . . .*

And she crept back to her friends, to tell them that she hadn't learned anything very useful at all.

CHAPTER 5

THE MOUNTAINS

MEANWHILE, ON THE MOUNTAIN TRACK, THE TRAVELERS WERE once again trying to turn Spindle around.

"We've gone far enough," said Papa. "If there was ever someone after us, they're not there now. Whoa, beastie. Whoa!"

Spindle took no notice.

"It's the rat," said Gwin, for what must have been the tenth or eleventh time.

And for the tenth or eleventh time, Papa sighed, "It can't be the rat, Gwinith. A rat doesn't give orders to an ox."

He flicked the whip, then cracked it loudly. But Spindle, usually the most amiable of creatures, plodded stubbornly northward with the tattered rodent sprawled between his ears.

"Maybe it's not a rat at all," whispered Hilde. "Look at those silver eyes. Maybe it's a demon. Maybe it was demons chasing us last night!"

Nat snorted.

Hilde said, "Don't you snort at me, Fetcher boy. You were asleep. You didn't hear what I heard."

"I didn't hear it either," said Gwin. "But I saw the rat."

"Shhhh!" Hilde put her finger to her lips. "We shouldn't be talking about it. Demons don't like that sort of thing."

"It's not a demon," Papa said wearily. "Someone has tamed it, that's all. Taught it a few tricks. I should have chased it away last night."

He cracked the whip a bare inch above the rat's head. But instead of diving for cover, it rolled its silver eyes and made that *tsk-tsk-tsk* sound again.

With a hiss of exasperation, Papa jumped down from the cart and grabbed Spindle's halter. "Whoa, you old fool! Whoa!"

The ox kept going. Papa coaxed and pleaded for all he was worth, and when that didn't work, he roused himself enough to throw his full strength against Spindle's shoulder and was nearly trampled for his pains.

And so they kept going into the mountains, with Spindle refusing to stop or turn, and the rat watching their worried faces with bright curiosity, as if the whole thing was a Fetcher performance put on for its benefit.

Papa raised his eyebrows occasionally, as if he was about to speak, then sighed and thought better of it. Nat scowled. Hilde chewed her lip until it was raw and kept a fearful eye on the rat whenever it wasn't looking in her direction.

As for Gwin, she skinned the rabbit, put the joints in a pot for later and began to scrape the hide clean. And all the while she watched the way ahead for signs of danger.

It was a dark, cold landscape they traveled through, even though it was spring. Cliffs rose up on either side of the track, and the mountains beyond them were forested and forbidding. Every now and again the cliffs made way for a ruined hamlet, so old that the stone houses were almost unrecognizable, and the only creatures that lived there were ravens, and maybe a fox or two.

Maybe the wild men have gone, thought Gwin. *Maybe the stories are just stories.*

But she didn't take her eyes off the track.

By the time Spindle stopped, the rabbit skin was pinned to the side of the cart for drying, and Gwin had been awake for so long that she was dizzy with exhaustion. The track stretched on ahead, and the cliffs were higher than ever. But Spindle was gazing over his shoulder at them, the way he always did at the end of the day, and when no one moved, he lowed mournfully.

Gwin put her hand over her mouth. "Papa! *Look!*"

"A demon," whispered Hilde. "I said so."

"No. No, someone has trained it," insisted Papa. "Someone has—"

He stopped. It was impossible to deny what was happening. The rat was unbuckling Spindle's harness, using its paws like tiny hands. When it saw their stunned faces, it rolled its eyes and pointed upward.

Gwin followed the direction of its claw, feeling as if she'd fallen into one of Papa's stories. "There's a hole halfway up the cliff," she breathed. "A—a cave."

The rat nodded approvingly and turned back to the harness. Spindle stepped out of the shafts and began to forage for bits of greenery around the base of the cliff, as if nothing was at all out of the ordinary. Wretched jumped down from the cart, nose to the ground.

Apart from a whispered explanation to Nat, no one said anything more about the rat. It was too strange, even for Fetchers. Instead, they turned their attention to the cave above their heads, feeling as if this at least was something they could understand.

"The top of the hole looks sort of smoky," murmured Gwin. "Maybe someone lives up there."

Hilde pulled a doubtful face. "Who'd live in a hole like that?"

"Wild mountain men?" As soon as the words were out of Gwin's mouth, she regretted them. *In a story, it's dangerous to call something by name. Especially when you're in its territory. . . .*

"S'empty," grunted Nat.

Papa was staring upward, looking almost like his old, endlessly-curious self. "I wonder if someone *did* live there once."

"I could climb up and see," Gwin said quickly.

Her father hesitated for the longest moment. But at last he nodded.

Three months ago, Gwin would've asked him to throw her up, and then catch her when she jumped down again. Three months ago, she would have trusted him not to drop her.

She spat on her hands and eyed the cliff face.

It wasn't a hard climb, not for a Fetcher. Gwin's fingers

found knobs and hollows in the rock; her toes dug into cracks and pushed her upward. She could hear Wretched digging somewhere below her, and her own breathing, and Spindle munching on whatever greenery he'd found.

When she reached the hole, she grabbed its lower rim and hung there for a moment, catching her breath.

"Are you all right?" cried Hilde.

Gwin didn't answer. She probed with her toes until she found a good strong foothold, then she pushed herself up and tumbled into the hole.

She found herself in a cave cut out of bare rock, with stones from the ceiling scattered over the floor. On one side there was an old hearth, with half-burned logs covered in dust and bird droppings. At the back was a pile of rubble, and right next to Gwin's feet was a crudely made rope ladder.

She stuck her head out of the hole. "Doesn't look as if there's been anyone here for years. But they left a ladder behind."

One of the rungs gave way when she tugged at it, but the others seemed strong enough. She slung the ladder over the rock posts on either side of the sill and tugged again, until she was satisfied.

"Come up," she called. "Bring a lamp."

Hilde climbed up first, scared but curious. She carried the lamp on her belt and eased her weight onto each rung until she was sure it would hold. Gwin dragged her into the cave, then called down, "Papa, aren't you coming? Nat?"

Nat came up slowly, as if he was interested but didn't want to show it. Papa followed him. Spindle watched them for a while, then went back to his grazing. The rat lay down and closed its eyes, and Wretched started digging another hole.

Gwin lit the lamp, using the flint she carried in her belt pocket, and inspected the pile of rubble. "There must've been a rockfall. But it's all right now."

She liked this odd little cave. If danger approached, she was high enough to see it coming. And rock walls would protect Nat and Papa far better than the cart. "We could sleep up here tonight," she said. "We could light a fire in the hearth."

"Mm," said Papa.

Which Gwin decided to take as a yes.

She climbed down the ladder and came up again with Wretched slung over her shoulders, and the frying pan and kettle tied to her belt. Then she brought up the rabbit and some of the mangels, as well as water, wood and bedding.

"You shouldn't have to do all the work," said Hilde, looking disapprovingly at Nat and Papa. "Here, give me that firewood. I'll help you."

Gwin felt her face redden. She didn't *want* help, not unless it came from Papa or Nat. She wanted things to be the way they used to be, with the little family of Fetchers so close and happy and hardworking that they didn't need anyone else.

"I don't mind," she said. "Really." And she turned her back on Hilde, set the fire and cut up the mangels for the rabbit stew, with Wretched watching every move she made.

No one said anything more about the rat, though Nat scowled occasionally, as if it was standing right there in front of him making a nuisance of itself, and Hilde inspected every corner of the cave before she would settle down to eat.

What if it won't let us turn around? Gwin thought later, as she wrapped herself in sacking and lay down by the fire. *What if it's brought us here for a reason?*

She tried to stay awake just a little bit longer, in case that reason was rushing toward them with disaster clinging to its tail.

I have to be ready for it. I have to protect Papa and Nat. . . .

But she was too tired. With a yawn, she closed her eyes and fell asleep.

MORNING CAME, AND TO GWIN'S RELIEF THERE WAS NO SIGN of the rat. She kindled the fire and reheated what was left of the stew.

"South again, Papa?" she said, and her father nodded. None of them wanted to stay in the mountains any longer than necessary.

But when Gwin tried to back Spindle between the shafts, he wouldn't go. He wouldn't stand for the harness to be buckled either, but kicked and turned until Gwin threw the straps to the ground in disgust.

"What's going on?" she demanded.

"Maybe he's tired," said Hilde.

Gwin shook her head. "He's faking. We'll have to go without him."

She didn't mean it, of course. Without Spindle, they couldn't take the cart, and there were things hidden in that cart that they must not abandon. Besides, Spindle was a member of the family, just as Wretched was, and they couldn't leave him behind just because he was being stubborn.

Gwin tried everything to get him into harness. She begged, she pleaded, she tried to trick him. She grew more and more desperate, but nothing worked. Spindle would not budge.

And so eventually, with the clouds low and threatening above their heads, they climbed back up the ladder into the cave.

"What do we do now?" asked Hilde.

Gwin looked at Papa, hoping he would smile, the way he used to. She wanted him to say that everything would turn out all right because they were Fetchers, and although they fetched trouble, they also fetched luck. And this was just a tiny setback, and maybe they should sing a song or two until they came up with a brilliant plan for getting Spindle to do as he was told.

But Papa's moment of being his old self was gone. So Gwin said the words for him. "We should sing."

Nat snorted, of course. Hilde said, "Sing? Here? Now?"

"Please, Papa," said Gwin.

"Gwinith—"

"*Please*, Papa!"

Her father sighed and picked up his fiddle. "I suppose it won't hurt."

"Play Ariel's song," said Gwin .

"Ariel's song it is." And Papa began to play. Three bars in, Nat picked up his clarinetto.

Ariel's song had always been Nat's favorite, which was why Gwin chose it. It told the story of the very first Fetcher, who was seven feet tall and rode a blue ox that could strike lightning from the earth with its hooves.

Gwin loved singing it, with her not-very-good voice.

"'No songs?' cried she, and her blue eyes blazed,
'No tunes for the ear?
No joy for the heart?
Then I will sing loudly for all of my days,
As I travel the land
With my ox and cart.'"

They were halfway through the fifth verse when Nat's clarinetto fell from his lips. "Someone's coming!"

The song faltered and died. Wretched tried to burrow into Nat's lap. Hilde whispered, "The wild mountain men!"

Papa's mouth opened and closed. But then he looked at Gwin and Nat, and with a trace of his old spirit, he said, "They will have heard us already. No use being quiet now." And he raised his fiddle to his chin once more.

Gwin could hardly remember what came next though she'd known this song all her life. She swallowed half a verse and sang the next one backward, but she didn't stop, though her heart was thudding with terror.

"They chased her east and they chased her west,
They placed a price
On her head and heart.
A hundred crowns in a wooden chest . . ."

Slowly, like a nightmare in the making, the rope ladder

began to creak and wobble. A hand slid above the rim of the hole.

The verses dried up in Gwin's mouth, and she sat there, trembling. Papa put down his fiddle. Nat looked defiant, though he was trembling too. Hilde pressed herself against the rock wall.

One by one, three wild mountain men stepped off the rope ladder and into the cave.

CHAPTER 6

THE ATTACK ON THE CITADEL

IN THE WEEKS LEADING UP TO THE ATTACK ON THE CITADEL, Dolph had naturally assumed she'd be part of it. Her mam, Orca, had been one of the best hand-to-hand fighters on the *Oyster*, and Dolph had imagined herself in there with the rest of the crew, helping to break the stranglehold the Devouts had on this poor broken country.

But so far all she'd done was stand around and watch.

Some distance from the Citadel's gate, the ram crew was readying itself for another run. Fifty men and women rubbed their hands together and bent to their ropes, which were woven around a massive tree trunk. With a shout and a heave, they lifted the tree to waist level and broke into a lumbering gallop.

Immediately, dozens of heads rose above the Citadel walls, and arrows began to rain down on the runners. At the same time, slings whirled and a fusillade of rocks flew in the opposite direction. One of the archers screamed and tumbled backward.

Two of the runners fell in their tracks. Everyone else ducked their heads and kept going.

Dolph crossed her fingers. "This time. Let it be this time!"

The ram hit the great wooden gates with a *thud* that echoed across the plateau. The gates shivered—and stood firm.

Dolph groaned. On her shoulder, Missus Slink said, "Patience, lass."

"I've *been* patient, Missus Slink. But nothing's happening, and when it does happen, I'm not allowed to take part!"

Because the fact was, there'd been hand-to-hand fighting at the very beginning. When the combined army of shipfolk and Sunkers had first marched onto the plateau, the Devouts had poured out through the Citadel gates, rank upon rank of brown-robed men, roaring with fury.

Dolph had been as eager as the rest of the *Oyster*'s crew to leap into battle, but First Officer Hump had stopped her.

"Not you, Dolph," she had shouted as she ran past. "Adm'ral Deeps and I have an agreement. No bratlings."

Dolph had just about fallen over with shock. "I'm not a bratling! I'm fifteen. I'm Third Officer!"

"Makes no difference," cried Hump.

"If the cap'n was here, he'd let me fight," Dolph shouted after her.

But Hump had disappeared into the melee.

The *Oyster*'s captain, a mechanical boy who had been terribly damaged by the Devouts, had vanished some weeks ago, carried off to unknown parts by Mister Smoke and a flock of pigeons. For as long as the captain was gone, Hump was senior officer, and so Dolph had done as she was told. She'd stayed on the sidelines, shouting warnings and advice, and swearing whenever she saw an opening where she might've made a difference. And just as she'd been about to join in anyway and take the consequences, the Devouts had retreated into their Citadel and barred the gates.

"They're used to folk cowering in front of 'em," Dolph muttered now. "They're used to half-starved villagers and townsfolk worn down by hard work. They can't stand up against the tribes of the *Oyster*."

"So you've said, a dozen times at least," Missus Slink remarked drily.

"And I'll say it a dozen more, Missus Slink. They outnumbered us, but we had 'em on the run in no time at all. They don't like proper fighters, 'specially not ones as fierce as us. That's why they don't dare come out again; they know we'll beat 'em. Which means we have to get that gate down." She scuffed her boots in the mud and sighed. "But it doesn't look as if it's going to crack any time soon."

Some of the ram crew seemed to be coming to the same conclusion. The moment they were out of arrow range, they dropped the tree trunk and walked away, wiping the sweat from their foreheads.

Head Cook Krill was one of them. He was a huge man, barrel-chested and bearded, and normally one of the most peaceable folk on the *Oyster*. But right now his face was dark, and he strode over to where First Officer Hump and Admiral Deeps, the leader of the Sunkers, were huddled in conversation by the side of the road.

"This should be interesting," muttered Dolph, and she hurried after him.

Dolph didn't mind the Sunkers. And she'd been prepared to like Admiral Deeps, a tall, hard-browed woman who reminded her just a little of her own murdered mam.

But then Deeps had turned her out of the planning meetings on the grounds that bratlings couldn't be trusted—which was because of Sharkey, of course. Dolph understood it, but that didn't mean she liked it.

And so, even though she no longer considered herself a bratling, she made sure she was well hidden behind a rope pile, where she could see without being seen. The last thing she wanted was to be sent back to the ship.

". . . losing folk with every run," Krill was saying, "and we've barely raised a splinter from those gates yet. They're too well built."

"Your Chief Engineer has plans to reinforce the head of the ram with iron," said Admiral Deeps. "And a mobile shield to protect the runners. That should make a difference."

"Our Chief Engineer," rumbled Krill, "would still be in the brig if I had my way. Just because he's a good fighter is no reason to forget his crimes."

First Officer Hump began to protest, but Krill hadn't finished. "And besides, he's busy trying to dig tunnels that don't go anywhere. I'm not holding my breath for shields and reinforcements."

Hump fell silent and stared into the distance.

"Tunnels were her idea," Dolph whispered to Missus Slink. "She didn't know the Citadel was built on such hard rock."

"I could've told her," said Missus Slink with a sniff.

"Don't reckon she would've listened. She's a good First Officer, or at least she was. But now she's trying to keep up with Deeps, trying to be all hard and superior, and that sort of thing just doesn't work with shipfolk."

"Thing is," continued Krill, "there's stuff we're forgetting with all this talk of tunnels and rams."

"If you've got useful suggestions, your First Officer and I are willing to hear them," said Deeps. "Speak up, man!"

Krill glared at her, unimpressed, and pointed to the hovels that lined the road farther down the hill. "It's them."

The first time Dolph had walked past those squalid little houses, she'd gagged. She was no stranger to strong smells; at the end of a long winter, the passages of the *Oyster* reeked of sour bodies and fish oil. But the stink of the hovels was different. There was something bitter and hopeless about it, something that had made Dolph want to turn around and march straight back the way she had come.

She was used to it now—hardly noticed it—and hardly noticed the townsfolk either, with their gaunt faces and hollow eyes.

Deeps looked puzzled. "What about 'em? They're no threat to us. If anything, they're on our side."

"So what are we doing for 'em?" demanded Krill, crossing his arms over his broad chest.

"Tearing down the Citadel and beating the Devouts," said Deeps, as if it was obvious.

"And how many of their bratlings are going to starve to death while we're tippy-tapping at those gates, like a seagull trying to crack open a boulder?"

Deeps stared at the Head Cook as if she didn't understand the question. But Hump nodded slowly and said, "I see your point, Krill."

"I can't stand by and do nothing while there are hungry bratlings about," said Krill. "I'm going to start feeding 'em. Just wanted to let you know."

He turned away, but Deeps stepped in front of him. For all her tallness, she was nowhere near Krill's great height, but she had such presence and such a habit of command that he stopped and raised a bushy eyebrow.

Dolph leaned closer, not wanting to miss a single word.

"The Devouts might be vicious, but they're not fools." Deeps glared at the small bones woven into Krill's beard. "Before we arrived, they stripped the countryside, which means there's hardly any food here except what we brought with us. If we feed those children, our own crews'll go hungry, and we'll have to abandon the siege. I will not fall into such a trap. And *you* will not give our supplies away."

"Oh dear," whispered Dolph. She grinned at Missus Slink. "This ain't going to end well."

Krill's beard bristled, and the bones trembled in the

morning light. "*Our* supplies?" he said, in a dangerously quiet voice. "I must be mistaken, Adm'ral. I thought all those dried fish, seaweed biscuits and slabs of portable soup we brought with us were from the *Oyster*'s stores."

Deeps realized she'd made a mistake. "Well, yes, I didn't mean—"

"And who's in charge of the *Oyster*'s stores?" continued Krill. "Why, I reckon that's me, and has been for the last nineteen winters since my da died. So if I want to feed a few bratlings, ain't no one going to stop me."

He turned back to what was left of the ram crew and bellowed, in a voice that was used to making itself heard over all the racket of a busy ship's galley, "Squid! Get some new cooking fires started! Back down the road apiece, in the town."

A young woman broke away from the ram. "Rightio, Da!"

As Krill strode off and the admiral fumed, Dolph headed back to her unofficial watch post. "I don't much like Deeps, Missus Slink, but she's got a point. I reckon the Devouts'd be pleased as penguins if we ran out of food. *They've* got plenty, from the sound of it, all those storerooms full of—"

She broke off midsentence, thinking about certain events that had happened on the *Oyster*. And about her mam, First Officer Orca, who'd taught her that the most important part of fighting was strategy.

Missus Slink eyed her curiously. "What is it, lass?"

Dolph didn't answer straightaway. Instead, she turned and watched the bustling array of shipfolk and Sunkers.

The ram crew was already rearranging itself. Several hefty

Sunkers were brought in to replace the cooks who'd left, and once again everyone spat on their hands and bent to their ropes. Closer to the Citadel, Chief Engineer Albie and his crew were hacking away at the bedrock with pickaxes and shovels.

"It's a good army," said Dolph. "Nice and strong, and everyone burning for vengeance. Even Albie's got into the spirit of it, which is an amazing thing. But at this rate it could take weeks. I know you say we have to be patient, Missus Slink—"

She broke off again and gazed up at the Citadel. Her eyes grew bright. "But what if we had a completely *different* sort of army?"

CHAPTER 7

THE WILD MOUNTAIN MEN

THE MOUNTAIN MEN WERE EVEN WILDER THAN GWIN HAD imagined. Their hair was tangled, their faces were filthy, and their clothes were a mix of animal skins and bracken. In their fists they carried crude stone blades.

For the longest moment, no one moved. Then one of the men grunted. There was nothing human about the sound he made, but his companions seemed to understand him. They grunted too, like wild pigs, and rubbed their bellies.

"Dear life, they're going to eat us," squeaked Hilde.

The three men stared blankly at her and grunted again, their eyes darting back and forth.

Papa said quietly, "Poor souls, I don't believe they can talk. What has the world come to?" And with trembling fingers, he raised his fiddle.

If anyone had asked, Gwin would have said that she couldn't remember another word of Ariel's song. But as the fiddle creaked out the shaky tune, she opened her mouth and sang the final verse.

"*I am the spark that will not go out,*
I am the life,
I am the song . . ."

The mountain men gaped like children. Gwin couldn't take her eyes off them. Despite the chill of the morning, she was dripping with sweat, and her voice wobbled. In Papa's stories, music could tame a wild beast. But would it tame the mountain men?

"*Loud is my voice and my heart is stout,*
And I'll travel the land
My whole life long."

The verse ended far too soon. Silence fell over the cave. Gwin felt as if she was about to faint with terror.

But as she sat there, waiting for the stone knives to do their work, Nat breathed, "They're not starving."

That made no sense to Gwin. Of course the mountain men were starving. Just about everyone in the country was starving.

All the same, her brother had always been able to hear things that no one else could, and when she looked past the beards and the bracken, she realized he was right. Even without the wildness, the men were nothing at all like the villagers she was used to. Their arms were solid with muscle. Their faces weren't plump, by any means, but neither were they hollow.

An ugly thought crawled into Gwin's mind. Perhaps there had been other travelers this way recently. Perhaps the rat had lured them here. Perhaps *that* was why the wild men were so well fed.

She felt sick. She was the one who'd been driving when Spindle had turned onto the mountain track. She was the one who'd wanted to sleep in the cave. Now they were all going to die, and it was her fault.

She cleared her throat, which didn't get rid of the sick feeling, and began to sing.

"We are F-Fetchers,
And here we stand . . ."

The men's eyes swiveled toward her. Gwin stopped singing for long enough to say, "If you're going to k-kill us, you should know who we are."

Papa whispered, "Well said, my love." He touched bow to strings. Nat licked his dry lips and raised his clarinetto. Gwin sang,

"Like a smile,
Like a laugh,
Like a bird cupped in the hand . . ."

If Mama were here, her voice would have stopped the wild mountain men in their tracks; it would have made them weep for joy, no matter how stony-hearted they were.

Gwin had never made anyone weep for joy. But this was probably the last song she'd ever sing, so she did her best. And when she finished, she closed her eyes and waited for death to come.

A deep voice growled, "Fetchers? Why dint you say so?"

Gwin's eyes snapped open, and she stared at the three men.

They still looked as wild as bears, but underneath that look, something had changed.

Another voice said, "Careful, Hob. Might be trick."

They were so hairy that it was hard to tell who was speaking. But the mere fact that they *could* speak gave Gwin hope.

Nat said hoarsely, "It—it's not a trick. We're Fetchers. It's who we are and what we do." Which was more words than he'd strung together in two months.

"Fetchers never come here," growled one of the men.

Another said, "If you be Fetchers, 'oo was your first?"

Papa leaned forward, white-lipped. "Our first? Y-you mean Ariel? We played her song."

The man grunted. "And 'oo was her friend?"

Papa hesitated. "I—I'm not sure what you mean."

There was little patience in the reply. "'Oo was her *friend*?"

"There are many stories," Papa said quickly, "but none of them mentions a friend. Except perhaps the blue ox."

The wild men looked at one another. "Don't mean they be wrong 'uns," said the one called Hob.

"But it might," growled one of the others. And that air of danger was back again.

It was then that Gwin had the inspiration. "Show them the heirloom, Papa."

Papa went very still. He never showed the heirloom to anyone outside the family. It was supposed to have once belonged to the great Ariel herself, and it was the sort of thing that could get people hanged, even if they weren't Fetchers.

"Why?" whispered Papa.

Gwin wasn't sure if she could explain. It was something to do with Ariel's song, which was about laughter and joy and all the other things that couldn't be measured. The heirloom, in contrast, ticked off the hours and minutes in a precise way that didn't sound at all like the first Fetcher.

"It's just—worth a try," she whispered.

Papa slid shaky fingers into his coat pocket, took out the heirloom and opened its cover.

It ticked quietly in his palm, a device from a long-lost world. The wild men leaned toward it as if pulled by strings.

Hob whistled. "It be Coe's watch. Rab, Bony, it be!" His beard parted, and surprisingly white teeth shone in an unmistakable grin. Then, before any of the Fetchers could stop him, he wrapped them, one after the other, in a stinking embrace.

Gwin tried to duck. Nat flinched. But Papa managed an uncomfortable smile, Hilde let out a gasp of relief, and Wretched's tail, poking out from behind Nat, thumped twice.

"You—ah—recognize it?" croaked Papa, brushing bits of bracken and filth from his shoulders.

The third man, Bony, wiped his hand across his face. He was grinning too. "Aye, we do. Property of Serran Coe hisself. Only mountain man 'oo ever went to university. They say he used to come home every holiday and bring liddle inventions with he. Last village you passed on way here? Nothing left but stones? That were Coe's village."

As he chatted away, telling them about Serran Coe, Hob whispered to Rab, then strolled across to the pile of rubble.

"Fetchers, you be called," he said, interrupting Bony, "'cos

57

you fetch things back from long past. Well, so do we." And he reached down between the rocks.

Gwin thought she heard a *snick*ing sound. Something groaned. Something else rattled.

"Hain't bin used much lately," said Rab, from the front of the cave.

No one so much as looked at him. They were staring at the pile of rubble, which was shaking violently, as if the rockfall that had caused it was starting up again. But then the shaking stopped, and with a rumbling sound the pile rolled sideways, all in one piece, leaving a gaping hole.

CHAPTER 8

THE BRING BACK

GWIN BACKED AWAY FROM THE HOLE AND BUMPED INTO NAT. "What was that?" he whispered. "What happened?"

"The rocks," hissed Gwin. "They've gone!"

Hob shouted into the hole, "They be Fetchers!"

For a moment, nothing happened. There was just an echo, and a sense of waiting. Then an enormous shadow fell across the opening. Papa drew in a sharp breath.

The shadow wavered and broke into pieces. And through the hole came a dozen children.

There was something strange about them, but Gwin didn't have time to work out what it was. The children fell on her and Nat, all chattering at once.

"Be you Fetchers, truly? You come to sing? Tell tales?"

"Big old cow, he with you? We heard he this morn, all snorty, but Hob wouldn't let we go see."

"That dog hiding under there—what name he?"

One of the children, a bandy-legged girl with a scar across

her forehead, said, "You been to Lower Thumb lately? Out west?"

"Here, let me ask. You visit Scoffle, Fetchers?"

"How about Dimbler? Big place, I bet you been there."

A woman stepped through the hole, holding her side and panting. "Sorry, Hob. Got away from we, they did. No problem, though?"

"No problem," replied Hob.

The woman sagged with relief. Hob put two fingers in his mouth and whistled loud and sharp. The children fell silent.

"Be this any way to treat visitors?" asked Hob, in his deep voice. "Gert, lead 'em through, nice and proper. No racing about, no questions, not till they settled."

The girl with the scar on her forehead grabbed Gwin's hand and said, with an air of great importance, "Welcome to mountains, Fetchers. Come with we."

She led them toward the hole, pointing to the row of rocks that still ran along the cave floor. "Mind toes. That bit be fixed in place."

Gwin took her hand back and stepped carefully over the rocks.

Nat sniffed the air. "Cooking oil?"

The girl nodded. "Got to keep wheels oiled. That be my job, every morn. Never miss it, me."

"Wheels?" asked Gwin, and the girl pointed to one side.

Hilde squeaked. Papa stopped dead, and Wretched bumped into him. Close to the rock wall, on the other side of the hole, were two great metal wheels with notched edges.

They looked like something straight out of the Forbidden Lands, only scraped clean of rust and age, and gleaming with oil.

Nat took a step toward them, following his nose. For the moment at least, he seemed to have forgotten how much he hated the world. But Gwin didn't trust it to last. She didn't trust the goodwill of the mountain men either. If there was treachery hidden under Hob's apparent friendliness, she'd be ready for it.

"This moves the rockfall?" asked Nat, laying his hand on the metal.

"It do," said Bony, from somewhere behind them. "Or at least, two of 'em together."

"But how—"

"Weights and counterweights. Pull one liddle lever and whole door moves. Hob's great-grandpa built it."

"Your great-grandfather?" said Papa, turning to Hob. "But the secrets of such things have been lost for generations."

"Not here." Hob grinned. "You wouldn't believe things we've got hid in these mountains, Fetcher. Great wonders, some of 'em, not seen in flatlands for three hundred years."

Gert tugged at the hem of Gwin's jacket. "Come on. Others be waiting."

Gwin followed the girl cautiously, still watching out for trouble. And there were plenty of directions it could come from. To her amazement, there was a whole village tucked away inside that cliff. Every cave opened into two or three others, with fireplaces and stoves, and chimneys disappearing up into the rock. There were floors that shone in the lamplight, and woven rugs, and beds piled high with animal skins.

Gwin saw faces peering around corners and heard children giggling, but Gert hurried her on, saying, "They be waiting."

And then, suddenly, they stepped out into daylight and found themselves right on the edge of another cliff. It was such a shock that Gwin almost kept walking, and was only saved by the other girl's arm stretched across in front of her.

"Easy now," said Gert.

Gwin gasped. So did Papa and Hilde. Wretched dived behind them with his tail between his legs, and Nat turned this way and that, trying to work out what he was hearing.

"It's . . ." Gwin wanted to describe it to him, but she couldn't find the words.

"It be our town," said Hob proudly.

It was like nothing Gwin had ever seen before. The cliff face curved around on both sides, like a giant arena. There were staircases cut into it, going up, down and across, and leading to so many doorways and windows that she couldn't count them.

The whole thing was so unexpected that it was a moment before she looked down. But when she did, she gasped again. Below them, on the floor of the arena, were several hundred people, all gazing up at them.

"How can this be?" asked Papa in a strangled voice. "The mountains were emptied out during the Great Cleansing. There was no one left alive. All those ruined villages we saw . . ."

Hob's face grew serious. "They was bad times, Fetcher.

You got your stories, we got ours, full of blood and sorrow. You'll hear 'em, right enough. But first, you've got folk to meet."

And he led them down one of the stone staircases.

Gert chattered all the way, skipping from one subject to another without pause. "Mind that step, there be great hole in it. There now, you missed it. See my cousin down there? With pidgie bird on shoulder? Wave to her, if'n you don't mind. You got songs ready for big feast tonight? There's good timing, you turning up at Bring Back. That dog of yours, he always so scaredy? Look, that be my foster ma smiling . . ."

It was then that Gwin realized what was so strange about these people.

They smiled. With no music playing to soften their harsh lives, they smiled, as if there were things in the world to be happy about. What's more, they didn't cower like the villagers Gwin knew. Their faces were proud, their arms were strong.

They looked like the people in the old stories.

Maybe their friendliness is real, she thought. But she didn't lower her guard, just in case.

In front of her, Papa was still asking questions. "Where did all the children come from? Are they yours?"

Hob laughed. "All of 'em? Not likely. Flatland villages smuggle 'em up here to stop Devouts taking 'em. Saves 'em from starving to death too. Started couple of years ago."

Hilde made a sound in her throat. When Hob looked at her, she mumbled, "Too late for some."

"Aye, missus." Hob nodded sympathetically. "We'd've started long before, but flatlanders was scared of own shadows. Wouldn't even talk to we. That's changed, which is something. There be anger in some villages that weren't there when I were boy. Only spark, mind, and easily snuffed, but it be better'n nothing." He grinned and waved his hand at the children. "Hain't worked out what we do when they grow up yet. Chuck 'em back or keep 'em."

Papa shook his head in amazement. "Surely I would've heard of such a thing."

"Villagers can be close-mouthed when it suits 'em," said Hob. "Now, come and meet folk. They awful keen to hear from Fetchers."

THE FEAST CALLED BRING BACK TOOK PLACE IN THE ARENA. All day, people poured in from higher in the mountains—most of them as ferocious-looking as Hob. Somehow, they'd already heard about the visitors and welcomed them gladly.

"You got treats ahead, Fetchers," they said. "Hain't no one but mountain folk told Bring Back for three hundred years. You got new stories coming."

Before long, Gwin's face ached from keeping up that Fetcher smile, and it was a relief when Gert suggested they go and move Spindle and the cart off the mountain track.

To Gwin's surprise, the old ox backed between the shafts as if he had never had a stubborn, difficult thought in his head. "Why wouldn't he do that this morning?" she asked as Gert led the way to a well-hidden stone corral, where a dozen cows munched on a pile of hay and a flock of pigeons circled over-head. "Did you people do something to him?"

"Not likely," said Gert. "Us thunk you lot *wanted* to stay. That be why Hob, Rab and Bony went in all hairy-man, try-ing to scare you. And if you didn't scare, well then, they was ready to murder, to keep mountain folk safe."

Gwin shivered, realizing just how close they had come to disaster. As for Spindle's stubbornness: "It must have been the rat," she said.

"Rat?"

"You know. The big one. The clever one. He brought us here."

Gert laughed, as if Gwin had made a joke. "Lots of rats in mountains, but none of 'em clever." She tossed a fistful of grain to the pigeons and said, "Come on, reckon bonfire be ready."

The fire was set in the middle of the arena. It was huge, with what looked like a whole dead tree dragged on top of it, and as night fell and the cold air closed in, everyone wrapped up in rabbit furs and took turns sitting close to the flames and holding their hands out to the warmth.

Gwin sat between Nat and Papa, with a respectful space around them. Nearby, Hilde was laughing and chatting with a group of mountain women as if she'd known them all her life, and Wretched lay on his back while the mountain children took turns scratching his tummy.

The celebrations began with Hob standing up to welcome everyone. "This be Bring Back number three hundred. Exact number, no more, no less. And I guess it be lucky, 'cos who come to join we, but Fetchers!"

Everyone cheered, and the people nearest to Gwin and Nat leaned toward them, saying, "Stand up and let's see you."

The two children and Papa scrambled to their feet, and Gwin smiled her widest Fetcher smile. Another cheer rang around the arena.

"And look what they brung with 'em." Hob had asked to borrow the heirloom, and now he held it high so that the light of the fire reflected off its silver case. "It be Coe's watch!"

When they heard that, the crowd erupted. "Coe!" they roared. "Coe, Coe!"

Hob raised his other hand for silence, then opened the heirloom and tapped the glass. "It be just like old stories too. Minutes, hours in big circle here. Aspect o' moon here. And liddle circle *here* be sun and moon together, when middle of day goes dark as night. What great-greats called eclipse. Hain't been one in West Norn for two hundred and seventy years, but see, there be one coming soon!"

"Eclipse," murmured the crowd.

"Day gets colder," said Hob, "and birds go to bed. Flatlanders fall on their faces with terror, but not we. We know all about eclipse, thanks to great-greats. And to Coe."

Papa leaned toward Gwin, looking more animated than he had for weeks. "I always wondered what that third circle was for. Eclipse, eh? I've never heard of such a thing. I wonder . . ."

But the rest of what he said was lost as all around them the cry of "Coe! Coe!" rose up again. A group on the other side of the fire burst into song. A woman leapt to her feet, shrieking, "Eclipse be sign! Change be coming!"

Hob watched with an expression of satisfaction on his face. And when things quieted down at last, he said, "No one can smell change like mountain folk. It be sign, all right. I tell you, this be Bring Back like no other."

He snapped the heirloom shut, handed it back to Papa and sat down with a *thump*. The Fetchers sat down too. The crowd fell silent, gazing upward.

On the cliff above them, a giant appeared.

The mountain people had obviously been expecting it, but still they gasped. So did Gwin.

"What?" whispered Nat.

"Where we stood this morning," breathed Gwin. "There's someone up there. He's *huge*."

The giant was bearded, like all the mountain men, and he wore a long coat edged with fur. The shadows danced across him, making him seem bigger than ever. He raised one massive arm.

"I. Be. Coe," he boomed, in a voice that echoed from one side of the arena to the other.

"Coe," whispered the crowd. "He come back."

"I be Coe," cried the giant again. "Hark to my remembering."

"Hark, hark," whispered the crowd.

Nat elbowed Gwin. "Sounds like Bony."

"No, he's way too big for Bony. It can't be—" Gwin stopped, realizing how caught up she'd been in the performance.

Shadows, darkness, a few tricks—that was all it took. When Papa took stones from children's ears, they thought he was a witch. This was the same.

She made herself look at the giant with Fetcher eyes. Then she leaned closer to Nat and whispered, "Might be stilts."

All the hair made it hard to see the giant's features, even without the shadows. But then the flames crackled up again, just as the giant roared, "I got rememberings of airships."

"Airships!" groaned the crowd. Wretched howled in chorus.

"And horseless carriages."

"Carriages!"

"And thousand moons lighting up night so it be bright as day."

"Moons!"

Gwin watched the giant closely. And before long, she thought she could see the trick. "There are two of them," she whispered to Nat. "A boy wearing a false beard, and a man. The boy's sitting on the man's shoulders, and both of them are covered by the coat; that's why he looks so tall. It's the man who's speaking—Bony, like you said. The boy's just mouthing the words, and every now and then he gets it wrong. But the sound—"

"A speaking trumpet under the coat," whispered Nat, "to make Bony's voice bigger. We should try something like that."

He sounded almost like he used to, working things out and looking for new ways of telling stories. Papa looked happier too, as if the shock of discovering this extraordinary place had jolted him back to life.

As for the mountain people, their welcome seemed completely genuine. What's more, they had a connection with Ariel, through Serran Coe. And like the Fetchers, they were the keepers of secrets, which separated them from everyone else in West Norn.

Gwin still didn't know where the too-clever rat had come from, or why it had brought them here. But perhaps it wasn't as important as she'd thought. Papa was happier, and Nat was talking to her again, and that was what mattered.

With a sigh of relief, she settled back to listen to the giant's stories.

They were well worth the attention. The giant described the world before the Great Cleansing as a place of such marvels that even the Fetchers were impressed. He told the audience that one day it would all come back, and they must be ready. He warned them about the treachery of the Devouts.

And then, in a flurry of sparks, he disappeared.

Before Gwin could draw breath, the people around her were on their feet and singing. Their songs were nothing like the ones she knew. Most of them sounded like instructions for building one thing or another; a few contained lists. She heard one that concerned weights and counterweights, and another about something called a zeppaleen, and another still that spoke of a ship called the *Oyster*, and a great secret hidden inside it.

Gwin was laying the songs down in her memory, using all her Fetcher craft, when an amazing thought struck her.

She elbowed her brother. "We could stay here," she

whispered. "For"—she wanted to say *forever*, but she didn't think Nat would agree—"for a few weeks."

"Mm," said Nat. It was a friendly sort of sound, as if he quite liked the idea.

Gwin's heart strummed like a fiddle string. *We COULD stay here forever. We'd still be Fetchers. We'd still sing and tell stories. We'd just be telling them to the mountain people instead of the villagers.*

And Papa and Nat would be safe.

CHAPTER 9

THE FETCH

As MIDNIGHT CRAWLED OVER WEST NORN, DOLPH STOOD outside a deserted farmhouse. The ground in front of her heaved with black bodies and long fleshy tails, and for a moment she felt as if she were back on the ice with Petrel and Fin, and Mister Smoke was bringing out the *Oyster*'s rats to save them.

That was what had given her the idea, and at first she'd thought it was brilliant. Now she was beginning to wonder.

She put her hand over her mouth to hide an uncertain laugh. *You always told me I'd be a leader one day, Mam. But I don't think this was what you had in mind.*

A voice at her feet jerked her back to the present. "Well, lass?" Missus Slink peered up at her. "That's all I could find, and they're not nearly as willing as the *Oyster*'s rats. But I should be able to keep them in line till dawn."

"That should do it," said Dolph. "As long as they can get in and out again."

"There's not many places in this world that a determined

rat can't get to," said Missus Slink. "And besides, I'll be show-ing them the way."

"Well then." Dolph felt as if she should salute or something. Her fingers twitched. "Good luck, Missus Slink. And"—she raised her voice, knowing the black rats couldn't understand her, but feeling as if she had to mark the occasion in some way—"and good luck, all of you! Go with—um—with my blessing."

She thought she heard a snicker from Missus Slink. Then the old rat whistled, and the heaving bodies stilled. Ears pricked, whiskers stiffened.

Another whistle—and the army of rats was on the move.

"I'll see you all a bit before dawn," whispered Dolph as the last tail disappeared into the darkness. "At least, I hope I will."

Gwin was used to getting up before the sun rose, so she was already awake when Hob came looking for them. Her mattress, stuffed with straw, was warm and comfortable, and she had slept better than she had for weeks. Hob winked at her, then set his lamp down and squatted next to Papa.

"Hey, Fetcher," whispered Hob. "You awake?"

"No," grunted Papa, and Wretched stuck his head out from under Nat's bedding and yawned.

Hob chuckled. "Message come up from flatlands. Someone looking for Fetch."

Gwin sat up very quickly. "Papa doesn't do them anymore."

"No?" The mountain man sat back on his haunches. "Why ever not?"

"He just doesn't."

Papa sat up too, rubbing his eyes. "A Fetch? Whereabouts?"

"East of mountain track turnoff and down a bit," said Hob. "Little village called Bale."

"I know it," said Papa.

"According to message, it be Fetch like no other. Big book, they say, buried for no one knows how long, and full of writing no one can read." He peered at Papa. "You sure you won't do it?"

"Of course he's sure," said Gwin.

On her other side, Nat shoved Wretched out of the way and rolled over. "What's this about a Fetch?"

"It's nothing," said Gwin.

"*Nothing?*" Hob raised one tangled eyebrow. "I'd like to see what you call something, if big old book full of writing's nothing. Devouts'll be after it quick smart, soon as they hear. They'll burn it, you know, and it'll be gone forever. Unless—"

Papa took a deep breath. "I'll do it."

And with those three words, Gwin's barely hatched dream of keeping her family safe in the mountains was shattered.

Because there was another side to being a Fetcher. If a villager somewhere unearthed an ancient book from a cellar or a stable, and didn't want to hand it over to the Devouts as they were supposed to, they'd put out a quiet word for a Fetch. And that quiet word would spread across the countryside like ripples on a pond, until it reached someone like Papa.

"But there are Devouts around," said Gwin. "It might be a trap!"

"Then I won't go as a Fetcher," said Papa. "You've seen me disguised—would *you* recognize me?"

"No, but—"

"We can't let a book like that be lost, Gwin. As it is, I've been too selfish for too long."

Hob raised that hairy eyebrow again, in an unspoken question.

Papa cleared his throat several times, as if there was something stuck in it. "There was a—a tragedy in our lives." For a moment he looked as if he might say more, might go on to talk about Mama, which none of them ever did these days. But then he shook his head and said, "Coming here seems to have woken me up a little. Reminded me that life goes on whether we like it or not."

Hob looked at him shrewdly and said, "Girl's right, though. Might be trap."

"Then all they'll see is a hungry old peasant going about his business. The Devouts aren't subtle people, in my experience. They see what they expect to see."

There was nothing more to be said. Papa packed his bedroll and a small amount of food. He dirtied his face, hunched his back and seemed to grow older and thinner in the space of three breaths.

Then he hugged his children, spoke quietly to Hilde, patted Wretched and set off, back down the track toward the village of Bale.

AS THE SKY ABOVE THE CITADEL BEGAN TO LIGHTEN, DOLPH kept watch. She could hear a chorus of snores from nearby shipfolk and, in the distance, a goat bleating. The Citadel, however, was quiet.

They know we're not going to get that gate down easily, she thought. *They're probably sound asleep, the whole lot of 'em. I wonder if—*

She stiffened. On the very top of the Citadel walls, something was moving. Could it be . . .

Yes!

A dark wave flowed down the high stone walls, then spread outward—at least that's what it looked like from where Dolph stood. But as it came closer, and the sky grew lighter, the wave broke apart into thousands of scurrying rats. They were working in teams of twenty or more, dragging hessian sacks, joints of beef, flitches of bacon, strings of sausages and salted herring, pumpkins, potatoes, rutabagas, hard biscuits, soft biscuits, loaves of bread, pigs' trotters, mangels, dried beans, mushrooms, wheels of cheese, and a hundred other foodstuffs across the rough ground.

Dolph heard running feet, and someone shouting, but took no notice. The food was piling up in front of her, so much of it that before long it entirely blocked her view of the Citadel.

A precise voice said, "You were right, lass." And there was Missus Slink, perched on a pumpkin high above Dolph's head, her green ribbon more tattered than ever. "The storerooms and larders weren't guarded. They weren't expecting an attack from the inside."

"Did they see you?" asked Dolph.

"They did not. They're going to get an awful shock when they go for their breakfast. There's not a scrap of food left in the whole Citadel."

It was such a relief—*It worked, Mam! My daft idea worked!*—that Dolph laughed out loud.

Missus Slink gave a most uncharacteristic wink. Then she whistled loudly and scurried down from the pumpkin. The horde of rats squeaked and swirled and dashed away down the hill.

It wasn't until they'd gone that Dolph realized the whole camp was awake, with rank upon rank of Sunkers and shipfolk staring at her in stunned disbelief.

Krill was the first to speak. He strode up to Dolph, saying, "What in the name of blizzards have you done, lass?"

"Um—this is from the Citadel," said Dolph. "It's for you, Krill. To feed the starving bratlings." She looked at the mountain of food. She'd never seen so much in one place. "I reckon there's enough for their parents too. For a year or so!"

Admiral Deeps appeared beside Krill. "This"—she pointed, almost speechless—"*this* is from the *Citadel*?"

"Aye," said Dolph. "They've got no food left. Not a scrap." A wave of glee swept through her, and she grinned at the admiral. "All we have to do is wait for a few days, and the siege'll be over!"

CHAPTER 10

WAITING

"WAITING," MUTTERED PETREL, WHOSE TURN IT WAS TO KEEP watch, along with Rain, "I hate it."

Two days had passed since Poosk and his men had rounded up the bratlings of Bale, and nothing had changed. The captives were still tied to a stump, with their parents sneaking them scraps of food whenever they dared. The Devouts sat in their cowhide tents when it rained, and sprawled outside on a meager patch of grass when it didn't. The mule dozed, its head lowered and its eyes half-shut.

"Me too," said Rain. "I cannot help worrying about Bran. Do you think he will be getting enough to eat?"

Rain's little brother had been left behind on the *Oyster*, along with all the other bratlings.

"He'll be as fat as a penguin chick by now," said Petrel. "You won't recognize him when we get back. They'll have to roll him out to meet us, like a barrel."

Rain laughed softly. Then she peeped over her shoulder, as

if she didn't want to be overheard, and whispered, "Petrel, do you really think we can save her? Fin's mama, I mean."

"Course we—"

"No, I mean, *really*. Because if we do not, Fin will blame himself."

"I know. Which means we have to save her, whether we like it or—" Petrel stopped herself just in time. Her throat felt tight, as if the loneliness was lurking nearby, waiting to pounce. She swallowed. "You know what I wish? I wish the cap'n was here. And Mister Smoke. But they're not, so we have to do this on our own. We *will* save—"

"Shh!" Rain's hand on her arm silenced her. "Is that the man who went to send out word?"

"Aye, it is," whispered Petrel. "And look, Poosk's coming out of his tent to talk to him. Keep your head down."

The two girls watched closely as the blunt-faced man took off his cap and clutched it behind his back. Poosk asked a question, and the man pointed with his chin in all the directions of the compass.

Another question. This time the man hesitated, as if he wanted to give the right answer but couldn't guarantee anything.

All the same, Poosk looked pleased. He shouted to his guards, "Cull! Bartle! Come!"

The blunt-faced man said something about the captive bratlings, and Poosk stared at them in a speculative fashion. Then he shook his head, and said, "I think not. We may need them yet."

The villager's fists clenched around his cap, and he looked as if he was building up courage to say something. But a woman broke away from the small knot of hovering parents and hustled him into the village. After a brief consultation with Bartle, Poosk and Cull set off toward the main road.

The two girls crept back to where Fin and Sharkey were sleeping and woke them with a hand over their mouths.

"That man came back," whispered Petrel, "and Poosk's leaving. Come on!"

She was expecting another long walk, but to her surprise, Poosk and Cull went no more than three-quarters of a mile along the track that led to the Northern Road. There they stopped and concealed themselves in a thicket of trees.

"Another trap?" breathed Sharkey.

"Aye," whispered Petrel. Fin was shivering as if he had a fever, and she quickly added, "Don't know who it's for though. Might be anyone."

But they all knew who Poosk was chasing, and they were all quite certain that *this* trap was for one person and one person only.

We're gunna save her, thought Petrel. *And I'm gunna be glad about it.*

Aloud she said, "Reckon we should split up. Sharkey, Rain, you stay here and keep an eye on Poosk. Me and Fin'll go farther along and watch for his mam."

"But you do not know what she looks like," said Rain.

"Don't matter," said Petrel. "We'll stop every woman we see coming down that track till we get the right one."

Rain and Sharkey made themselves comfortable in an overgrown ditch, and Petrel checked that they couldn't be seen, even if Poosk and Cull came out of their hidey-hole. Then she and Fin circled around the Devouts, crept back toward the track and set up their own hidey-hole in the long grass, closer to the Northern Road.

"More waiting," grumbled Petrel, brushing grass and tiny white flowers out of her hair, and wondering why her nose was suddenly so tickly.

They sat there for most of the day, with Petrel trying not to sneeze in case she was overheard. But they saw no one except the birds and insects that darted in and out of the trees and hovered over the flowers. Once, Petrel went to check on Sharkey and Rain and to make sure Poosk hadn't moved. She returned with the news that the trap was still set, only now it was Cull watching, while Poosk took a nap.

"Reckon your mam'll come soon," she said to Fin as they chewed on seaweed biscuits.

Fin didn't answer. He hadn't said a word since they'd left Sharkey and Rain, and his face had that distant expression that Petrel hated.

Guess he's worried she won't remember him, thought Petrel. *Or that he won't remember her, even when he sees her. If it was my mam walking down that track, I'd be scared stiff.*

It was still an hour or so till sunset when Fin jerked upright—then slumped down again. Someone was coming down the track at last, but it was an old man, not a woman. Petrel didn't know whether to be disappointed or relieved.

The newcomer looked like every other old man in West Norn. He shuffled along as if he were so tired that he could hardly lift his feet. On his shoulder, he carried a ragged bundle.

"Think we should warn him about Poosk?" whispered Petrel.

Fin shook his head.

"I spose you're right," Petrel said reluctantly. "If Poosk questions him, he might give us away. Best to keep quiet."

But a few minutes after the old man had disappeared around the corner, Sharkey came looking for them. Petrel stuck her head out of the grass. "What's up?"

"Did you see that old man?" asked Sharkey. "Poosk and Cull nabbed him and tied him up. Doesn't look as if they were chasing Fin's ma after all."

"But they were. They are!" It was the first time Fin had spoken in hours, and his voice was cracked and harsh.

"Then why'd they take some poor old man?" asked Sharkey.

None of them could answer that.

"Rain's following 'em back to the village," said Sharkey. "She thinks the man must know something about your ma, Fin. Or maybe Poosk's going to use him in some way, like he used the village children."

"We'd best go and see," said Petrel.

But when they caught up with Rain, they discovered that this time there was to be no eavesdropping, no matter how quiet and clever they were. Poosk had dragged the man into his tent, and the other two Devouts stood outside with their arms crossed and their eyes watchful.

Petrel hissed with frustration. "What're we sposed to do now?"

Fin shifted his feet.

"What?" asked Petrel.

"Nothing," said Fin.

Petrel scowled at the distant tent, wishing that Poosk would speak up nice and loud and tell them exactly where Fin's mam was, so they could go and save her.

Fin shifted his feet again.

"*What?*" said Petrel.

"I could use the robe." Fin swallowed. "Initiates are some-times sent out to the villages to carry messages that cannot be taken by pigeon. I could pretend to be one of them."

"No," said Petrel. "They'd recognize you—"

"I do not know them, and I do not think they know me," said Fin. "Poosk was not at the Citadel when I was chosen for the expedition to the ice, and Cull and Bartle do not look at all familiar. And besides, what else can we do? I do not want to find Mama—"

He broke off, but they all knew what he had been going to say. *I do not want to find Mama too late. I do not want to find her dead.*

Petrel gnawed her lip. "What would you say to 'em?"

"I will ask them what they are doing. It is a common enough question between Devouts."

"What about between Devouts and Initiates?" asked

Sharkey. "Seems to me that's different. Maybe *I* should go. I could cover my face so Poosk doesn't recognize me and roll into the village all scared and wanting to help." He put on a ridiculous voice. "D'you need another informer, Masters? What's that you're doing?"

"The Devouts are not fools," Fin said coldly.

Sharkey bristled, just a little. Petrel said, "I'm sorry, Sharkey, but you don't look like one of those poor villagers. You're not starved enough."

"And if Uncle Poosk realized who you were," said Rain, "he would kill you on the spot."

Sharkey shrugged. "He could try."

"Look," said Fin, "we have the robe; it has worked so far, and I am willing to do it. I do not see what the problem is."

"And it is your mama, after all," said Rain. Then she quickly added, "I do not mean you *should* go. But if it was my mama, I would want to go."

Rain had a way of cutting through to the heart of things. Petrel sighed. "Aye, me too."

Before they could change their minds, Fin pulled the robe over his head and settled it around his shoulders. He was breathing in quick shallow gasps, as if he couldn't quite get enough air.

"You sure you want to do this?" asked Petrel. "You don't have to."

"I am sure." With an effort, Fin settled his breathing. His face grew distant and proud, and with an abrupt nod he slipped away from them, back to the last bend before the village. Then he brushed himself off and strode around the corner toward Bale, his head so high and confident that he looked as if he owned the world.

Petrel's heart thumped painfully. It was hard to believe that such a pompous-seeming boy was her best friend. But that pomposity was what would protect him.

At least, she hoped it would.

CHAPTER II

A PROPER CONVERSATION

GWIN'S PAPA LEFT THE MOUNTAIN VILLAGE VERY EARLY IN the morning. Late that same day, another message came up from the flatlands. But this one had traveled by such a complicated, fearful route that it arrived too late to do any good.

"It was a trap?" breathed Gwin, hardly recognizing her own voice. She felt as if someone had punched her.

Beside her, Nat said nothing. Wretched tried to press against his knee, but the boy pushed him away.

"Aye," muttered Hob. "Sorry I am that I even told your pa about that Fetch."

"We have to go after him," said Gwin. "We have to stop him!"

"Reckon he's there by now, girl. If'n they're going to take him, it's probably done already."

"Then—then we'll go and save him. Won't we, Nat?"

Her brother laughed. It wasn't a happy sound; all his anger was back, only now it was laced with scorn. "Of course—why didn't I think of that? The brave Fetcher twins, the girl and her *blind brother*, ride in on Spindle and snatch Papa out of the Devouts' clutches. They won't know what's hit them. Good thinking, Gwinith." And he stalked out of the room, his hand scraping along the wall.

Gwin stared after him, wondering if she was going to be sick. Then she turned back to Hob and said in a small voice, "I'll go by myself."

Hob shook his head. "You're not going anywhere, girl. If'n cow walks off cliff, you don't let calf jump off after her, do you?"

"But—"

"Just 'cos there be trap don't mean your pa's fell into it. And if he has fell, might be he can climb out again. I'll send Bony down road a bit, see what he can learn. 'Oo knows, he might meet up with Fetcher coming back."

Gwin nodded and wiped the tears from her eyes. She didn't trust herself to speak. But at that moment she made a silent promise to her father. *If Bony doesn't find you, Papa, I'm coming after you. No matter what anyone says.*

FIN HAD LIED WHEN HE SAID THAT CULL AND BARTLE DID not look familiar. He remembered them from his days as an Initiate, remembered their casual cruelty and the way they had regarded the villagers of West Norn as less than human.

He did not think *they* would remember *him*. He had been just another Initiate until the night when Brother Thrawn had chosen him for the voyage to the southern ice. And after that, no one but his fellow expeditioners had seen him.

All the same, his stomach clenched with nerves as he marched up to the two guards, and there was a moment when all he wanted to do was turn around and run back to his friends.

Which would not save Mama.

To his relief, the men greeted him with no sign of recognition. And before half a minute had passed he found himself pushed into the tent—which was where he both wanted and did not want to be.

"Brother Poosk," said Bartle. "This boy has been out west carrying messages. Can we use him for anything?"

The tent was high in the middle and low at the edges, with patches of hair where the cowhide had not been scraped completely clean. Poosk was standing in the high part, next to the pole that supported it. The prisoner sat on a wooden box, with his hands and ankles bound so tight that the rope cut into his grubby flesh.

Up close like this, Brother Poosk looked small, mild and not the least bit dangerous. He dismissed Bartle and handed Fin a piece of paper and a quill pen. "Record our conversation please, boy," he said quietly.

Then he turned his attention back to the prisoner and said in that same quiet voice, "I will be honest with you, Fetcher. I was sent to find you and bring you back to the Citadel."

What? thought Fin. *I thought he was sent to find Mama!*

Poosk ran his hand over his chin. "I have been on many such excursions, and until a few months ago I have done my duty without question. But now"—he studied his fingers, which were fine-boned and clean—"now I am questioning that duty, Fetcher."

Fin stared at him. Rain had described her uncle as ruthless and manipulative. But this man seemed so straightforward that it was hard to believe he was the same person.

The prisoner looked as bewildered as Fin felt. "I'm sorry, gracious master, you mistook me for someone else. Me name's Bunt, not Fetcher. Bunt, son of Gall the potter."

"Of course," said Poosk. "Where did you say you came from?"

The man blinked. "Been all over, gracious sir, tryin' to trade me little toys." He nodded toward the unrolled sack on the floor, which held a couple of mangels and two pitiful dolls made out of sticks and rags. "Now I'm on me way 'ome. To Cramby."

"Mm-hm," said Poosk. He glanced at Fin. "Do you know Cramby, boy?"

Fin paused in his writing. "A little, Brother."

"An impoverished village, would you say? A *hungry* village?"

Fin had never been asked such a question in his life, not by one of the Devouts. They preferred words like *lazy* and *stupid*.

"I—yes," said Fin.

Poosk turned back to the prisoner. "Truth from the mouths of children, eh? You would not find one of my brothers answering the question so plainly. They think that as long as they are well fed and comfortable, the world is as it should be. But it is not, is it, Fetcher? And some of us can no longer ignore the problem."

"But I'm *not* Fetcher, sir, beggin' your pardon. I'm just a poor man on 'is way 'ome."

Outside the tent the sun was setting. Brother Poosk lit a lamp, set it on a second box and continued talking, always addressing the prisoner as "Fetcher." But Fin was beginning to wonder if there had been some mistake. Surely the man was who he said he was, and the real Fetcher was off somewhere else.

It seems I have made a mistake too. This has nothing to do with Mama. I will leave as soon as I get the chance.

But the chance did not come. Poosk talked late into the night. At one point he said, "Sometimes I feel as if my life has been small and ignorant. I wish I knew more about our country's past. Will you not tell me one of your stories, Fetcher?"

Fin was tired and hungry. *Brother Poosk is not at all like the Devouts I knew,* he thought sleepily. *Nor does he seem like the man Rain described. Perhaps something has happened to change him.*

"No?" said Poosk. "Well, I cannot blame you for not trusting me. Sometimes I think that the Devouts will have to be overthrown before change can come."

His captive gazed at him with terrified eyes. "If you say so, Master. S'not my place to judge."

Brother Poosk nodded sympathetically. "You are right. It is *not* your place to judge." He slipped his hand into his pocket, and suddenly all the niceness vanished, and his next words were harsh and triumphant. "But neither is it your place to have something like *this* hidden in your baggage!" And he thrust a round silver object, no bigger than a baby's fist, in front of the startled prisoner.

89

The man's eyes widened, and he began to wail. "Oooooh, I knew it, I knew it'd get me into trouble! I should've 'anded it in straightaway soon as the man give it to me in trade, but 'twas so pretty, I'd never *seen* anythin' so pretty, and I thought, I'll just keep it till I get 'ome and show me wife, and *then* I'll 'and it in. Is it important, Master? Little silver stone like that? Is it somethin' you wanted?"

This was clearly not the reaction Poosk had hoped for. He seized the man by the throat and snarled, "Tell me the truth or I will kill you on the spot. You *are* a Fetcher. I know you are."

The man trembled. "If you say so, Master. You know best. But please don't kill me! What would me wife do without me?"

With a curse, Poosk flung the man down. Then he seized the lamp, jerked his head at Fin and strode outside.

As soon as they were well away from the tent, he said, "What does it matter if he will not confess? I could haul him back to the Citadel anyway, for execution. And what a coup that would be, to hang a Fetcher. They are as rare as hen's teeth these days. Eh, boy?"

Fin couldn't answer; he was still reeling from the sudden change in tone. *I believed him. Despite all those warnings from Sharkey and Rain, I thought he was sincere. But the whole thing was a performance.*

Poosk held up the round object, so the lamplight fell upon it. "Do you know what this is?"

"N-no, Brother."

"A *timepiece!*"

Fin shuffled his wits into some sort of order and said, in

what he hoped were shocked tones, "From before the Great Cleansing, Brother?"

"Indeed," said Poosk. He pressed something, and the lid of the timepiece flew open.

There were a number of ancient clocks on the *Oyster*, so the glassed circle and the little hands and numbers were nothing new to Fin. There were smaller circles, however, that he did not understand, and he longed for a closer look. But in the end, he did not need one.

"It is in perfect order," murmured Poosk. "Look, this tells us the hour of the day, and this, I believe, gives the stages of the moon. I am not sure about *this* one, but still, what a useful device."

Fin watched him, more puzzled than ever. As a Devout, Poosk should have loathed the timepiece as much as he loathed the Fetchers. He should have smashed it to pieces so it would not contaminate him. He certainly should not have studied it with such gloating interest.

Except Poosk was the one who ordered the use of the spotter balloons. And the catapults and bombs. He pretended it was Brother Thrawn giving the orders, which bothered me when I heard about it. The Brother Thrawn I knew would never have allowed such things, not for any reason.

Which raised some interesting questions about Brother Poosk.

"Will it steal our souls, Brother?" whispered Fin, still playing his part.

Poosk chuckled. "I doubt it, boy." And he snapped the lid

shut, put the timepiece in his pocket and raised a hand for Bartle and Cull, who came hurrying over.

By the tree stump, one of the captive children cried out in her sleep, and her parents, dozing nearby, sat up with a jerk.

"Go back to the main road, Brother Bartle," said Poosk, "and wake up a few peasants. Find someone who saw the 'old man' pass earlier. I want to know where he came from."

Bartle nodded and went to find a lamp.

To Cull, Poosk said, "We will let the Fetcher stew for the rest of the night. Tie him to a tree and make him as uncomfortable as possible. In the morning, he will crack."

BUT WHEN MORNING CAME, THE PRISONER SEEMED MORE frightened and confused than ever, and Brother Poosk could hardly get a sensible word out of him.

It was not long before the Devout said, "Well, you have brought it on yourself, Fetcher. I did not want to do it, but I cannot stand another day of this I-am-just-a-simple-peasant nonsense."

He turned to Fin. "Bring the smallest child to me. And a sharp knife. Let us see if he will cling to his ridiculous story when the life of a village brat is at stake."

The prisoner did not seem to understand what Poosk had said. But Fin felt as if the ground had been ripped out from under his feet.

I will sneak away, he thought as he left the tent. *I will go back to Petrel and the others and tell them that Poosk has forgotten about Mama and become obsessed with Fetchers. Then whatever happens here will be nothing to do with me.*

But that was a weaselly way of thinking, and he knew it.

I will hide the smallest child so Poosk cannot find her.

Except that was no good either. If the smallest child disappeared, Poosk would simply take another. And even with the best of intentions, Fin could not hide *all* the children.

So in the end he did as instructed, knowing that although his friends were watching, they might as well have been miles away and could not help him.

The children's parents were still hovering. When they heard Fin ask Brother Cull for the smallest child and a sharp knife, one of the women set up a dreadful keening and fell to her knees, rocking back and forth, while her husband begged Fin not to hurt his baby.

Their distress tore at Fin's heart, but he did his best to look as if it meant nothing to him. He unfastened a girl no more than three years old and marched her away. She sobbed and twisted her neck to keep sight of her parents.

Fin's hands tightened on the girl's shoulders. He wanted to whisper, "Do not be afraid. I will not let him hurt you."

But I cannot make any such promise.

So he kept silent, wondering if he was being wise or just cowardly.

As soon as he entered the tent, Brother Poosk took the knife from him and dragged the girl in front of the prisoner, with the blade at her throat.

"Now," he said, his eyes sparkling. "Now we can have a proper conversation, can we not? Where did you say you came from, Fetcher?"

Under the dirt, the prisoner's face was as pale as parchment, and his throat convulsed. But all he said was, "Gracious sir, please don't harm the littlie. I've told you everythin' I know. I come from Cramby, and me wife's waitin' for me."

Poosk smiled and pressed the knife harder. The girl whimpered. A trickle of blood ran down her neck.

Fin felt sick to his stomach. *He will kill her. I cannot stand here and watch it. I must do something.*

He knew that any attempt at persuasion was hopeless. Which meant he had to either distract Brother Poosk somehow or take the knife from him. He braced himself, knowing that this would probably be the end of him.

But before he could move, the prisoner heaved an enormous sigh and said, in a voice completely different from his previous one, "You can let her go. I'm the one you're looking for. I'm the Fetcher."

CHAPTER 12

A SMALL, ROUGH VOICE . . .

On the day when Papa was due back from the Fetch, Gwin sat in the mouth of the cave room waiting for him. She hadn't slept since the second message arrived, and her eyes were gritty with tiredness.

Hilde and Gert kept her company all day, with Gert chatting about nothing in particular. But as night fell, the younger girl said, "No sign of your pa. I expect he's fell into that trap."

"Might not have," Hilde said. "Maybe he stopped off to snare a rabbit. He could be just a couple of bends away."

"Mm," said Gert, unconvinced. "Come and get supper, afore someone else eats it."

Gwin didn't sleep that night either.

By morning, Papa still wasn't back, and neither was Bony. Gwin couldn't bear the thought of sitting in the cave again, watching the track. Something inside her felt like a river in flood, backed up for miles and threatening to burst its banks.

If she had to sit and wait for another day, she thought she might die.

I'm going after Papa.

She wanted to set off straightaway, before Hob could stop her. But she couldn't go without checking on Nat.

She found him in the stone corral, practicing his leaps with such ferocious concentration that he didn't hear her approach. The mountain cows were bunched in the middle of the corral, and Wretched was asleep in one of the mangers. Gwin stopped just inside the entrance and watched her brother.

As Spindle cantered around the circle, his hooves kicking up mud, Nat jumped on and off the old ox's back. It was a sight that should have been as familiar to Gwin as her own hair beads.

But there was something wrong with Nat's timing. It was too fast, too reckless. When he jumped, it was too high. When he threw himself at the ground, it was too hard, as if he was daring it to hurt him.

"Nat, stop!" cried Gwin.

He heard that, all right. With a nudge of his toe he brought Spindle to a halt, and sat there with his chest heaving and his face defiant.

Gwin felt a burst of uncharacteristic anger. "How's it going to make things better if you hurt yourself? How's that going to help Papa?"

Nat didn't answer. But a small, rough voice somewhere near Gwin's feet said, "You got a minute, shipmate?"

Gwin almost jumped out of her skin. She looked down—and there was the rat with the silver eyes, peering up at her.

But it couldn't have been the rat who'd spoken. *It's some sort of trick*, she thought, and she glowered at the walls of the corral. "Gert, is that you? Stop playing tricks. Gert?"

"Nah, it's me, shipmate," said the rat.

Wretched poked his head over the side of the manger and wagged his tail. Nat sat very still. "Who's that? Who're you talking to, Gwin?"

She couldn't answer him. The words would not form in her mouth. She tried to edge away from the rat, but it trotted at her side like a miniature dog. "Shoo!" she whispered.

"Who're you talking to?" Nat said again.

Gwin managed to croak, "No one," then immediately wished she hadn't because the rat said, "Now that's a straight-out lie, shipmate. Name's Mister Smoke, though some call me Adm'ral. Take your pick. I've got a favor to ask."

"Mister . . . Smoke?" said Nat, turning his head first one way, then the other.

"Don't talk to it," hissed Gwin.

"Why not?"

"Because—because it's a rat. I mean, it's *the* rat. The one that brought us here."

Nat snorted in disbelief.

Gwin said, "I know, Nat. But it *is*!"

"Well spotted, shipmate," said the rat. "Now about this favor . . ."

Gwin shook her head. None of this made sense, but it didn't matter. All that mattered was Papa. Talking rat or not, she had to go and find him.

She headed for the entrance, but the rat got there first. "Where're you goin', shipmate?"

"Nowhere."

"Then you won't mind doin' this favor," said the rat.

"No!" Gwin tried to walk around him, but he was always there, right where she wanted to tread.

Nat slid down from Spindle's back and made his way carefully across the corral. "A rat?" he said, still not believing it.

"That's me, shipmate. *Rattus rattus.* Sort of."

Gwin glared down at the creature. "Get out of my way. I have to go."

"Where?" This time it was her brother who asked.

She didn't answer.

"You're going after Papa?"

"Maybe."

"Not without me," said Nat.

Now Gwin glared at *him*. "Day before yesterday you said I was stupid."

"I didn't!"

"That's what you meant." She imitated him. "'Good thinking, Gwinith.'"

Nat flushed. "I just—"

"Thing is, shipmate," interrupted the rat, "I've been trying to get you by yourself for the last few days, and this is the closest I've come. You can argue all you like as long as it's on the move.

This way." And he set off out of the corral, clearly expecting Gwin to follow.

When she didn't, he looked over his shoulder. "What's the problem? Busted gaskets? Rusty valves?"

"I'm not going with you. I'm going after Papa."

"So am I," said Nat.

"Does Hob know?" asked the rat, in a conversational tone. "No? Thought not. Would 'e stop you?"

Gwin felt as if she had stumbled into a nightmare. First Papa, now this. She didn't want to believe that a rat could talk, much less bargain. But there was the evidence, right in front of her.

And Hob *would* stop her, without a doubt. Which meant . . .

"What is it?" she demanded. "This—this favor."

"Easier to show you, shipmate."

"How long will it take?"

"Not long." The rat cocked its head. "So, you're comin'?"

"I haven't got much choice, have I?"

"Anchors aweigh, then, shipmate," said the rat, at which Wretched began to scramble out of the manger.

"Stay, Wretched," said Nat. "Stay there."

The rat led the way out of the corral and onto the mountain track. There he turned north, but not for long. Before they could run into Hob or anyone else, he climbed off the track and onto a side path that looked as if it hadn't been used in years.

Nat hesitated, then put his hand on his sister's shoulder in an unspoken truce.

Gwin guided him over the rough patches, whispering directions. "First bit's steepish. Then there are five steps. Mind your head, there's an overhang."

The rat peered over its shoulder at them, but said nothing.

The path twisted and turned, climbed and fell. With every step Gwin took, her heart tried to drag her back the other way. *Papa, we're coming for you. Soon . . .*

"How much farther?" she called.

The rat waited for them to catch up. "We'll be there by six bells of the mornin' watch."

"What's that mean?" asked Nat.

"It means not long." And the rat set off again.

At last they came to a place where the rock face was pitted with caves. Some of them were no deeper than a foot or two; others disappeared into the darkness.

The rat waved a paw at one of the darkest holes, as if inviting them to enter. "There you go, shipmates."

"What's in there?" asked Gwin.

"Nothin' that'll 'urt you."

Gwin swallowed. "You go first."

The rat led them into a cave very similar to the one where the Fetchers had spent their first night in the mountains. Except this was even more derelict. Nat touched the worn walls. "It's old."

"Been deserted for a century or so, shipmate, which makes it a good place for 'idin' things that don't wanna be found. Foller me." And the rat headed for a gap in the back wall.

It was dark on the other side of the gap, and for once it was

Gwin who was at a disadvantage. She and her brother swapped places, and Nat followed the sound of the rat's paws, his fingers trailing along the rock wall.

Through one cave, ducking their heads at the far side. Down a short tunnel, with rubble underfoot. Into another cave.

"Hang on a bit," said the rat from somewhere in front of them. "Don't want you trippin' over anythin' important."

Gwin heard a scratching sound and a lamp flickered to life. Shadows sprang up all around her.

"There we are, shipmates," said Mister Smoke. And with an oddly shy gesture, he pointed to the far corner of the cave.

Gwin picked up the lamp, took three steps forward—and stopped. "There's someone lying on the ground," she whispered. "A boy."

"No," said Nat. "I'd be able to hear him breathing."

"Look closer, shipmate," said the rat.

Gwin raised the lamp and crept forward until she was almost touching the boy's feet.

It was then that she saw his face. One side of it was finely formed and beautiful. The other side was crushed, as if something had fallen on it.

But it was neither the beauty nor the injury that made Gwin gasp and almost drop the lamp.

"Nat," she breathed, and for a moment all thought of Papa vanished. "He's made of silver!"

CHAPTER 13

THE SINGER AND THE SONG

"*SILVER?*" NAT SHUFFLED FORWARD UNTIL HIS TOE NUDGED the boy's leg, then he knelt down and ran his hands over the still body. Gwin tried to breathe slowly and sensibly, but it wasn't easy.

Nat's fingers found the boy's face. "Who is he? *What* is he?"

"'E's the cap'n," said Mister Smoke. "'E's a mechanical boy from the old times."

"A mechanical boy?" Gwin's eyes widened, and a thrill of excitement ran through her. This was like Papa's heirloom, only a hundred times better. This was—

She stopped. *Papa.*

"Cap'n's clever as can be," said the rat, "only 'e got smashed by a rock, and now all that cleverness is tucked away inside somewhere. I've mended what I can, with the materials I've got, and 'e's woke up twice. But 'e won't stay woke, which is why—"

Gwin interrupted him. "We can't help you, Mister Smoke.

We don't know anything about mechanicals." She turned to Nat. "We have to go after Papa."

Her brother touched the silver boy's face one last time and stood up.

But Mister Smoke said, "It's not mechanics I want you for, shipmate. It's somethin' else. Won't cost you more than another minute or two. Then you can go." He winked up at Gwin. "With no one the wiser."

Gwin hesitated. That wink suggested there was still time for the rat to tell Hob what she was planning. A delay of a minute or two might be worth it, to get away unnoticed. "What is it?"

Mister Smoke gestured toward the still figure. "I want you to sing to 'im."

It was so unexpected that Gwin almost choked. "You dragged Nat and me here to *sing*? When Papa is—"

"Not exactly," said the rat. "I can see that your brother's a bratlin' of taste and distinction. But you're the one that counts. I want *you* to sing."

"Why?"

"'Cos," said the rat.

Gwin pulled her rabbit-skin jacket more tightly around her. One song couldn't do any harm. "I'll sing about Ariel—"

"Nah," said Mister Smoke. "Give us the one about the tree."

"You mean the Hope song?"

"Aye, that's it."

"And then we can go? You won't try and stop us? You won't tell Hob what we're doing?"

"You 'ave my word, shipmate."

Gwin stared at her bare toes for a moment. Then she closed her eyes, cleared her throat and began to sing.

"How tall the tree,
The first to fall . . ."

Her voice might not be as beautiful as Mama's, but it was just as strong. It filled the little room and drifted out to the cavelets on every side.

"How wise to flee
The worst of all . . ."

She opened her eyes to draw breath—just in time to see the mechanical boy open *his* eyes.

"The song," he said.

His voice was sweet and true, and it made the words dry up in Gwin's mouth. Nat whispered, "Keep going!"

So she did.

"But hear the song
The singer gives.
The trunk is gone,
The root still lives."

The silver face didn't move, but the mechanical boy seemed to smile. "The Singer," he said. Then he closed his eyes—and all that sense of life and brightness was gone.

Mister Smoke patted the boy's forehead. "Cap'n? Cap'n?"

There was no response.

A small tool appeared in the rat's paw. "I'm gunna 'ave to take 'im apart again, though I don't know what good it'll do. Now if I 'ad a Baniski coil, that'd be a different matter." And he began to turn something on the silver boy's neck.

"What did he mean, *the song* and *the singer*?" asked Nat.

"Before 'e was 'urt," said Mister Smoke, without looking up, "'e was searchin' for a coupla things that'd 'elp us change the world. 'E found the Song a while back, but that wasn't enough; 'e 'ad to find the Singer too. Now 'e's done it."

"You mean *Gwin* is the Singer? She's going to change the *world*?"

"That's the idea, shipmate."

"*Me?*" Gwin couldn't believe she'd heard him right. She was barely managing to hold her own family together—in fact, she wasn't holding it together, because Papa was missing and she had no idea how she and Nat were going to save him. And now someone expected her to change the world? She would have laughed if she wasn't so horrified.

"This captain of yours has made a mistake," she said.

"Don't think so, shipmate." The rat raised a curved piece of silver, exposing a tangle of shiny string.

"Of course he has. Look at him, he's broken! He—he didn't know what he was saying."

"Broken or not, shipmate, Cap'n always knows what 'e's sayin'."

The lamp swung in Gwin's hand. The shadows danced grotesquely. *We should never have come here.* "Nat, we must go. Now!"

"Wait," said her brother. His face wore that reckless gleam again, as if he wanted to throw himself against something and dare it to break him. "If you're going to change the w—"

"I'm not. Come away, this is nothing to do with us."

"But don't you want to know how—"

"*No!* Come on! Or I'll go after Papa by myself."

Nat didn't move straightaway. And when he did, his face was closed tight against her.

For once, Gwin didn't care. She just wanted him out of that cave. She wanted them *both* out of there. The mountains no longer felt safe.

If anything, they were even more dangerous than the lowlands.

CHAPTER 14

HE'S BEEN TOOK

THE TWO CHILDREN WALKED BACK TOWARD THE MOUNTAIN village with Nat's hand stiff and angry on Gwin's shoulder.

I don't care, she thought. *It's all nonsense. Or maybe the mechanical boy mistook me for someone else. Either way, I don't want anything to do with it.*

When Nat spoke, however, it was nothing to do with the mechanical boy. "Something's happening farther down the track. People. Lots of them."

Gwin quickened her pace. As they rounded the last bend, Wretched came running to meet them, his tail wagging furiously even as he whimpered.

Hilde, Hob and a couple of others were hurrying up the track too, their faces grave. Behind them, the mountain people were pouring out of their little village, like ants from a nest. They carried bundles on their backs, with babies tied to some, and saucepans, ladles, pickaxes and spades to others. The younger children ran ahead with their own bundles, while the older ones drove cows or carried baskets full of pigeons.

"What is it?" said Gwin as soon as she reached Hilde and Hob. "What's happening?"

Hob glanced at the man beside him—and Gwin realized it was Bony.

Her stomach lurched. "Did you find Papa?"

Bony shook his head sorrowfully. "He's been took."

Gwin had been expecting this news for the past two days, but still it hit her like a hammer blow. "No," she whispered.

"Devouts catched him before he even got to Bale," continued Bony. "He dint admit to being Fetcher, not till they threatened to kill young 'uns, and even then he dint tell 'em 'bout us. But someone saw him coming off mountain road and spilled to Devouts. Now they's coming here. Three grown men and a boy."

"So we's clearing out," added Hob unnecessarily.

"The Devouts are coming here?" Nat's fingers bruised Gwin's shoulder. "Then you can't go. You must stay and—and frighten them, like you did us. Perhaps they'll run and leave Papa behind."

"And if they don't run," said Gwin, "then you can fight them."

Before Hob could reply, the crowd reached them, and Gwin found herself separated from Nat and Hilde by a sea of clanking, chattering people. A ladle swatted her across the cheek. A baby tried to grab her hair beads. Men and women nodded as they passed and shouted over the noise, "Sorry 'bout your pa, Fetcher girl!"

Gwin yelled at Hob over the ruckus, "Why are you all leaving? You can fight! There's only four of them."

Hob shook his shaggy head. "If we fight and don't kill 'em, they know we here. If we *do* kill 'em, other Devouts'll come looking, to see where they got to. It's not worth it." He raised his voice. "I said, '*Not worth it!*'"

"It *is* worth it," cried Gwin. "It's *Papa!*"

More cows came along, and a horde of children. Before Gwin could be swept away, Hob picked her up and set her down next to Nat and Hilde in a sheltered spot by the cliff face.

Then he bent over and said in her ear, "Three hundred years we been doing like this. Strangers come, maybe we hide, maybe we frighten 'em. But Devouts be different. Always go deep into mountains when Devouts come, so they can't find we. Our grandmas and grandpas did so, and our great-grandmas and grandpas, and all the great-greats, right back to beginning. It's kept us free, it has. Not gunna do different now, not even for Fetcher."

"But—but you said you could smell change coming," began Gwin. "At the Bring Back, you said there were signs."

"It's no use," said Hilde. "I've tried everything. They're leaving, and we can't stop them."

"You three best come with we," said Hob. "Bring liddle dog and ox too. Hide till Devouts give up and go away."

"No," said Nat and Gwin together.

Hob eyed them. "And if Devouts take you too? What then? You gunna babble 'bout mountain folk? Hand over our lives in exchange for yours?"

Nat shook his head. "We're Fetchers. We don't betray people."

Hob stared at him for a long moment, considering. Then he nodded and turned to Hilde. "How 'bout you? Come or stay?"

Hilde tried to smile but bit her lip instead. "I—I can't leave them here alone. That'd be poor payment for them saving me from the Masters. I'll stay too."

"Well then," said Hob. "Wish you luck, and lots of it." He glanced up. "Here come your ox. You go anywhere, take him with you. Corral's all closed up and hid."

He touched his finger to his forehead, as if that was the end of it. But then he looked at Gwin and hesitated. He and Bony whispered to each other. The smaller man hurried away.

Gwin couldn't think of a thing to say. Spindle trudged up the road toward them, pulling their cart. The mountain people parted on either side of him, then surged back together. The old ox stopped right in front of Nat and pushed his nose into the boy's chest.

Nat didn't move. Neither did Gwin, who was trying very hard not to panic. She hadn't been able to save Mama. What if she couldn't save Papa either?

Bony came striding back with a pigeon in his hands. "This here bird," he said, "ain't one of ours. We found her a while back, and she settled in nicely, so we kept her. She'll fly to we, I reckon, if you loose her. She'm clever liddle thing."

He addressed the pigeon, saying, "You stay close to Fetchers. Hear me? Only fly back to us if'n they send you. Go on, now."

The bird hopped onto Gwin's fist. She stared at it. "But what—"

"P'raps signs are right," said Hob. From his pocket, he produced a scrap of cloth, a broken stylus and a stub of ocher. He handed them to Gwin. "P'raps there *do* be change comin'. If that be true, if you see other folk ready and willin' to fight, and change roarin' down like avalanche, then you loose bird, with message tied to leg. Not sayin' for sure we'll come. Not sayin' we won't."

And with that, he and Bony hurried away with the rest of the crowd.

The last of the mountain people trickled past Gwin, brushing the road with straw as they went, so as to leave no sign of their passing. Slowly the noise lessened, until nothing remained but the shrike thrushes and the wind.

And then it was just Gwin, Nat, Hilde and the pigeon, with Wretched groveling at their feet, and Spindle in his harness.

And somewhere below them, coming up the mountain track, the Devouts. And Papa.

Dolph had hoped that the Devouts, used to high living and regular meals, would cave in straightaway. But two days had passed since the rats had emptied the Citadel's storerooms and larders, and there was no sign of surrender.

"Two days is nothing," said Krill, standing by her shoulder as she watched the gates. "You know that, lass. And besides, they've still got water. Folk can go a long time without food if there's water."

"I should've asked Missus Slink to do something about the well," Dolph said miserably. "I didn't think of it."

Her moment of triumph had passed all too quickly. Krill was pleased with her because he could spend his time doing what he loved—feeding hungry folk. And the town bratlings had taken to addressing Dolph very respectfully as "Witch," and bringing her hand-polished stones and plaited reeds, which were the only gifts their grateful families could afford.

But Admiral Deeps, after that first moment of astonishment, had grown less and less impressed.

"Maybe there were other storerooms that Missus Slink missed," said Dolph. "They're probably sitting in there laughing at us as they eat their breakfast."

Krill looked at her shrewdly. "The adm'ral been having a go at you, has she?"

"She said this morning if I'd only talked to her, instead of going off on my own, she'd have made sure of the well and a dozen other things I didn't think of. Except I couldn't talk to her, Krill, she wouldn't listen to me. And I wasn't trying to escape my duty or get glory for myself; I really wasn't. I know she and Hump are in charge, and that's fine. I just wanted to speed things up a bit."

"Hmph." Krill folded his arms across his chest. "I've got a lot of respect for the adm'ral, but Sunker ways are different, that's for sure. It was a clever thing you did, lass, and don't let anyone tell you different."

"Not clever enough," said Dolph.

"We don't know that yet, do we? Wait and see, lass. Wait and see."

CHAPTER 15

THE DREADFUL IDEA

THE DAY WAS MILD, BUT GWIN WAS SO COLD THAT SHE COULD hardly feel her hands. She kept trying to make some sort of sensible plan for rescuing Papa, but all Nat would talk about were wild strategies that would only have worked if the three of them were each ten feet tall and as strong as a team of oxen.

Gwin shook her head as he outlined yet another impossible scheme. "They'll be *armed*, Nat. They'll have cudgels. Maybe bows and arrows—"

"We've got a skinning knife," said her brother. "I'll use it if you won't."

"But—" began Hilde.

"But we're not fighters," Gwin said quickly, just in case Hilde had been about to say something about Nat's blindness. That was what was driving him, and any mention of it would only make him worse.

She wished Hilde had gone with Hob. Gwin didn't want

to have to think about anyone else, not right now. Papa was the only one who mattered.

"We can't save him by force," she said. "We have to do something clever."

She'd known this from the beginning, but it didn't help. In the old stories, the villains always had some sort of weakness, and the heroes used it to defeat them. But what weakness did the Devouts have? They were armed, strong and brutal. If it had been anyone except Papa in their clutches, Gwin would have . . .

Beside her, Nat tensed. "They're coming. I can hear them!"

It was like a bucket of cold water thrown in Gwin's face. She shook herself and said, "Then we must hide."

"The cave," said Hilde. "The one where we spent the first night."

Gwin shook her head. "We have to hide Spindle and the cart too. Maybe up the track further? How far will the Devouts go?"

None of them knew the answer to that, any more than they knew why the Devouts were coming this way instead of heading straight back to the Citadel with their prisoner.

"Nat," said Gwin, "will you and Hilde take Spindle up the track? A mile or so?"

She was afraid her brother would say no. But although the shadow of recklessness still flickered across his face, he nodded.

"You'd better take Wretched too," she said. "And the pigeon. I'll hide somewhere near here. Perhaps I'll spot a weakness. Then we can . . ." Her voice trailed off.

Then we can what? Sneak up on them? Bargain with them?

Hilde pushed her pale hair behind her ear. "Why don't you come up the track with us? We can keep ahead of the Masters. They'll have to give up sometime."

"Then we'll learn nothing," said Gwin. "It's not enough to stay ahead of them. We must save Papa."

"Yes, of course," said Hilde, "but—"

"Go," said Gwin. "Just go."

Nat drove Spindle up the track, with Gwin sweeping away the hoof and wheel marks. When they reached the path that led to the mechanical boy, she gave the broom to Hilde, saying, "Don't leave a single mark."

She kissed Spindle's ears and Wretched's nose. Then, as the oxcart rolled away, with the pigeon perched on Hilde's shoulder, she scrambled up the steepish section of the path and found a spot where she was hidden from below.

Countless heartbeats later, she heard the distinctive sound of stones crunching under someone's boot.

Gwin had never worn boots in her life, and neither had anyone she knew. Boots were a luxury that only the Devouts could afford; they were a sign of wealth and viciousness. Gwin trusted bare feet in a way that she would never trust boots.

The crunching sound grew louder. She crept forward and peered over the edge of the path.

It was all she could do not to cry out when she saw Papa. His face was bruised, his hands were bound behind his back, and he was gagged with a length of filthy cloth. A rope circled his neck so he couldn't escape, and he was surrounded by three

Devouts, an Initiate who looked no older than Nat, and a heavily laden mule.

One of the Devouts was small and ordinary, but the other two were almost as big as Hob. They strode along with cudgels in their hands and Papa squeezed between them, as if they and their boots owned the world.

Gwin shrank back. There was no weakness there. If she tried to sneak up on such men, they'd catch her. If she tried to bargain, they'd surely cheat her. Besides, what did she have to bargain with?

It was then that she had the dreadful idea.

She knew right from the start that she shouldn't do it. She tried to think of another plan, but her mind was blank. She wasn't strong enough to beat the Devouts in any sort of struggle. All she had was her desperate need to save Papa. Because if she didn't get him away from these men, they would . . . he would be . . .

Gwin couldn't say the words, even to herself.

She waited until the small party was well past, then she scrambled quickly and silently down the path and trotted after them. She had almost halved the distance when the man leading the mule heard her and spun around. Gwin stopped, careful not to get too close. The big man said something, and they all turned, dragging Papa with them.

Gwin saw her father's eyes widen with shock. She looked away, knowing that he wouldn't approve of what she was about to do. But she had nothing else.

"Sirs!" she cried. Despite her anguish, her voice was strong, and she stood the way Papa had taught her, as if she too owned the world. "I wish to make a bargain with you. For your prisoner's release."

The Devouts laughed. At least, the two big men did. The Initiate's face was unreadable.

But the small man tipped his head to one side like a bird and studied her. He glanced at Papa, then back at Gwin, as if he could see the likeness.

"A bargain?" he said mildly. "For your father's release? This *is* your father, is it not?" He took a step forward, but when Gwin retreated, he gestured apologetically and stopped. "What are you offering?"

"A—a relic. Something from before the Great Cleansing."

"We have any number of relics," said the man. "We are up to our ears in them. Why would we want another?"

Gwin had thought she'd be able to say it straight out, to make that dreadful bargain and be done with it. But she couldn't.

She knew it was wrong; that was the trouble. She could see the dismay in Papa's eyes, even though he didn't know what she was talking about. She could hear Nat saying, *We're Fetchers. We don't betray people.*

She swallowed. "Because it's like no other relic you've ever seen."

To her dismay, the small man chuckled. "Ah, children." He nudged Papa with his elbow, as if they were the best of friends. "They find a scrap of rusty iron in the fields and think it will pay a Fetcher's ransom. Such innocence!"

Still chuckling, he turned on his heel and continued up the

track. One of the big men jerked at Papa's rope. The other smacked the mule on the rump to get it moving. Only the Initiate continued to stare at Gwin, with an odd expression on his face. But when Gwin caught his eye, he spun around to follow the men and the mule.

Gwin was left standing there, feeling like a fool. "But it's not a scrap of rusty iron," she whispered.

She thought of Papa's bruises. She thought of what would happen to him if the Devouts took him back to the Citadel, and a shaft of panic shot through her.

Before she could change her mind, she shouted, "It's a mechanical boy!"

The words seemed to bounce off the cliff like pebbles. The Initiate spun around first, his face a mask of horror, but the other three were no more than a whisker behind him.

"A mechanical boy?" The small man's eyes glittered. "How . . . interesting."

"Then we have a bargain?"

"If you are telling the truth," said the Devout. He nudged Papa again. "That is quite a daughter you have, Fetcher. Not as foolish as I thought, eh? No, indeed, she is a girl to be reckoned with."

To Gwin he said, "Perhaps I should introduce myself. Brother Poosk, at your service." He made a little bow and cocked an eyebrow.

Gwin didn't want to give him her name. But she didn't want him to know how frightened she was either, so she stood tall and said, "Gwinith."

"Very well, Gwinith. Tell me, is this mechanical boy whole or broken?"

"He—it's broken."

"In that case, yes, we have a bargain. You give us the mechanical boy, and we will free your father. How does that sound?"

Papa was trying to speak, but the gag stopped him.

"No," said Gwin. "The other way around. You free my father, and *then* I'll give you the mechanical boy."

Brother Poosk threw back his head and laughed. "Fetcher, what a daughter you have. She does not trust me, and who can blame her? The trouble is—and I am sure you will understand me, Fetcher—*I* do not trust *her*. So who will give way, hm?"

"Not me," Gwin said quickly.

Brother Poosk sighed. "A stubborn bunch, you Fetchers. Ah well, it would have been nice to have had a mechanical boy to take back to the Citadel. I would have made the exchange gladly, once the creature was in our custody, but if we cannot have it, we cannot. At least we will not go back empty-handed. And of course, there is the other matter. Come, brothers."

Gwin stood dumbfounded. She'd been sure that the mere mention of the mechanical boy would be enough to seal the bargain. But now Brother Poosk was walking away from her, up the mountain track.

He's bluffing. He's waiting to see if I'll give in. And I won't!

Except then she heard Poosk say, "You know, I do not really want to feed an extra person all the way back to the Citadel.

Brother Thrawn will be just as happy with the Fetcher's corpse as with his living body. What do you think, Brothers? We have plenty of rope for a noose. Shall we look for a tree?"

Gwin put her hand over her mouth, to stop herself from crying out. The Devouts were almost out of sight around the next bend, and she still didn't know why they had come this way, or what the *other matter* was. But she no longer cared. All she could think of was a tree. And a noose. And Papa.

The air in her lungs felt like fire. "Forgive me, rat," she whispered. Then she ran after the Devouts, shouting, "I'll take you to him! I'll take you to the mechanical boy. And *then* you'll free Papa."

FIN WANTED TO STOP THE GIRL BEFORE SHE COULD DO any more damage. But he could not get near her. None of them could. She led them along the narrow path, sure-footed and nimble, with a good distance between her and Brother Poosk.

Behind Poosk came Fin, then Bartle with the Fetcher. Cull had stayed behind on the main track to look after the mule.

Fin wished he knew how far away Petrel, Rain and Sharkey were. He was sure they would have followed him from Bale, and if they were close enough, they might be able to do something. Except he had no way of getting word to them, not without arousing Brother Poosk's suspicions.

And what about Mister Smoke? He must be here somewhere—he would not leave the captain unprotected. But what could a mechanical rat and an ex-Initiate do against Brother Poosk and his guards?

The path narrowed further. *Make her slip*, thought Fin. *Make her twist her ankle so she cannot go on.*

But the Fetcher girl did not even stumble. Instead, she stopped at the entrance to a cave and held up her hand. Her face was bloodless, but Fin felt no sympathy for her. The captain was the hope of humanity. Without the knowledge he carried, the world would be stuck in ignorance for generations to come.

Even more important, he was Fin's friend.

"He's in here," said the girl, and she ducked her head and disappeared into the cave.

Fin stepped forward, knowing he must do something before it was too late. "Brother Poosk, we do not know what is in there. It could be a trap. Will you let me go first, so I can take the risk instead of you?"

Poosk smiled gently, as if there were nothing more interesting in that cave than another pile of rocks. It was an act, of course. Beneath that nonchalance, he must be quivering with excitement. "Do you value my life so much, Initiate?" he asked. "Hmm?"

"Yes, Brother, I—"

"Or is it that you want the glory of catching the demon for yourself?"

"No, Brother, I just—"

"Do not worry on my account. If there is one thing I know,

it is human nature. And the girl will not trick us." Poosk's smile broadened. "No. *She* will not trick *us.*"

He ducked his head to enter the hole. "Bring the prisoner in. Let him see what his daughter has found."

The girl was waiting for them with a lantern in her hand. "This way," she said. And she led them into the darkness.

CHAPTER 16

BETRAYAL

THE MECHANICAL BOY WAS LYING JUST AS GWIN HAD LEFT him. She glanced at him once, then looked away.

It's not as if he's a real person, she told herself, trying very hard not to think about that sweet, true voice.

To Brother Poosk she said, "That's my side of the bargain. Now you must keep yours."

She might as well not have spoken.

"Look how still it lies," whispered Poosk, tiptoeing toward the mechanical boy. "There is no power left in it, none at all. It is defeated."

"We should burn it," said Bartle, staying well back. "It is a demon, and we should burn it on the spot."

Poosk nodded. "Perhaps you are right, Brother Bartle. Mm-hm. Perhaps you are. Though it seems a pity."

It was then that the Initiate spoke up. His eyes were white in the lamplight, and his fists were clenched so tight that they looked as if they might never open again. But his voice was calm. "The safest thing is not always the one that brings the greatest reward."

Poosk turned to him. "What was that?"

The Initiate repeated his words.

"Mm," said Poosk. "So what would you do with the demon if you were in my shoes?"

A muscle in the Initiate's cheek twitched. "I would take hi—I would take it back to the Citadel, Brother. Burn it here, and there will be nothing to show for what you have done. No one will believe your story; why would they? But take it back and burn it there, and they will fall at your feet with gratitude."

Bartle spluttered in horror. "It—it is not worth the risk! We all know what the demon is capable of."

Poosk ignored him. "That is an interesting idea, Initiate."

"Thank you, Brother."

Poosk clapped his hands, and everyone, including Gwin, jumped. "Bartle, bring the demon." And he strode toward the cave entrance.

"Me?" cried Bartle. "I will not touch the creature!"

Brother Poosk swung around. "You will if I say so."

"I will not. I will do anything else you tell me, Brother, but I will not touch that thing."

His leader leveled a finger at him. "You will regret this, Brother. I have a long memory."

"I will carry hi—I will carry it," said the Initiate.

Once again, Poosk turned that searching gaze onto the Devout boy. "Are *you* not afraid?"

"No. Yes. But"—the Initiate sounded as if he was repeating a lesson—"but orders are more important than fear."

"And ambition," murmured Poosk, "is a great driver. I will have to watch you, boy, I can see that. But for now at least, you are useful. Pick up the demon."

"Yes, Brother."

It seemed to Gwin that the Initiate picked up the mechanical boy with a certain tenderness. *No, I'm imagining it*, she thought, and when she looked again, the tenderness was gone, and the Initiate was hauling the limp figure over his shoulder with an expression of disgust on his face.

Gwin glanced at Papa, but his eyes were so sorrowful that she quickly looked away. "You have the—the relic," she said to Brother Poosk. "Now you can release my papa."

"And have the two of you run off and leave us here, unable to find our way back?" Brother Poosk raised his eyebrows. "I think not. You will be reunited with your father when we are back where we began, and no sooner."

Gwin didn't like it, but there was nothing she could do about it. Reluctantly, she led the way out of the cave and along the cliff path. There was no sign of the rat, which was a relief. She didn't want those silver eyes judging her.

I had to do it, she thought. *There was no other way. I'm sorry, rat.*

As soon as they reached the mountain track, she stopped and put her hands on her hips. "Now," she said, mustering that air of confidence. "You must let Papa go."

"Wait, wait." Brother Poosk waggled a finger in her direction.

Then he turned to the Initiate. "Put the demon down, boy. There, next to Cull."

The Initiate didn't seem to hear him. He stepped down onto the track and kept walking, his back stiff, his eyes straight ahead.

Poosk shouted at him. "Initiate! I said, 'Put the demon down.'"

The Initiate hesitated, and for an odd moment, Gwin thought he was going to run off, taking the mechanical boy with him.

"Put it *down*!" yelled Poosk.

The Initiate swung around, red-faced. "My apologies, Brother. I was deep in the Spire Contemplation and did not hear you." And he laid the mechanical boy on the ground.

Brother Poosk pursed his lips. "Do not get too keen, boy. It is dangerous to be too keen." He turned to Bartle. "It is also dangerous to be too reluctant. Pick up the demon."

"But—" said Bartle.

"If the Initiate can carry the creature unharmed, so can you. Pick it up."

Gwin stepped forward. "What about Papa? You said you would let him go."

But they were still ignoring her. The Initiate sidled up to Poosk and said, "Brother, do you want me to run ahead? I will run all the way to the Citadel, if you wish, and tell them you are coming with the demon. That way they will have time to—to plan a great celebration. By the time you get there, they will be lining the roadway."

"Hmm," said Poosk, sounding pleased. He nodded. "Go!"

And without a backward glance, the Initiate sped off down the road.

"Now!" Gwin said loudly. "You promised!"

At last Poosk turned toward her. "Ah, yes. The little Fetcher girl. We made a bargain, did we not, that you would be re-united with your father? And so you shall."

There was something about his words that raised the hair on the back of Gwin's neck. Without consciously thinking about it, she found herself up on her toes, as if she were about to leap onto Spindle's broad back.

Poosk snapped at Cull, "Take her!"

For all his size, Brother Cull was fast. But Gwin was faster. She had run and leapt and somersaulted all her life, and even though she was nowhere near as good as Nat, the big man didn't have a chance against her. As his hands closed over her arm, she sprang backward and scrambled up the little path. Cull labored after her, but she was too quick, and the path was too narrow, and it wasn't long before he gave up and went back to his fellows.

"Useless, Brother Cull," grumbled Poosk. "Completely useless."

"How could I have caught her without breaking my neck, Brother? Tell me that."

From her perch, high on the path, Gwin shouted down at them. "You promised! You promised to let him go!"

Poosk didn't even look up. "I suppose it does not matter. We have two big prizes—the Fetcher and the demon. We cannot complain." He laughed.

Gwin thought she might be sick, right there and then. "They never meant to free you, Papa," she cried. "They tricked me!"

But in her heart she knew that she'd tricked herself. She'd known from the start that the Devouts were not to be trusted, but she'd been so desperate to save her father that she'd refused to listen to her own wisdom.

She'd traded away the mechanical boy for nothing.

CHAPTER 17

EVERYONE SHE LOVED

FIN WAS NO MORE THAN A FEW HUNDRED YARDS DOWN THE road and running hard when he heard a low whistle from somewhere above him. He skidded to a halt, his eyes searching the cliff top.

Petrel and Sharkey scrambled down the rock face to meet him. Rain stayed where she was, watching the track.

"They . . . have him," panted Fin. He put his hands on his knees and tried to catch his breath. "They have . . . captured him!"

"Who?" asked Petrel. "What's happened? Fin, are you all right?"

Fin pressed his fingers to his side and straightened up. "Yes. No! Brother Poosk has . . . caught . . . the captain!"

His friends stared at him in shock. "The cap'n's *here*?" said Sharkey.

"Yes. There are caves. He was . . . hidden in one of them."

"How did Poosk find him if he was hidden?" demanded Petrel. "Did you talk to him? Was Mister Smoke there?"

Fin just about had his breath back by then, enough to explain about the Fetcher girl and what she had done. "The captain looks just the same as when we last saw him. When I was carrying him, I whispered to him, told him we were here, but he did not answer. I thought of running off with him, but I would not have got far. And now Poosk has him. I could not think of anything to do except come and tell you."

The horror on Petrel's, Sharkey's and Rain's faces reflected Fin's own dismay. In their search for his mama, none of them had forgotten the captain. But they had believed he was tucked away safe somewhere and would come back to them when he was mended. Now that belief was shattered.

"What was Mister Smoke doing?" asked Sharkey. "Why didn't he stop them?"

"He was not there." Fin dragged off the hated Initiate robe and threw it to the ground. "Perhaps he was hiding. But there was nothing he could have done anyway."

"We could've helped, if we'd been there." Petrel looked around wildly. "We could've—we could've grabbed that Fetcher girl before she said anything, and—and tied her up. How could she betray the cap'n like that? How *could* she?"

Up to that point, Rain had been silent, watching the road. But now she called down, "She was just trying to save her papa, Petrel. I do not think we can blame her for that."

"*I* can blame her," cried Petrel. "I don't care about her papa. He's not nearly as important as the cap'n."

"And I doubt if she *did* save him," said Fin. "A Fetcher is too fine a prize to let go, no matter what Poosk promised."

"Serves that girl right." Petrel dug her toe under a rock and kicked it to the other side of the track.

"So what now?" asked Sharkey. "What's Poosk doing?"

Fin shrugged. "I suspect he will go straight back to the Citadel."

"Well, that's something," said Petrel, brightening. "It means your mam's safe, for a while at least, and—and we don't have to rush to find her. I mean, we *will* find her, but we've gotta save the cap'n first, don't we? Fin, can you go back, d'you reckon? You might be able to sneak the cap'n out while they're all asleep."

Fin shook his head. "I am supposed to be running to the Citadel with the news. If they see me now, they will know something is wrong."

"Then we'll have to find another way," said Petrel.

Rain called down to them again. "Uncle Poosk will see the captain as his ticket back to power and influence." She clasped her hands together, the knuckles white. "He will not let him go easily." And she began to sing, the way she always did when she was frightened.

Sharkey smiled up at her. "We've already beaten your uncle once, remember? We can beat him this time too."

"Aye," said Petrel. "Course we can, can't we, Fin?"

"Yes. Of course." Fin wished he could be as certain as Petrel. But he was not certain, not even a little bit.

Rain is right to be afraid, he thought. *I am afraid too.*

GWIN HAD BELIEVED THAT THINGS WERE AS BAD AS THEY could possibly get. That was before she looked north and, from her high perch, saw a familiar figure hurrying down the mountain track toward the Devouts.

It was Nat, his left hand trailing along the rock face, while his right shoved Hilde away. Wretched was with them, and Spindle and the cart trundled along some distance behind. The pigeon flew in circles over their heads.

Gwin almost fell from her perch in horror. "Nat!" she whispered. "What are you *doing*?"

She couldn't understand it, not until she saw the rat trotting beside her brother. Then she knew. Mister Smoke had discovered what she'd done. Maybe he'd even been there, watching from a dark corner.

This was his revenge. A boy for a boy. With Nat in such a reckless mood, it wouldn't have been hard to persuade him that he was needed. That he and the skinning knife could somehow tip the balance and free Papa.

At the bottom of the path, Brother Poosk was issuing orders. "I see no need to continue with the other matter. This is far more important. We will go straight back to the Citadel. . . ."

Gwin wanted to scream, *Nat! Stop!* But she couldn't, not without giving his presence away. She couldn't do a thing except bite her knuckles, hard.

And then, just a few steps from the corner, Hilde managed to seize Nat's arm. He tried to shake her off, but she wouldn't let go. Gwin held her breath. She could see them arguing in whispers.

Neither of them noticed Wretched until it was too late.

He must've caught Papa's scent. With a yelp of delight, he raced around the corner—and stopped, with his tail tucked between his legs.

Brother Poosk glanced up and beamed. "A dog," he murmured, kneeling down in the middle of the track. "A *fine* dog. Where did you come from, I wonder. Here, doggie. *Nice* doggie."

Wretched's ears went back and forth, trying to work out who this stranger was and whether or not he could be trusted.

Poosk raised his voice. "I have heard," he crooned, directing his words toward the corner, "that dog meat is very tasty."

He knows, thought Gwin, and a terrible chill ran through her. *He knows there's someone else there.*

"And now I can try it for myself," Poosk continued. "Cull, Bartle, step away from the prisoner, if you please. But keep hold of the rope, and be ready with your cudgels. *Fine* dog. *Nice* dog. Come closer, now, doggie."

Cull and Bartle raised their cudgels. Wretched inched forward. "Nearly there," Brother Poosk said loudly. "Just a few steps further . . ."

"Wretched, no!" shouted Nat, and he tore himself away from Hilde and ran around the corner after his dog.

Gwin groaned out loud, as did Papa. Wretched backed away from Brother Poosk and hid behind Nat's legs.

Bartle and Cull grinned and started forward. Nat slid the skinning knife from its sheath, and they paused.

They don't know he's blind, thought Gwin.

Nat wasn't acting blind; that was the thing. He never did.

He knew where the two men were, from the sounds their boots made as they shifted on the track, from their whispers, from their breathing. His knife turned toward Cull, and then toward Bartle.

But it wasn't going to be enough.

Gwin started to creep down the path, hoping against hope that she might be able to do something.

But she was only halfway down when Brother Poosk said cheerfully, "Stay where you are, Gwinith, or I will slit your father's throat."

Gwin froze. Nat turned his face toward Poosk and cried, "If you kill him, I will kill you!"

In that moment of distraction, Cull nodded to Bartle. Gwin cried, "Nat, they're going to rush you!" And then, because her brother didn't have a chance against those two huge men, she screamed, "Hilde, help him!"

She wasn't entirely sure what happened next. She thought she heard Poosk shout, "Bartle, up the track!"

But by then Cull was upon Nat, lashing out with his cudgel, and Nat was fighting with all the anger that had consumed him since Mama died, and Wretched was leaping around them, barking.

Gwin couldn't take her eyes off them, hoping for a miracle.

It didn't come. In a fight like this, neither Nat's anger nor his astonishing hearing were enough. As Gwin watched, a sly blow from the cudgel knocked the knife out of her brother's hand, and Cull kicked Nat's legs out from under him. He kicked Wretched too, and the dog yelped and ran for cover.

Bartle came back around the corner dragging Hilde. "I have her, Brother Poosk. And there's an ox and cart to go with her, if we want them."

"An ox and cart?" said Poosk. "How fortunate we are!"

And so it was that fifteen minutes later Spindle set off again, back down the track toward the lowlands, with the mule tethered to the cart. Cull wielded the whip, with a very satisfied Brother Poosk sitting beside him. Bartle was crammed in the back, keeping an eye on Papa, Nat and Hilde. Not that he needed to—they were trussed up so well that they couldn't have escaped in a year of trying. The mechanical boy lay silent and unmoving at their feet.

The only one left behind, apart from the pigeon, was Wretched. He sat at the bottom of the path, gazing up at Gwin with eyes that begged for comfort.

Gwin didn't have a scrap of comfort to give him. She felt as if someone had ripped her heart from her body and cut it to pieces.

Everyone she loved was being taken away. Her whole life was disappearing down the mountain track toward the Citadel.

CHAPTER 18

IT CANNOT BE HER

WHEN PETREL HEARD THE CART COMING, SHE AND SHARKEY hauled Fin back up the cliff and hid. She didn't think it was Brother Poosk and his men—they only had a mule—but her old habits of caution were always with her.

Just as well. There was Poosk, riding on the front of an oxcart with a smirk as wide as a glacier. His guards looked equally pleased with themselves, probably because of their prisoners.

"I do not know where the woman and boy came from," breathed Fin. "Poosk must have caught them after I left."

"Prob'ly the Fetcher's wife and son," whispered Petrel. She felt no sympathy for the captives, not after what the Fetcher girl had done. The only one she cared about was the captain. And Fin's mam, of course, but she wasn't there, which was like a secret weight removed from Petrel's shoulders.

She peered up at Rain, who was in a slightly better position. "Can you see the cap'n?"

"Yes. He is in the bottom of the cart."

They waited until the cart had disappeared around the next bend; then Sharkey and Petrel helped Fin and Rain down the cliff, and they ran after the Devouts.

They had not gone far when a voice hailed them. "Ahoy, shipmates!" A large gray rat wriggled out from between a couple of rocks.

"Mister Smoke!" cried Petrel. She was so pleased to see her old friend that she scooped him up and kissed his nose. "Where've you been?"

"I been waitin' for yer, shipmate. Got a ride in the cart. You wouldn't believe the things Fetchers've got 'idden in there."

"Tell us about the cap'n," said Petrel. "Fin reckons he's still broken. D'you think we can get him away from Poosk? That man's a nasty piece of work, and those two thugs he's got—"

Sharkey interrupted her. "We should keep walking. We don't want to lose the cart."

"Don't reckon you'll lose it, shipmate," said Mister Smoke. "Poosk's aimin' for the Citadel. Might take a bit of runnin' to catch 'im, but 'e won't be makin' detours. And besides, there's someone you need to meet. If my calculations are right, she'll be comin' down the track in just a few minutes."

"Who?" asked Petrel. "Not—not Fin's mam?"

Fin turned white, but Mister Smoke shook his battered head. "It's the Singer."

All four children gaped at him. "You found the *Singer*?" said Rain.

"But that's *wonderful*," cried Petrel. "If we've got the Singer and the Song, we can do anything!"

"Can we, shipmate? We'll see. You just keep yer eyes open till she gets 'ere."

"Aren't you staying with us?"

"Nah. Don't wanna leave the cap'n by 'imself for too long."

Petrel found it hard to stand and watch Mister Smoke trotting away down the track when she'd only just found him again. It was even harder waiting for the Singer.

She wriggled her toes and breathed on her hands. She shifted position one way, then the other.

Fin was sitting back against the cliff with his eyes closed, as if nothing bothered him. But Petrel could see the pulse beating in his temple and knew what he was thinking about.

"That woman in the cart," Rain said suddenly. "Could she be your mama, Fin?"

Petrel froze. She hadn't thought of that.

But without even opening his eyes, Fin laughed sourly and said, "I think I would know if my parents had been Fetchers. Or if I had a brother and sister."

"Oh," said Rain. "Yes. Of course."

Petrel shifted position again. "Wish the Singer'd hurry up. Maybe Mister Smoke was wrong. Maybe she's not coming."

Sharkey squinted into the distance. "*Some*one's coming."

Fin sat up quickly. Rain put her hand on Sharkey's shoulder. Petrel stood next to them, peering at the girl who was hastening down the track toward them with a dog at her side.

This was the mysterious Singer the captain had been search-ing for. This was the person who would help them change the world.

Maybe everything's gunna turn out right after all, thought Petrel.

She was about to call out when Fin seized her arm. "No!" he hissed. "It cannot be her. She is the one who betrayed the captain!"

IT WAS WRETCHED WHO WARNED GWIN THAT THERE WERE people about. He stopped suddenly and cowered against her legs, which forced her to stop too.

She heard voices raised in argument, but didn't bother looking up. There was no room in her mind for anyone but Papa and Nat.

I have to save them, she thought. *I HAVE to save them!*

The voices, however, were too loud and insistent to ignore for long.

"I tell you, it cannot be her," said a boy.

"Course it can't," replied a girl. "Except Mister Smoke reck-oned it *was*."

"Perhaps there is someone else walking behind her." That was a different girl.

"Can't see anyone." And that was a second boy. "It's her. It has to be."

"But it *cannot* be."

And they started all over again.

Gwin looked up at last.

A little way down the track stood four ragged children. They were about Gwin's age, and when they saw her staring at them, they approached cautiously.

Two of them—a small, dark girl and a taller boy with white hair—were glaring at her as if they hated her on sight. Like the Devouts, they wore boots, and so did the pale-haired girl who hung back a little, watching the track. The boy with the patch over his eye had bare feet, but Gwin wasn't going to trust him, not when she saw the company he kept.

Wretched, however, wriggled a welcome. He liked children, and if Gwin had given the slightest sign, he would've trotted forward to meet them.

Gwin didn't move. *I have to save Papa and Nat. . . .*

The small girl put her hands on her hips. "You betrayed our cap'n. He's the hope of the world, and you gave him to Poosk. If we were on the *Oyster*, shipfolk'd chuck you overboard without thinking twice."

The other girl, the one who'd hung back, said, "Petrel, ask her about—you know."

Wretched's tail thumped against Gwin's leg.

"I don't want to." Petrel's whole body radiated anger. "What if she says yes, what do we do with her then? We'd have to take her along with us, and I can hardly bear to look at her as it is."

"Ask her anyway," said the boy with the eye patch.

Petrel grimaced and said, "Hey, traitor. Are you the Singer?"

I have to save Papa and Nat, thought Gwin, and she stepped around Wretched.

Petrel dodged in front of her. "I *said*, 'Are you the Singer?'" Gwin didn't answer.

Petrel glowered, worse than ever, and turned to the boy with the white hair. "Fin? What d'you reckon?"

It was only when the white-haired boy spoke that Gwin realized he was the Initiate, without his robes. "You know what I think." He was as angry as Petrel. "She cannot be the one."

"Sharkey?" said Petrel.

The boy with the eye patch shrugged. "Mister Smoke sounded pretty sure of it."

"Rain?"

The quiet girl was on her knees by then, with her hand out to Wretched. She studied Gwin for a long moment. "I think I remember you," she said at last. "You were part of the circus that came to my village when I was seven. You sang the Hope song, and your brother could hear the world breathing. Why will you not talk to us?"

"Because she's bad through and through." Petrel turned away in disgust. "But if she's the one who sang the Hope song, we'll have to take her with us. Sharkey?"

The boy with the eye patch was much quicker than Brother Cull. He grabbed hold of Gwin's arm, just above the elbow. And almost before she realized what was happening, her hands were tied in front of her, and she was a prisoner.

CHAPTER 19

THE HIDDEN PATH

The children hurried south for the rest of the day, first running, then walking, then running again. At first Wretched clung to Gwin's side, but before long he was sniffing Rain's hand, then wagging his tail and bouncing along as if this was just another day on the roads of West Norn. Whenever they slowed to a walk, Petrel or Sharkey questioned Gwin or asked her to sing the Hope song.

Gwin didn't answer. The rope chafed her wrists, and all she could think of was how she might escape from it, and use Ariel's Way to get ahead of Papa and Nat.

I have to save them. I HAVE to save them.

But no matter how she twisted and flexed her hands, the knots stayed firm, and Sharkey kept a tight hold on the other end of the rope. So Gwin stopped trying to escape and started listening to her captors' conversation.

According to Petrel, the Citadel would be under attack by now. There were people called Sunkers, and others called shipfolk, and they were trying to bring the Devouts down. To defeat them. To free West Norn from tyranny.

In any other circumstances, Gwin would've laughed. The Citadel under attack? Someone trying to defeat the Devouts? It was like the old stories; everyone loved listening to them, but no one was silly enough to believe them.

Still, it made her look twice at the other children. Three of them might wear boots, but from the sound of it, they loathed the Devouts almost as much as she did.

She tried to gather her thoughts. *What if I can't get away from them? What do I do then? Take them with me on the secret paths?*

She flinched away from the thought, then slowly circled back to it. There was still no sign of the oxcart, which meant that Cull must be driving Spindle hard.

We won't catch them, thought Gwin, *not if we stick to the road. And we have to catch them. I have to save Papa and Nat. I have to!*

She didn't say anything until after they had passed the turnoff and were heading along the Northern Road toward the coast. They were all flagging by then, and Gwin's throat felt as if it were lined with knives.

"We won't . . . catch up with them . . . like this," she croaked.

"What?" Petrel didn't slow her pace. "What're you talking . . . about? Mister Smoke said we *would* catch 'em. And I'd trust him—a lot more than I'd trust you."

"He's wrong," croaked Gwin. "Papa says"—she wanted to howl like a lost dog, but if she started she might never stop—"Papa says Spindle's . . . descended from the same line as the blue ox, which means he's faster and stronger . . . than any other ox in West Norn. They might drive him all night. But we'll have to . . . rest some time."

The four children looked at each other and slowed down a little. Sharkey said, "We've gotta catch them. Otherwise the cap'n's done for."

And so were Nat and Papa. "There's a . . ." Gwin swallowed. She'd never imagined saying these words to anyone except another Fetcher. But today her whole life had been turned upside down, and the old rules no longer applied.

Besides, she thought, *if I don't save Papa and Nat, there won't BE any other Fetchers.*

"There's a shortcut," she said. "If we take it, we should catch them at Quorky."

Fin stared at her. "I have never heard of a shortcut on the Northern Road."

"And even if there is one," Sharkey pulled a face, "wouldn't Poosk take it?"

"It's a trap," Petrel said bluntly. "She's gunna try and sell us, like she did the cap'n."

Rain was more out of breath than any of them, partly because she insisted on singing as well as running. "Mama once told me that Fetchers can . . . disappear . . . from right under the noses . . . of the Devouts. Perhaps it is . . . a *secret* shortcut."

Fin shook his head. "The Devouts would have found it. I agree with Petrel. It is a trap."

"Devouts don't find everything," said Sharkey. "Didn't find us Sunkers for three hundred years. I say we give it a try."

Gwin wanted to scream at them, *Make up your minds. Quickly!*

But screaming wouldn't help Nat and Papa.

At last Petrel nodded, without losing her hostile expression. "We'll try your shortcut, traitor. But don't you get tricksy. You lead us straight, or else."

It was another couple of miles before Gwin saw the signs. Night was falling by then, but she picked out the telltale scattering of rocks, the scuff mark on the trunk of a tree and the scraping of sheep's wool. By themselves they meant nothing, but together—she drew a ragged breath—together they were as clear as written directions.

She wished she could blindfold her companions, as she'd done with Hilde. But they would never agree to such a thing, and besides it would slow them down too much. So she just whispered, "Forgive me, Ariel. But I have to save Nat and Papa." Then, feeling horribly sick at what she was about to do, she dragged Sharkey up the bank.

It wasn't easy to unweave the hedgerow with her hands still tied, especially in the growing darkness. But Sharkey caught on quickly, and between them they bent the branches back until there was a small gap.

Wretched was the first one through. As soon as the other children followed him, Gwin wove the branches back together as best she could. Then she led four strangers—unblindfolded—onto Ariel's Way.

This particular part of the Way was what Mama used to call a "rale," though there were two of them, rusty iron lines that were completely buried in some places, while in others they ran along the top of the ground like upside-down wheel ruts. The trees grew over them in an arch, as if to protect them from prying eyes.

"I never knew such a thing existed," whispered Rain.

Sharkey looked up at the moonlight that filtered through the trees and murmured, "It's almost like being in the Undersea."

Fin and Petrel didn't say a word. But they watched Gwin closely, as if they expected nothing from her but wickedness.

The rale took them down into a valley and through a cutting in the hills. They passed blocks of stone tumbled willy-nilly across the landscape, and brick walls that only stood upright because of the vines that had grown around them, and hoops of rusty iron that looked as if they had burrowed up from beneath the earth and were waiting for someone to find a use for them.

By midnight they were all limping, and so tired that Petrel and her friends were holding each other up.

No one held Gwin up. She lurched along at the end of the rope, clenching and unclenching her fists. And when they stopped in the early hours of the morning for a brief sleep, she wrapped her arms around her brother's dog and whispered, "Tomorrow night, Wretched. We'll be in Quorky by then, and Brother Poosk will have to stop for the ferry. That's where we'll catch them. That's where we'll save Papa and Nat."

BECAUSE OF THE FERRY, QUORKY WASN'T QUITE AS POOR AS the villages around it. No one except the Devouts had any money, of course, so most people paid their fees with cabbage seeds or fish heads or a wizened old apple that had been hidden from the quarterly tithe. In a hungry land, cabbage seeds and apples were riches.

Sharkey untied Gwin's wrists, so as not to attract unwanted attention, then the five children stumbled, exhausted, down to the river bank. There was already a crowd of forty or so waiting for the night crossing. But there was no sign of the oxcart.

Gwin looked around frantically. Could Poosk have crossed already? Had she missed her only chance?

She could feel something building up in her throat, but before she could make a sound, she heard Spindle. Or rather, she heard the cart.

She stumbled back a few steps and saw the old ox trotting down the road toward the ferry, his chest lathered with sweat. Bartle was driving, with Poosk beside him, while Cull guarded Papa, Nat and Hilde. The mule followed behind on a long rope.

Gwin's relief was so great that her legs wouldn't hold her, and she slumped down on the trampled grass, feeling as if her bones had melted. Wretched stood next to her with his nose twitching in the direction of the cart and a whine starting in his throat.

"Hush!" whispered Gwin, and she grabbed the scruff of his neck and dragged him behind a couple of old women so that Brother Poosk wouldn't see them.

The other four children sprawled around her, pretending a

complete lack of interest in the Devouts and their prisoners. Gwin listened to their whispering.

"Can you see the cap'n, Fin?"

"Not yet."

"Reckon he's still there?"

"Yes, I do."

"How are we going to rescue him, Petrel? Uncle Poosk will not . . ." Rain's voice trailed off in a whisper of song. *"How tall the tree, the first to fall . . ."*

"Don't know yet," said Petrel.

"Attack 'em midstream," whispered Sharkey. "All those people on board, it'll be chaos. We dive overboard in the middle of it and take the cap'n with us."

Fin shook his head. "I cannot swim."

"Neither can I," whispered Rain. And there was the Hope song again. *"How wise to flee the worst of all . . ."*

None of them said anything about saving Papa and Nat. But Gwin didn't care. She was making her own plans.

"Perhaps we could—" Fin began.

Petrel interrupted him. "Shhh! They're coming."

Rain ducked behind Sharkey, her face pale. The oxcart rolled through the crowd, with Poosk talking loudly, as if the watching villagers did not exist.

"I have caught the demon, Brother Bartle; I have done what no one else could do. Which means there will be changes at the Citadel. You will see." His eyes were bright and hard, and he looked like a completely different man from the one who had made that false bargain for the mechanical boy.

Wretched growled softly. Gwin stroked his ears and whispered, "Shhh!"

"They will not treat me the way they used to," continued Brother Poosk. "I will not tolerate it. They will not say *no* to me. They will not slam doors in my face, and tell me to *wait*. . . ."

The ferryman had been in his hut. Now he came hurrying out, bowing and smiling and wringing his hands. "Kind sirs, *gracious* sirs! You wish to cross the mighty River Quor? We'll be happy to oblige, if you'll just wait a little while."

It was an unfortunate choice of words. Brother Poosk turned his hard, bright eyes on the man. "*Wait?* No, I will *not* wait. You will take us across now."

The ferryman's smile froze on his face. "But it's too dangerous, gracious sir. The tidal b—"

"Are you deaf?" said Poosk.

"No, grac—"

"Stupid?"

"No, gr—"

"Wilfully disobedient to an order from your betters?"

The ferryman blanched. "No, no! We will take you across, gracious sir! Right now!"

Brother Poosk sat back with an air of satisfaction.

But the ferryman had obviously dealt with Devouts before. He dragged a filthy scrap of paper out of his jerkin and said, "If sir will just sign here, proof that he insisted? See, when we all drown, Citadel's going to come down hard on my wife and children, and blame *me* for—"

"*When* we drown?" interrupted Cull, leaning forward.

"Yes, sir. When the tidal bore comes through, we'll be dragged under. You will have seen it on your way west, yes? How the wave rushes upstream at the turn of the tide, like a maddened bull? Nothing can stand in its way, gracious sir, particularly not my little barge."

"Brother Poosk," said Cull. "A short wait will make little difference."

Poosk glared at him, then turned back to the ferryman. "When does this tidal bore come?"

"Main wave should be through shortly after sundown, gracious sir. But then there are the following waves, which we call ruffles—"

"We will go directly after the main wave," snapped Poosk.

His prisoners took no notice of this exchange. Papa and Nat were leaning against each other, as if that was the only comfort they could find. Hilde sat beside them with her face in her bound hands.

I'll save her too, if I can, thought Gwin. *I hope she can swim.*

The ferryman was protesting again, as strongly as he dared. "Sir, the ruffles are not to be treated lightly—"

"Do you wish to keep your pathetic little ferry?" snarled Poosk.

"Y-yes, gracious sir! Directly after the main bore, of course, sir!"

Gwin nibbled the edge of her collar. *If it's dark and everyone's watching out for the ruffles, it'll make my job easier.*

And for the briefest of moments she felt as if this unspeakable day might end better than it had begun.

That is, until Brother Poosk waved his hand at the waiting villagers and said, almost as an afterthought, "It will be too crowded with this riffraff on board. Leave them behind. We will have the ferry to ourselves."

CHAPTER 20

THE FERRY

GWIN WAS HAVING TROUBLE BREATHING. *I have to go on that ferry!*

All around her, people were whispering more or less the same thing.

"Leave us behind?" said one old woman, in a horrified voice. "But we're burying my poor daughter and her baby first thing in the morning. I've got to get across!"

"Don't start fretting yet," said her companion. "Maybe the Master'll change his mind."

The man directly in front of them said over his shoulder, "Masters only change their minds when they might gain from it."

"They'll gain all right if I miss my daughter's burial," muttered the old woman, crossing her arms. "They'll gain a clout over the head! See if they don't!"

The man said, "You need a hammer, missus? I'll lend you mine."

"Shhhh!" murmured the companion. "Don't say such things! You'll get us all sent away."

"I'm past caring," said the old woman. "They take everything we've got, and still they want more." But she fell silent all the same.

Petrel turned to Rain. "Will he change his mind? What d'you reckon?"

"I do not think so," whispered Rain, who was still hiding behind Sharkey. "Uncle Poosk does not care about other people."

"Then what do we do?" Petrel's face was desperate. "How can we save the cap'n if we can't even get on the stinking ferry?"

No one had an answer for her.

Meanwhile the ferryman was almost falling over himself in his desire to be agreeable. "Leave them behind? Certainly, sirs! Should we leave the quarterly tithe behind, too, to give you more room? No rush for it, after all."

Poosk eyed him. "Where is it?"

The ferryman pointed with his chin. "That pile of boxes and bags, gracious sir. Forty percent of produce, going to the Citadel as required. There's grain from last year's harvest and cabbages and winter apples—we'd never say no to the Citadel. I'm sure they need it more than we do."

The old woman hissed, so quick and sudden that only the people around her could tell where it came from.

A shiver of excitement ran through the waiting crowd. Everyone knew that the Citadel had no need of extra grain or cabbages. The Devouts had too much already; they grew fat on it while the villagers starved. But no one dared protest, not where they might be overheard. Not usually.

Poosk scanned the crowd, his face hard. Then he turned back to the ferryman. "There are carts waiting for the tithe on the other side?"

"Yes, gracious sir."

"You may load it."

"Yes, sir!" And the ferryman shouted to his crew, "Get the tithe on board."

Night fell fairly quickly at this time of year. As the sky lowered and the villagers whispered, Gwin heard a flutter of wings overhead, and a small feathered body landed on her shoulder.

The pigeon. She'd forgotten all about it. It must have been following her ever since she left the mountains, flying high above the rale until it came to Quorky.

If only I could send it for help, thought Gwin. *If only Hob and Bony and their friends would come striding down from the mountains to rescue Papa and Nat.*

Except they'd already told her they wouldn't. They'd only come if change was roaring down like an avalanche, which was about as likely as the Citadel being attacked, or Ariel and her blue ox coming back from the dead. The pigeon was as useless as it had ever been.

Which meant Gwin had to get on the ferry.

"Scroll?" said Petrel, behind her. "Is that *Scroll*?"

The pigeon cooed softly.

Petrel grabbed Gwin's arm and dragged her around so they

were nose to nose. "What're you doing with Scroll? Betraying the cap'n not enough for you? You had to steal his pigeon as well?"

"W-what?" stammered Gwin.

"The pigeon," Fin said coldly. "She belongs to the captain. Where did you get her?"

Gwin opened her mouth—and shut it again. She was sick of these children treating her as if she was no better than the Devouts, especially when there was so much else to worry about.

"Here, you can have her," she snapped, and she thrust the useless bird into Petrel's hands. Then she stood up, turned her back on them and watched the men loading the tithe.

She was still trying to work out how she could get onto the ferry without being seen when the tidal bore came surging up from the coast, like a wave going the wrong way.

Within the blink of an eye, the river went from peaceful to roaring. The ferry, which was really just a barge with a pole at each corner, began to spin and jerk at its ropes. Its crew leapt for safety just in time, but a sack of grain, not yet secured, splashed into the water and was whisked upstream.

The water curled up the banks, higher and higher, louder and louder—then fell back with a groan.

The main bore was past. It was time for the crossing.

"All aboard!" cried the ferryman, before remembering that only the Devouts and their prisoners were taking this particular trip. He coughed a couple of times to cover his mistake, shook his head at the waiting crowd, then bowed obsequiously to Brother Bartle. "If you'd care to drive onto the ferry, sir. Mind the edges. And hold on tight; there's always ruffles to come, not as bad as the main bore but tricksy all the same."

A murmur rose, beginning with the old woman and spreading in all directions, as people realized that the Devouts *weren't* going to change their minds and that everyone else would be left behind, no matter how important their business. It was an ugly sound, not quite loud enough for Poosk and his men to hear. But the ferryman's hands patted the air behind his back, as if to say, *Don't make a fuss. We don't want trouble.*

If it had been broad daylight, the crowd would probably have done as they were told. But night had fallen, and the old woman's tiny protest seemed to have made people bolder than usual. That shiver of excitement ran through them again, and as the oxcart inched down the long bank toward the ferry, lit only by a couple of flickering torches, the crowd followed.

Is this change? thought Gwin. *Is this the beginning of an avalanche?* And for a heartbeat or two she wondered if she should grab the pigeon back from Petrel.

But a few people pushing forward on a riverbank wasn't the sort of change Hob meant, and she knew it. There were small rebellions like this every year in West Norn, and they all ended badly. The only real question was whether Gwin could take advantage of this one.

She edged away from the other children, then bent over

Wretched and stroked his ears. "You'll have to stay here," she whispered. "Stay with Rain; you like her, don't you?"

The dog whined and pressed closer.

"I'd take you with me if I could," whispered Gwin. "But I can't. We'll come back for you, once Nat and Papa are safe." She swallowed. "Stay here, Wretched. Stay!"

She had almost caught up with the crowd when someone seized her arm. "Where are you going?" demanded Petrel. "You've got an idea, I know you have. What is it? How're you gunna get on that ferry?"

Gwin didn't answer. Farther down the bank, the murmur of protest was swelling. The ferryman patted the air harder than ever, his eyes wide with alarm. Cull turned around at last and saw the crowd pressing forward, almost within reach of the cart. His face grew thunderous, and he raised his cudgel in what was clearly a threat.

The people at the front came to their senses and tried to stop but couldn't. Those behind them were pushing and shoving, still driven by that dangerous sense of excitement.

Then, inevitably, someone slipped on the muddy bank. He managed to scramble up again before he went under the wheels, but Cull leapt to his feet with a shout and began to lay into the man with his cudgel. The mule brayed and kicked, the man screamed for mercy, and everyone else surged one way and then the other, trying to escape.

As the noise reached a crescendo, Gwin tore away from Petrel's grasp, dived past the mule and slipped beneath the oxcart.

When she and Nat were small, they used to play under the cart, clinging to the struts and braces, or scratching at the boards until Mama declared, laughing, "I do believe we have an infestation of mice."

It was those same struts and braces that Gwin grabbed hold of now, swinging her feet up as the cart rolled forward above her. It wasn't an easy position to hold, not with the cart still jolting down the long bank, and the shouting and cursing all around her. But she didn't move, even though her whole body ached with exhaustion.

There was a thump and a jerk as Spindle stepped onto the ferry, then another thump as the cart followed. Gwin eased her hands into a better position.

The ferryman wasn't taking any chances with the hostile crowd. As soon as the mule was on board, he slammed the back of the barge into place, bolted it shut and shouted to his crew, "Lay off quick now. Banks away. Poles to portside."

The ferry edged away from its mooring.

"Watch the bow," cried the ferryman. "Mizzle, Bosh, get round here! There's the first ruffle."

As the ferrymen labored, and the ruffles nudged at the barge in a testing sort of fashion, Gwin took one hand off the strut and scratched twice at the boards above her head. So quietly that only a boy who could hear the world breathing would notice.

There was a heart-stopping pause, then something scraped out a reply. A toenail. Once. Twice.

Gwin swallowed. Nat knew she was here.

"Hey-up, here comes the next one," cried the ferryman, and the barge began to jerk and tilt.

Spindle snorted. The mule stamped uneasily. Brother Poosk said in tones that were a little too high and tight, "Note that I did not sign your piece of paper. If anything happens to us, your wife and children will suffer, I guarantee it."

The ferryman cleared his throat. "It's always a risk, gracious sir, crossing before the ruffles are done. If you and your men could come over here and help us watch out for logs, I'd be most grateful."

For far too long, the Devouts didn't move. Gwin clung to the bottom of the cart, hardly daring to breathe.

Go! she begged silently. *Go and watch!*

But it was not until something thumped against the barge and spun away into the darkness, that Brother Poosk cursed and climbed down from the cart, followed by his two men.

"Downstream side, sirs, if you please," said the ferryman. "That's where the danger'll come from."

The Devouts edged over to the downstream side of the barge. The crew were on that side too, with their poles. The water fretted and surged.

As the ferry began to shake more violently, Gwin dropped to the deck and crawled out on the upstream side of the cart, next to the mule.

She knew she didn't have long. As soon as the ruffles were past, Poosk and his men would return to the cart. Papa and Nat—and Hilde—must be freed before then.

She went straight to Papa, who had his back to her. He flinched when she touched him, but then his fingers tightened briefly over hers, and he shifted so she could get at the knot that bound his wrists.

Gwin was so wound up that when a small paw patted her hand she almost cried out. She stared at Mister Smoke, who had appeared out of nowhere and was teetering on the edge of the cart.

Mister Smoke, whose mechanical boy she had betrayed.

"You takin' the cap'n with you, shipmate?" he whispered.

Gwin almost said yes. She was taking Hilde, so why not take the mechanical boy as well and make up for that useless betrayal?

But then she saw the lights looming on the far side of the river and realized that they were already more than halfway across.

Panic flared up inside her. "I won't have time," she whispered. And she turned back to Papa.

The rat darted in front of her. "You gotta take 'im, shipmate. You're the Singer."

"No, I'm not. Get out of my way."

"That's the worst of them, sirs," cried the ferryman. "Just a couple more to go, then you can rest."

Gwin's heart thumped frantically against her ribs. She shoved the rat to one side. She didn't see where it went, but even as her fingers tore at Papa's ropes, the mule began to bray in protest, as if something—or someone—had pinched it.

The sound brought Bartle spinning around. In the light of

the torches, he saw Gwin, and with a shout he leapt onto the cart with his cudgel raised.

Gwin thought she heard a small voice say, "Sorry, shipmate, but the cap'n and the Singer gotta stay together."

Then Bartle's cudgel clouted her across the temple and everything went dark.

CHAPTER 21

THE FIRST TO FALL

"She got away from me," Petrel said bitterly. Scroll was perched on *her* shoulder now, head tucked under wing. "I think she made it onto the ferry."

"Then Brother Poosk will catch her," said Fin.

"Not if she is hidden," murmured Rain, her eyes dreamy and unfocused.

Sharkey looked at her. "What's the matter?"

"Nothing." And Rain started to sing the Hope song again, very quietly, as she'd been doing on and off all day. "*How tall the tree, the first to fall . . .*"

"There's her dog," said Petrel, pointing.

The dog trotted up to Rain and collapsed on her feet with a sigh.

"Then she's on the ferry all right," said Sharkey. "She's gone after her parents and her brother. Question is, will she muck things up for us? And for the cap'n?"

"How far ahead of us will they get?" said Fin. "If there are more shortcuts, I don't know them."

Petrel turned to one of the villagers, who was scowling across the water. "'Scuse me. D'you reckon the ferry'll come straight back, once it's dropped that lot? Will it make a second run tonight?"

The man shrugged. "We all need to get across, and ferryman'll want our fares."

"Will you wake us when it comes?"

"Don't worry, I'll give you a nudge." And the man went back to watching the river.

"You're not going to *sleep?*" said Sharkey.

"Can you think of anything better to do? I ain't shut my eyes for a month—least that's what it feels like." Petrel yawned and lay down on the muddy bank, with her head pillowed on her arm and Scroll tucked in beside her elbow.

I've had worse beds, she thought, *and there's no one trying to kill me. Not right at the moment, anyway.*

Rain curled up beside her, still singing under her breath. The dog turned in circles, then squeezed in between the two girls. It stank, but then so did they all.

Sharkey and Fin stood for a little longer, trying to pretend that they weren't about to fall over from sheer exhaustion. But before long they lay down too, on either side of the girls.

Petrel closed her eyes—and opened them again. "Where d'you think Scroll's been all this time?" she whispered to Fin. "She's too well fed to have been hiding in a cave with Mister Smoke and the cap'n."

"I do not know," replied Fin. "Does it matter?"

Rain's quiet voice drifted between them. "*The trunk is gone, the root still lives . . .*"

"Mmm. Prob'ly not." Petrel smoothed the pigeon's feathers with gentle fingers. "Wish I knew how shipfolk are going against the Citadel. I bet they're showing those Devouts a thing or two."

"If the attack went ahead."

"Course it did, Fin! Shipfolk ain't gunna just walk away and forgive what happened, and neither are Sunkers. Who knows, maybe the Citadel's fallen already. Maybe Brother Poosk'll get there just in time to hand over the cap'n to Krill and Dolph. Wouldn't that be good?"

Fin shook his head. "The Citadel will not fall so easily."

On Petrel's other side, Rain suddenly sat bolt upright. "I have it!" she cried.

Folk up and down the bank stopped talking and turned to stare at her. Rain blushed and lowered her voice to a whisper. "The Song. I know what it is about. At least, I—I think I do."

Petrel, Fin and Sharkey sat up and crowded closer. Rain whispered, "The captain said it was a code, remember? Which means we have to read behind the words. So *the first to fall* could be"—she hesitated—"I might be wrong. If we follow my idea, we might make things even worse."

Sharkey rolled his eyes. "What is it, Rain?"

"I think it is the Grand Monument."

"Never heard of it," said Petrel.

"It is an important memorial," said Fin.

Sharkey said, "It's on the coast road, where Poosk tried to trap me after *Rampart* was sunk. It might've been important once, but there's nothing there now except a huge pile of stones."

Rain nodded eagerly. "It is where the Great Cleansing started. Don't you see? Where it *started*. There was a building there, and now there is not. The *first* to *fall!*"

"I spose it could be," said Petrel, nibbling her thumbnail. "But what's the point of it if there's nothing there except stones?"

"There is nothing we can *see*." Rain's eyes were growing brighter by the second. "It must be hidden, so the Devouts would not find it. *The trunk is gone*—that's the building that used to stand there. *The root still lives.* Which means that some part of the building remains, though we cannot see it."

Petrel desperately wanted Rain to be right. *We've got nothing else*, she thought. Aloud she said, "So we have to get the cap'n there?"

"Yes." The excitement vanished from Rain's eyes, and her voice faltered. She glanced at the river, where the dark shape of the returning ferry was just coming into sight. "Somehow, we have to get the captain there. *And* the Singer."

DOLPH SHOULD'VE BEEN ASLEEP; INSTEAD, SHE WAS WATCHING the Citadel. "Those gates just ain't going to open, Missus Slink," she said gloomily. "For all the good it did, we might as well not have bothered with the rat army."

"It's the water," said Missus Slink. "We should've done something about their water."

"I suppose it's too late now?"

"Aye, lass. I crept back in two nights ago, just in case, but they've got that well so closely guarded even I couldn't get near it."

All around them, night sentries strode up and down, or gathered in small groups, talking quietly. When a couple of them passed Dolph and Missus Slink, they nodded, and one said, "Got any more clever tricks up your sleeve, Dolph? Going to get us out of here before next winter?"

Dolph grinned in a halfhearted fashion and leaned against an empty barrel. "I should go to bed, Missus Slink. No use sitting here night after night. I should—"

Somewhere to their right, a man shouted.

Dolph shot upright, with Missus Slink clinging to her shoulder. Another shout—and there on the face of the Citadel was a sliver of torchlight that hadn't been visible a moment ago. The gates were opening.

Dolph grabbed her knife and banged out a message on the barrel, in general ship code. *Gates opening. Gates opening!*

All around her, sentries were bellowing the same thing, but the clanging of the barrel rose above them all. Within seconds, every single crew member of the *Oyster* was on his or her feet, with the Sunkers only a few steps behind.

By the time the first Devouts set cautious foot outside the Citadel, with flaming torches to light their way, there was an army wide awake and ready to accept their surrender.

Except they weren't surrendering.

Dolph was one of the first to realize. "Stay back!" she cried. "Don't rush 'em, they've got bratlings with 'em."

So they had. Every brown-robed man pushed a bratling in front of him. And every bratling, however small, had a knife at its throat.

Krill shoved his way through the crowd to stand beside Dolph and Missus Slink. "We should've guessed they'd try something like this," he growled. "I've been chatting to the townsfolk; this is how the Devouts keep 'em in order. They take away their bratlings for Initiates and servants, and if anyone steps out of line, it's the bratlings that suffer." He shook his head in disgust. "Even Albie'd never pull such a low trick."

"But what do we do?" asked Dolph. "We can't just let 'em stroll past. We can't let 'em escape."

"What d'you suggest, then? Rush 'em, and see every one of those bratlings murdered?"

"They'd do it too," said Missus Slink.

"Aye, they would," growled Krill. "Look at their faces."

It was only the second time Dolph had seen the Devouts up close. The first time had been when they'd attacked the *Oyster*, months ago and thousands of miles away, and so much had happened since then that the main thing Dolph remembered was how quickly the Devouts had scuttled away when they saw the captain.

They weren't scuttling now; they didn't have the strength. Some of them limped; others wore bloodstained bandages. One man, close to the front, rode in a wheeled chair, with a protective cordon around him.

Every one of them, man and bratling, showed signs of

hunger. But the Devouts' faces were still grim with purpose, and the bratlings looked as if they had fallen into a nightmare and didn't know how to wake up.

As they came closer, someone behind Dolph cried out, "There's my Dovesy! *Dovesy!*"

One of the smaller hostages sobbed in distress. A townswoman pushed past Dolph and fell to her knees, crying, "Gracious sirs, don't hurt her, I beg you!"

She might as well not have spoken. The Devouts stumbled past her, four abreast.

"Where are they going?" whispered Dolph. "They must know we'll follow 'em."

"Maybe there's food somewhere," said Krill. "I've heard they collect it from the villages every quarter. Maybe it's on its way. And if they've got food *and* hostages, I'm not sure what we can do."

The Devouts drew level with the watching army, and shipfolk and Sunkers fell back with a groan and let them pass. The mountain of food that the rats had stolen from the Citadel was still where it had been dropped, and although Krill had been feeding the townsfolk from it for days, it looked no smaller. When the Devouts saw it, they surged toward it, snatching up bacon, biscuits and salted herring, and stuffing them into their mouths, then filling their arms with whatever they could carry. They seized water bottles from the camp too, and bedrolls, and loaded them onto the bratlings.

The watching army groaned again, and so did the townsfolk, but there was nothing they could do. Even Admiral Deeps wouldn't order an attack, not when the lives of so many bratlings were at stake.

But as the last of the Devouts came out of the Citadel, Dolph and Missus Slink fell in behind them. So did a couple of Sunkers, then more and more of both crews, until the entire army was shuffling along at the same snail's pace as the Devouts. Krill and his cooks brought up the rear, rolling barrels of supplies.

"Devouts'll have to stop sometime," Dolph said to Missus Slink. "They'll have to sleep sometime. And when they do, we'll get 'em."

CHAPTER 22

DO YOU THINK ME SO GULLIBLE?

GWIN WOKE WITH A HEADACHE, AND THE SUN GLARING IN her eyes. It hadn't been so bright for days, and her first thought was that it would be good traveling weather, which might cheer Papa up a little.

Her second thought was that Nat and Papa must have got up early because the cart was swaying and rattling beneath her and she could hear Spindle's hooves on the road.

She felt a wave of relief. For weeks she'd been the one to wake up first, to cook breakfast, to make sure they set off at a reasonable hour. She'd sung when she didn't feel like it, struggled to make things work the way they were supposed to, carried the burden of being a Fetcher almost entirely by herself.

And now at last Papa and Nat were doing their share. Which was just as well, because Gwin's head was so sore that she wondered if she was sickening with something. Her wrists were sore too, which was odd. Perhaps she wasn't sick; perhaps she'd just slept in the wrong position.

She tried to sit up.

Somewhere above her a deep voice said, "The Fetcher cub is awake, Brother Poosk. Shall I toss her out of the cart to walk with the others?"

Gwin was used to walking great distances, but not like this, with a rope around her wrists and despair in her heart.

She'd fought for so long to hold things together, to keep her family safe. She'd tried and tried with all her strength, and it had come to nothing.

That was bad enough. But then she overheard Brother Poosk congratulating himself on having captured Hilde, the woman he'd been sent to find. "And such good fortune," he crowed, "that I also stumbled across the Fetchers and the demon."

At which point Gwin realized the awful truth. The Devouts hadn't been chasing her little family at all, not at the beginning. They'd been hunting Hilde, who Gwin had rescued. In trying to make things work the way they were supposed to, she had doomed them all.

It was too much to bear. By the end of the first day, she had retreated into a merciful numbness, where she didn't have to think or feel or care about anything.

It was a long way down the coast road to the Citadel. With the prisoners walking, Brother Poosk could no longer push Spindle so hard, but neither was he willing to rest more than necessary. They set off before sunrise every morning, and kept going far into the night.

As the days passed, Brother Poosk grew more cheerful. Once, he turned to his prisoners and cried, "Make the most of what time you have left, Fetchers. Dance! Sing! Tell your stories to the birds and the stones."

Cull and Bartle sniggered, but Papa looked at Gwin, then cleared his throat and began to sing in a voice that was little more than a croak,

"There once was—a girl, a blue-eyed girl,
A girl with a song
And a bold, bold heart—"

He hadn't even finished the first verse when Brother Poosk interrupted him. "Enough! I have never heard such rubbish."

And that was the end of that.

Some time later, Nat twitched as if he'd heard something unexpected. "Bird," he whispered.

Gwin plodded along beside him, too numb to even wonder what he was talking about.

"Pigeon," murmured Nat.

And that was the end of *that*.

Except it wasn't. Not quite. That night, Gwin's exhausted sleep was interrupted by a rough whisper. "Wakey, wakey, shipmate."

"Nnnh," mumbled Gwin.

A tiny paw raised one of her eyelids, and a long whiskered nose peered at her. "You in there, shipmate? Still got all your circuits? Listen, Petrel and crew've caught up with us. They're worn to the bone with runnin', and could do with a good meal, but they've got news. D'you know the Grand Monument?

They're gunna trot ahead and wait for us there. So when you see a big pile of rocks on the seaward side, you be ready to move."

And he dashed away, leaving Gwin to close her eyes and go back to sleep.

Next morning, as usual, the Devouts ate a lavish breakfast while giving little to their hungry prisoners. But even Gwin couldn't help noticing that Brother Poosk was not happy.

"I tell you, there was more bacon left," he snapped. "And now there is barely enough for a single meal. How do you explain that, Brother Bartle? Hmm? You were on guard last night. Did you think I would not notice?"

"It was not me, Brother," protested Bartle as he buckled Spindle's harness. "I did not go near the bacon. Perhaps there was not as much as you thought—"

"I do not make mistakes."

"Then it must have been Cull."

But Cull swore it hadn't been him, and they argued for half the morning, as the cart creaked onward.

Gwin wondered if she should be watching out for a pile of rocks. But it felt like too much effort, and as the hours wore on and nothing happened, she knew she was right.

No one's going to save us. It's the end of three hundred years of Fetchers.

Nat edged closer to her and whispered, "You all right?"

Gwin said nothing.

Nat left her alone for a few minutes, then edged back. This

time his whisper was even quieter. "I can hear something. Under the cart. Like someone sawing wood."

Gwin couldn't hear a thing over the rattle of the wheels. She considered telling her brother about Mister Smoke, but if she did, he'd only be disappointed when nothing happened. So she kept her mouth shut.

As the sun sank over West Norn, Brother Poosk dug in the pocket of his robe and pulled out Papa's heirloom. "Ah, Fetcher, I had almost forgotten. Come up here and tell me about your timepiece. Quickly now, before the last of the light disappears."

Bartle, who was driving, raised the whip, and Papa shuffled forward at the end of his rope.

"What is this?" asked Brother Poosk, stabbing his finger at the face of the heirloom.

Exhausted though he was, Papa was still a Fetcher, and as he limped along beside the cart, he did his best to explain. "It predicts the . . . aspects of the moon. When it will be . . . new. When it will be . . . full."

Gwin thought she saw something in the gloom ahead. A great pile of stones, as big as five or six village huts set one on top of the other.

The cart rolled toward it. Brother Poosk interrupted Papa's explanations to say, "I am not stupid, Fetcher. I know that is the moon. I was talking about this bit here." And he poked at the heirloom again.

"I believe that is when . . . the moon and the . . . sun come together," croaked Papa. "And turn . . . the middle of the day . . . into night."

"Turn day into night?" said Brother Poosk, his voice rising in disbelief. "I have never heard anything so ridiculous. This is just one of your stories. Do you think me so gullible?"

Papa shook his head. "It is called . . . eclipse. There is one . . . coming very soon. In fact"—he appeared to be counting the days in his head—"I think . . . it is tomorrow. At noon. It is getting too dark to see . . . but in the morning . . . you will notice how the little hand . . . points."

"Hmm," said Brother Poosk, with a thoughtful expression on his face. "Cull, light a torch so I can see."

By the time the torch was lit, and jammed into its bracket on the side of the cart, they were passing the Grand Monument. Poosk studied the heirloom curiously, then turned back to Papa. "How does the timepiece know about this . . . eclipse?"

Halfway through an uncertain explanation, Papa stumbled over a rut in the road and almost fell.

"Keep *up*, Fetcher," said Brother Poosk. He twisted in his seat. "Woman, come and help him. I have more questions."

Hilde hesitated, and Cull, who was walking close by, raised his cudgel in a halfhearted fashion, as if he was sick to death of the prisoners but would still beat them if they gave any trouble. "Move," he grunted.

Hilde limped forward and put her arm around Papa's waist.

"Tiny wheels, you say?" prompted Poosk. "What makes them go?"

Behind them, the Grand Monument was almost lost in the darkness. *I was right*, Gwin thought numbly. *No one's going to save us.*

A heartbeat later, Nat leaned toward her and whispered, "Someone's coming. Up ahead."

The figure was almost upon them before Gwin saw it. "Brother!" cried a boy's voice. "Brother Poosk!"

It was Fin, and he was panting as if he'd been running hard. As he came into the torchlight, Gwin thought she heard a sound from Hilde.

"Brother, I am so glad . . . to have found you," gasped Fin. "I must tell you—no, do not stop, I will walk along with you— the most amazing . . . thing has happened."

Brother Poosk leaned forward, saying, "What is it, boy?"

"I am sorry, I have a . . . a stitch," panted the Initiate, clutching his side.

"Never mind your stitch, what is your news? Is it from the Citadel? You did reach the Citadel, did you not? Cull, come here."

Cull hurried toward the front of the cart. Nat hissed through his teeth, as if he'd heard something else—

With an earsplitting crack, the cart's axle snapped.

Poosk and Bartle were thrown off the cart and onto the roadway, where they sprawled, cursing at the tops of their voices. The mule kicked Cull and sent him flying.

Petrel and Sharkey dashed out of the darkness.

"Treachery!" screeched Poosk.

A knife appeared in Fin's hand, and he slashed right through

Spindle's harness. Bartle scrambled to his feet and brought the whip down on the Initiate's arm. Fin cried out and dropped his knife, but before Bartle could grab him, Spindle bellowed and galloped off down the road, knocking the Devout back to the ground in the process.

Nat's head swiveled back and forth, trying to follow what was happening. Sharkey leapt into the broken cart and grabbed hold of the mechanical boy. At the same time, Petrel sawed through the ropes that tied Gwin and Nat to the cart.

Gwin didn't move. The shock of the rescue had ripped the numbness away, like a scab off a wound. But now she found herself paralyzed by self-doubt. In saving Hilde she had brought disaster upon her family. What if she did the wrong thing again? What if she made things worse? What if people died because of her?

Beside her, Nat gasped, "Papa? Hilde?"

"We'll get 'em." And Petrel ran forward.

But Bartle was on his feet again, and now he wielded the Initiate's knife. Poosk screamed instructions. Cull staggered toward the cart and seized the mechanical boy's legs. A desperate tug of war began.

Petrel left Papa and Hilde and raced to help Sharkey with the mechanical boy. But the two of them were not enough. With a shout, Cull jerked the limp body out of their grasp.

Petrel and Sharkey hesitated. Bartle roared and raced toward them. The children dodged away from him, but at the last minute, Petrel dashed back and grabbed both Gwin and Nat by the hand.

Nat cried, "Papa!"

"Run!" shouted Papa. "*Run!*"

And with that, the two Fetcher children were dragged off the road and into the darkness, leaving Papa, Hilde and the mechanical boy in the clutches of the Devouts.

CHAPTER 23

THE GRAND MONUMENT

PETREL COULD HARDLY BELIEVE IT. She and her friends had driven themselves to the point of exhaustion and beyond to catch up with the oxcart. They had cut across country several times, never sure if they would be able to find the road again. They had scoured the area around the Grand Monument to find the right place for the attack and chewed their fingernails almost to the quick while they waited for the cart. And after all that, they had failed to rescue the captain.

She was furious with herself and furious with the Fetcher bratlings too, but she said nothing, just hustled them through the undergrowth as fast as she could, with Sharkey and Fin bringing up the rear. She'd scouted this route earlier, while there was still light, going over it until she knew it almost as well as she knew the passages of the *Oyster*.

There was a cry of triumph in the distance, followed by a barrage of cursing. The Fetcher boy jerked to a halt so suddenly that Fin almost ran into him. "What was that?"

It was probably Mister Smoke leading the Devouts astray, but Petrel wasn't going to say so. She hadn't forgiven the boy's sister for betraying the captain, which was why they were in this mess in the first place. "Get a move on."

The boy didn't budge. "What about our father?"

"Nothing we can do about him," said Sharkey, from somewhere in the darkness. "*Or* your ma."

"She's not—"

"Count yourselves lucky that we got you two away," snapped Petrel. "Now are you coming, or do you want to wait for Poosk and his bully boys?"

They didn't go directly to the Grand Monument. Instead, Petrel took a devious path, avoiding the soft ground that would mark their passing. By the time they reached the monument, the Fetcher bratlings were flagging badly.

"How much farther?" whispered the boy.

At the sound of his voice, there was a whine from the bushes, and the dog came barreling toward them.

"Keep him quiet!" hissed Fin, and the Fetcher boy fell to his knees, whispering, "Hush, Wretched! Yes, Gwin's here too. Hush!"

Somewhere nearby, Rain murmured, "Sorry, Petrel, the dog wriggled away from me. Have you got the captain?"

"No!" Petrel's frustration spilled out in a stream of words. "All we've got is the Singer and her brother, and now Poosk and his men'll be on high alert, and I don't see how we're gunna get near the cap'n again, *and* they'll be after us as soon as they stop running in circles."

"The dog found a little shelter," whispered Rain. Petrel could just see Scroll, asleep on the other girl's shoulder. "We could hide there while we work out what to do next. If we can get far enough in, we might be able to light the lantern."

The place the dog had found was really just a crevice between two of the stones that made up the Grand Monument. It was a bit of a scrabble even for Petrel, who was the smallest of the six. Sharkey, who was the biggest, had to take off his jerkin and wriggle and twist and squirm until he came out the other side scraped half raw.

They found themselves in a narrow space, surrounded by stones piled upon stones. Water dripped from a point above Petrel's head, and puddled on the ground at her feet. "How do we get farther in?" she asked the darkness.

"Here." A cold hand grasped Petrel's and tugged her closer to the ground. "I have not been through because I was afraid. But the dog went through and back again, and he did not come to any harm."

The gap in the stones was so close to the ground that Petrel had to lie on her belly to inspect it. She couldn't see a thing, but her questing fingers told her that she'd probably fit through, though it'd be another tight squeeze for Sharkey.

"Come on," she said. And she wriggled head-first into the narrow space, feeling as if she were back on the *Oyster*, trying to hide from Chief Engineer Albie.

She could hear the others behind her, whispering to each other. At one point, Fin hissed with pain. Rain was singing, so quietly that only the occasional note reached Petrel.

Scroll woke up and cooed in protest. The Fetcher girl's beads clacked against stone, and her brother murmured something to the dog.

Wish we'd left those two behind, thought Petrel. *Wish we'd gone for the cap'n straight off, all three of us, and got him away before Poosk and his mates knew what was happening.*

The tunnel was longer than she'd expected. She crawled on and on, groping ahead to make sure she wasn't about to run into anything nasty. When at last she emerged from the hole, she sighed with relief, brushed the dirt and cobwebs from her face and helped the others to their feet, one by one.

Rain lit the lantern with shaking fingers. "We will not have to go back that way, will we? Scroll did not like it, and neither did I."

"Hope not," said Petrel, and she took the lantern and held it high.

The first thing she saw was a rusty iron door, buckled under the weight of the enormous stones that had fallen on top of it. There was a pool of dark water on one side, and an iron ladder hanging broken in midair on the other. Beyond the water, the end of a pipe gaped from a heap of debris. There were smashed iron wheels and crushed gauges, and bolts and clamps and cables, all of them cobwebbed and useless. Petrel thought she could feel a faint draught from somewhere overhead.

"Is this it, Rain?" she whispered. "Is this what you were talking about? The first to fall?"

Rain nodded, her eyes white and scared in the lantern light. "It was a building once—or so I was told." She turned around slowly. "They smashed it at the beginning of the Great Cleansing, then piled up the stones to make the monument."

"There's part of the old wall," whispered Fin, pointing. "See? Where the stones are still square on top of each other?"

A shiver ran down Petrel's spine. This was what the Devouts would have done to the *Oyster* if she and her friends hadn't stopped them. It was a level of hatred she didn't understand, built on superstition and ignorance, and it made her even more afraid for the captain.

"So we're in the right place," she said. "Least, I hope we are. What do we do now?"

"Waste of time trying to surprise Poosk twice," said Sharkey. "We'd just get ourselves caught."

"And we cannot use Fin again," said Rain.

Fin grimaced. "Unless I pretended you made me do it. If I told them you threatened me—"

"No," said Petrel. "Poosk'd kill you."

Since coming out of the tunnel, the Fetcher bratlings hadn't said a word. But at Petrel's bald statement, the boy straightened up and said, "He'll kill Papa if we don't get him away."

"What about your mama?" asked Rain. "Are you not worried about her?"

"She's not our—" The boy bit his lip and started again. "She's not our mama. She's only been traveling with us for a little while, but"—his brow creased and he nodded in Fin's direction—"but I think she knew *him* from somewhere. Her name's Hilde."

Fin's face lost every scrap of color, and he looked as if he might fall. Petrel grabbed his arm, still too busy thinking about the captain to make sense of her friend's reaction. "Are you all right, Fin? What is it?"

"I had"—his voice was that of a stranger—"I had forgotten. But . . . Hilde. That was Mama's name!"

CHAPTER 24

THAT DREADFUL VOICE

THE INITIATE'S FRIENDS LOOKED ALMOST AS STRICKEN AS HE did. Gwin watched them, but said nothing. That awful paralysis still had her in its grip. *Leave it to them*, she thought. *They won't get everything wrong, the way I did. They won't get us all killed.*

"That was your mam?" whispered Petrel.

"We must go back." Fin's eyes glittered. "We must go back right now. We must get her away before Brother Poosk kills her."

"We can't," said Sharkey. "You know we can't, Fin. They'll be waiting for us."

Rain touched Fin's arm. "You are hurt."

"It is nothing," said the Initiate, shrugging her off.

"But you are bleeding—"

"It is *nothing*!" And before anyone realized what was happening, Fin had dropped to his hands and knees and was crawling into the tunnel, back the way they had come.

Nat whispered in Gwin's ear, "We should follow him. If he's going after Hilde, we must go after Papa."

Gwin didn't move.

"What's the matter?" hissed Nat. "Don't you want—"

An exclamation from outside the Grand Monument interrupted him.

"Here, Cull!" It was Bartle, his voice hollowed out by its passage through the stone tunnel.

Fin's boots, the only part of him Gwin could still see, stopped abruptly.

Bartle said, "Bring the torch over this way. See? There is the blood trail. I told you I got the boy a good whack."

"But where did they go from here?" asked Cull.

"Through this little crack in the stones, I would say. There is more blood around the edges."

"Too small for either of us to get through," said Cull. "I do not think Brother Poosk would fit either."

Bartle laughed. "There are more ways of getting a periwinkle out of its shell than squeezing in after it. Go and tell Brother Poosk we have them."

Fin backed silently out of the tunnel and stood up. None of the children said anything for several minutes. Then Petrel whispered, "They don't know for sure that we're here. If we can wait 'em out, they might go away."

"But we *cannot* wait them out," whispered Fin. "If they go, they will take . . . Mama." He sounded as if he barely knew how to say the word, as if he'd had no practice in it. "Or perhaps they will just . . . kill her."

Silence.

Then, "How d'you get a periwinkle out of its shell?" breathed Petrel.

"With a knife," whispered Sharkey.

A longer silence, that was eventually broken by a quiet voice from outside. "Initiate? Can you hear me? I have your mama, Initiate. She is very keen to talk to you."

Rain whispered, "Uncle Poosk!" Wretched tried to tuck his head under Nat's foot.

"Amusing, is it not," said Poosk, "that we spent those days together, and I did not know who you were? But I know now, Initiate, and so does your mama. According to Citadel records, it is nine years since she last held you in her arms. Such a long time, and she has missed you for every minute of it. I wonder if you have missed *her.*"

"Don't listen to him, Fin," whispered Sharkey. "He'll turn you inside out, that's what he's good at."

But it was impossible *not* to listen. To Gwin, that dreadful voice seemed to sour the air; it made the darkness beyond the lamp seem alive and ugly.

"She thinks you do not care about her, Initiate, saving the Fetcher cubs and leaving her to hang. Not that *I* wish her to hang. I would give her to you, right now, but I am tied by my vows—and, I confess, by my fondness for my own neck. I must take *someone* back to the Citadel, or my superiors will hang *me.* I have the demon, of course, though the creature appears to be dead already. And I have the Fetcher. But Brother Thrawn will still ask questions if I do not return with your mama. Now, if I could offer him *an entire Fetcher family*, in place of your mama, that would be different."

Fin's eyes flickered toward Gwin and Nat.

Rain put her hand to her mouth. "No, Fin. You cannot!"

But Brother Poosk was still talking. "Your mama is right here with me, you know. Will you not do this one little thing for her? The Fetcher cubs will not come to any serious harm; we Devouts do not hang children. A few months in the reeducation camp, that is all, to teach them the error of their ways."

In the uncertain light of the lamp, Gwin could see a pulse beating in Fin's throat.

Sharkey whispered, "You can't trust him, Fin. He'll cheat you. And besides, we still have to get the cap'n back. We'll get your ma at the same time."

"The captain is dead," Fin said bitterly. "You heard Brother Poosk."

"Course he's not dead," said Petrel.

Fin rounded on her. "He *is*! You know he is. We have failed at everything we set out to do, and all that is left is—is Mama's life. Why should we not hand over these two"—he jerked his chin at Gwin and her brother—"to save her?"

Beside Gwin, Nat said, "Your captain isn't dead. He spoke to us."

Four pairs of eyes fixed on Gwin's brother. "He *spoke* to you?" hissed Petrel. "And your sister still betrayed him?"

"Yes." For the first time in two months, Nat fumbled for Gwin's hand and held it tightly. "I would've done the same, if I'd thought it would save Papa."

Petrel's face darkened. "Then maybe we *should* give you to Poosk. Both of you. Right now!"

Sharkey shrugged uncomfortably. "We can't, Petrel."

"You heard what he said. They're traitors, both of 'em—"

"What would you have done, Petrel?" asked Rain. "Your papa's name was Seal, was it not? What would you have done if it had been him?"

Petrel shook her head. "I wouldn't've—"

"Or your mama. Quill."

"I don't know what I would've done, all right?" said Petrel. "But I wouldn't have given up the cap'n."

"That is because you know him," said Rain. With one finger, she stroked Scroll's sleeping head. "But you would have thought about it. We all would, if it was *our* papa."

Gwin swallowed. She hadn't expected any sort of understanding from these children. They'd seemed so self-sufficient, so determined and clever.

When Gwin was small, Mama used to say that her daughter was as strong-willed as Ariel herself and as stubborn as the blue ox. Gwin didn't feel strong-willed, not anymore. But it must have been there inside her somewhere because she felt the paralysis shift a little.

She tried to stop it. She didn't trust herself, not anymore. She didn't want to be the one who got people killed.

But Nat's hand was warm and alive in hers, and that old stubbornness was working away inside her, whether she liked it or not.

What if, she thought, *what if the mechanical boy is as important as Petrel believes? What if there's something big happening in
West Norn?*

What if change is coming?

She didn't say a word, but Nat heard her anyway. "What is
it, Gwin?"

Before she could answer him, the whisper started up again.
"I hope you will not take too long to decide, Initiate. Bartle
has a knife at your mama's throat, you see, a good sharp knife.
And he is notorious for his clumsiness. His hand might slip,
and once a throat is cut it cannot be uncut, however much we
might regret it. So are you thinking hard, Initiate?"

Fin groaned. He was bent almost double with the need to
do something and to do it quickly.

Gwin knew exactly how he felt. She leaned toward Nat and
whispered, "The pigeon."

It was hardly more than a breath of sound, but Nat heard
it. She saw the realization dawning on him. He turned to the
others and said, "There are people in the mountains who might
help us. We could send a message with the pigeon!"

No one moved. "The mountains?" said Sharkey. "What
good's that? It'd take 'em too long to get here. We need help
now." He rubbed his forehead. "We could rush Poosk, maybe.
He won't be expecting it."

"We couldn't squeeze out of that little crack in the rock
quick enough," said Petrel. "They'd pick us off one by one and
cut Fin's mam's throat at the same time."

191

Nat shook his head. "Poosk's lying. Hilde isn't with him."

"What are you talking about?" snarled Fin. "You cannot know that."

"But he can," whispered Rain. "I told you, Fin, I have seen them before. He is the blind boy who can hear the world breathing."

"He's *blind*?" said Petrel, at the same time as Nat said, "Two people sound different from three. There are only two outside, Poosk and Bartle." He hesitated. "No, wait. There's someone else. Someone very small—"

"That'd be me, shipmate," said a voice at floor level.

"Mister Smoke!" cried Fin, and now all the bitterness was gone, and the only thing left was a desperate hope. "Is Mama—"

"She's back where you left 'er, shipmate. It's Poosk and Bartle outside, no one else."

Fin looked as if he might collapse with relief. Petrel slipped her arm around him. "There, see? Things ain't as bad as we thought."

"They're bad enough, shipmate," said Mister Smoke. "I'd like it better if that door over there"—his whiskers twitched in the direction of the rusty metal—"was standin' open, with a little signpost directin' us to where we're sposed to go. But the only signpost we've got is the Song." He peered up at Gwin. "'Ow about you sing it for us? Nice and quiet so that lot outside can't hear."

"*Now?*" said Fin. "But—"

"Can you see any other course, shipmate? Your mam's in

mortal peril, and so's the cap'n. But they're out there, and you're in 'ere, which don't add up to much of a rescue in my opinion. We need to do somethin' else, quick as we can."

Rain said, "He is right, Fin. We cannot go at Uncle Poosk straight on. We should hear the Song."

"But we know what it says," protested Petrel. "That stuff about the tree's dead and the root's not. That's why we're here, to find the—the root thing." She gazed dismally at their surroundings. "Though it's not jumping out at me."

"There is another verse," said Rain. "I could not remember it, but the Singer will know it." And she looked expectantly at Gwin—

Who was so shocked that the last scrap of paralysis melted away, and she said, "You mean . . . I really *am* the Singer?"

"Told you so, shipmate, didn't I?" said Mister Smoke. "Thought I made it clear enough."

"But—but *me*?"

"Why not you?" said Nat.

"Because . . ." There were so many reasons that Gwin didn't know where to start. But all she said was, "I'll sing. But I want to send a message first."

"There's no point," said Sharkey. "Like I said, it'd take too long."

"But maybe it won't!" Gwin squeezed her brother's fingers. "Nat, remember what Hob told Papa? He said they've got great wonders hidden in the mountains, things not seen in West Norn for three hundred years. What if they've got a—a machine that makes their legs go faster? Or a—an airship!"

She wasn't at all sure what an airship was, but the idea gripped her and would not let go.

"They could save Papa!" she said, imagining something like a fisherman's boat flying through the air with its ragged sails flapping. "And Hilde and the captain. And—and get us out of here!"

The other children looked as doubtful as ever, but Mister Smoke said, "Right you are, shipmate. It's always good to have a backup plan. And with any luck, Scroll'll be able to get past Poosk before he knows what's 'appenin'."

Gwin dug into her pocket for cloth, stylus and ocher. Her fingers felt as unwieldy as tree trunks, but she spat on the ocher then rubbed the end of the stylus against it and wrote as neatly as she could:

<u>BIG</u> CHANGES!
COME QUICKLY!
GRAND MONUMENT COAST ROAD.
GWIN FETCHER

Then, while Mister Smoke tied the scrap of cloth to the sleepy pigeon's leg and led her out through the tunnel, Gwin began to sing, very quietly.

"How tall the tree,
The first to fall.
How wise to flee
The worst of all . ."

With every note she sang, hope seemed to trickle back into her.

"But hear the song
The singer gives.
The trunk is gone,
The root still lives."

"Something hidden, like I said," whispered Rain. "What does the second verse say?"

"How bright the sun
The first to fade,
The world undone,
The work unmade—"

"That's the Devouts," murmured Sharkey. "The Hungry Ghosts, smashing everything that had gone before."

"But hear the song
The singer gives,
The sun is gone,
The moon still lives."

As the last note died away, there was silence. The air felt sullen and heavy. Gwin thought of Papa, out there in the darkness with a sentence of death hanging over him.

It's all right, she told herself. *Hob will come and save him.*

"*The first to fade*," murmured Rain. "It still sounds like the Grand Monument. But the rest of it—it is not really telling us anything new."

Petrel's shoulders slumped in disappointment. But Nat turned toward the low tunnel that had brought them there. "Smoke," he said.

"He's taken Scroll out," said Sharkey. "He's not back yet."

Nat shook his head. "I don't mean him. Can't you smell it? The damp leaves? The fire?" His blind eyes traveled around the little cave. "I think Poosk has given up on persuasion. I think he intends to smoke us out."

CHAPTER 25

WITCH

DOLPH WAS NO LONGER AT THE BACK OF THE COLUMN. She'd tried waiting for the Devouts to fall asleep, but when they did they set guards, and no one could get near them without risking the lives of the hostages.

So now Dolph was out in front, with her eyes peeled for opportunities. She wasn't sure what those opportunities would look like, but she'd know them when she saw them.

Missus Slink was with her, and a dozen of the bolder towns folk. They were more or less toothless, most of them, and Dolph had assumed they were old men and women. But when she'd talked to them, she'd been horrified to discover that some of those haggard figures were younger than she was.

That might have explained their boldness. Or maybe it was that they had full bellies for the first time in their lives and that they'd seen the Devouts crawl out of the Citadel like wounded dogs. Whatever the reason, it worried Dolph.

"Don't you try anything stupid," she said. "Devouts'll kill those bratlings if we get too close."

"Might be worth it," muttered one of the boys.

"You shut your mouth, Gant," said the girl next to him. "My little sister's there."

"And my brother," said another boy. "I seen 'im when they come out o' the Citadel. Scared out of 'is wits 'e was, poor mite. We won't do nothin' stupid, Witch, don't worry."

All the same there was a breathlessness to them, a wide-eyed skittish look that kept Dolph awake at night, worrying that one or two of them might creep off and attack the Devouts on their own.

"It's like trying to herd seals," she whispered to Missus Slink. "They keep slipping away from me, and I lose count of who's where. That boy Gant, have you seen him? He was asleep last time I looked, and now he's gone."

"There," said the old rat, pointing into the darkness.

Dolph sat up quickly. Gant was creeping round the outside of the little camp, whispering to his mates. One by one they stood up.

"What're you doing?" hissed Dolph.

Gant half turned, and the moonlight caught his eyes. "None o' your business, Witch. You're not in charge 'ere."

"Never said I was." Dolph yawned, nice and casual, as if she was at the end of a fishing shift and not worried about anything much except how soon she could get to her hammock. "Just thought I smelled a fight, that's all. And since I've been fighting since I was nine years old, and am reckoned to be one of the quickest and fiercest on the *Oyster*, I thought you might want my help. Course, if you don't, I'll go back to sleep. It's all the same to me."

Gant and his mates whispered to each other. Then, "It's a Master on 'is own," said Gant, "with oxcart 'n prisoners. I seen 'im up the road a step."

"Did he see you?"

Gant laughed scornfully. "What if 'e did? 'E's not gunna call the alarm if 'e sees a starlin', is 'e? Or a 'alf-starved fox? That's 'ow they think of us. Vermin, we are." He glanced at his fellows again. "Least, we was. Not anymore."

"Sounds good to me," said Dolph. "Let's scout it out. Work out what we're going to do."

"No need to work out nothin'." Gant thumped his bony chest. "I done that already. We rush 'im, all of us at once, that's what we do, and if you don't like it, Witch, you don't 'ave to come." And he set off into the night with his mates, all of them bouncing on their toes and whispering to each other.

Dolph groaned, "They're going to get 'emselves killed, Missus Slink." But she followed them all the same, watching the boasts and the excitement with a wary eye.

It was just as well she did. The oxcart was lit by two flaming torches, and by the time Gant and his friends reached it, they'd worked themselves into such a frenzy that they'd lost all common sense. They shouted their intentions at the tops of their voices, along with promises that the reign of the Masters was over. Then, having warned the Devout that they were coming, they shambled toward him in twos and threes.

The Devout, of course, had plenty of time to get ready for them. He threw his two prisoners into the bottom of the oxcart. Then he climbed up onto the driver's seat and thwacked his cudgel against the palm of his hand.

"Come on, scum!" he roared, so loudly that the flames of the torches wobbled. "You think the Devouts are done? Come and see what I've got for you. I'll show you *done*."

Gant and his friends hesitated.

"Idiots!" hissed Dolph, running up behind them. "You don't stop halfway. Gant, you take two around the back of him. You and you, attack from starboard—no, not that way. *That* way." She pushed them into position. "You two go round the other side, and you come with me; we'll go straight ahead. And watch out for those torches."

She didn't give them time to think about it. They were wavering already—any longer and the habits of fear and obedience would get the better of them. She set Missus Slink on the ground, took out her fighting knife and said, "Now go!"

And with a battle cry that made them all flinch, she raced toward the cart, low and fast.

She was pretty sure that not all of them would follow her. It didn't really matter; Dolph'd back herself against one of the Devouts any day. Even now, this man was laughing, as if he was looking forward to smashing her head, then going back to whatever he'd been doing.

She went straight on, as she'd promised. But at the very last minute, she dodged sideways, away from the cudgel, and slashed at the Devout's ankle. *Just like you taught me, Mam.*

The man yelled with shock and pain and swung around. But by then, Dolph was slashing at his other ankle, and Gant was there too, with at least three of his mates, swarming over the cart with desperate grins on their faces. They threw themselves onto the Devout's back, like mice trying to take down a cat, and he roared and shook them off, lashing out with his cudgel and dropping several of them to the ground.

Dolph leapt in close again—only this time she went for the man's hand. It wasn't easy, not with Gant and his friends jumping and screaming all around her, and the torchlight making everything waver. But Dolph had been trained by the best knife fighter on the *Oyster*, and before the Devout knew what was happening, he had dropped his cudgel and was clutching his bleeding fingers.

It was the shortest battle Dolph had ever been in, which was just as well because she'd seen something from the corner of her eye while she was darting in and out. Something that had almost stopped her in her tracks.

The cap'n.

He was lying in the bottom of the cart next to the human prisoners, bound so tight that Dolph had to look twice to make sure it was him.

She didn't waste time wondering how he'd got there; she knelt beside him and started to unknot the ropes. Over her shoulder, she said, "Tie that man well. Don't want him getting loose."

There was no answer. Instead, she heard an ugly sound that brought her back to her feet. The Devout was lying on the ground, and the town bratlings were kicking him. Some of them were picking up rocks—

"Stop!" shouted Dolph, in her most commanding voice. She jumped down from the cart. "You don't *kill* your prisoners. You *use* 'em."

Gant was one of those with a rock in his hands. "Use them for what? Fertilizer?"

His mates laughed, and Dolph smiled to show she was on their side. "No, I mean use 'em to bargain, to get what you want. Trade 'em for something. The other Devouts'll want this bloke back, won't they? So what've they got that you want?"

The town bratlings stared at each other. "My little sister," said one of them.

"My brother," said another.

"And mine."

"Don't know if they *will* trade," Dolph said hastily. "They might decide they don't want him back, not when they're in such desperate straits. But it's worth a try. Now tie him up so he can't get away. I'll let the prisoners go."

Gant tossed his rock from hand to hand. "Maybe we shouldn't let them go, not just yet." He mumbled something to one of his fellows, who trotted off into the darkness. "Maybe we should use *them* for trade too."

"Not the cap'n," Dolph said quickly. "You don't get to use him for anything. He's coming with me."

"If you say so. Which one's the cap'n? That boy with the silver face? I seen 'im when we was grabbin' the Devout." Gant tipped his head to one side. "He a witch too?"

"Aye," said Dolph. "If you touch him, your fingers'll fall off."

"Weren't gunna touch 'im. Just askin', that's all. Why's 'is face silver? Is it a mask? I suppose it must be. Is 'e 'orrible underneath? No nose, and—and black lumps all over? Is that why 'e wears it?"

Dolph narrowed her eyes. She didn't trust Gant one bit—didn't trust all these questions and the way he kept glancing off into the darkness as if waiting for a signal.

Better get the cap'n out of here quick smart, she thought. And she turned back to the cart.

Behind her, Gant shouted, "Pin, you got it?"

"Got it," came the reply, and Pin trotted into the torchlight with a rope in one hand and a rock in the other. At the end of the rope, dragging along the ground, was a tightly tied bundle. It was a moment before Dolph realized that the bundle had whiskers and a long tail.

"Missus Slink!" she cried. "What—"

"Told it the witch wanted it," smirked Pin. "Offered to carry it. The rest was easy."

"But—"

"You keep back, Witch," shouted Gant. "Or 'e'll smash it, won't you, Pin?"

Pin nodded and raised the rock.

"And *they'll* smash your witchy friend."

Dolph glanced over her shoulder. And there were four of the town bratlings, standing over the captain with rocks in their hands and the same gleeful expressions as Pin.

It took all her self-control to shrug, as if the whole business wasn't nearly as important as Gant seemed to think it was. "I thought we were on the same side."

Gant sneered. "No one's on our side except us. You want to tell us what to do, just like the Masters. *Let the prisoners go, Gant. Do it this way, Gant. Do it that way, Gant. You're an idiot, Gant.* And maybe we *was* idiots for lettin' the Masters run our lives all that time. But not anymore."

"But the cap'n isn't—"

The boy interrupted her. "You 'n your friends might've winkled the Masters out of the Citadel, but they're still strong, and they don't like witches. So maybe they'll give us somethin' good in exchange—*Don't you move!*"

Dolph eased back on her heels and let the knife fall to her side.

Gant smiled. "We don't want to kill your friend, Witch. Don't want to kill your little rat neither, or those two prisoners. Much better to use them, like you said. But if you try 'n free them with some of that fierce fightin' you're so proud of, if you do anythin' we don't like, we'll smash their 'eads in."

CHAPTER 26

DOWNWARD

Inside the Grand Monument, the six children crouched close to the ground, with smoke swirling about their heads. They had all wet their jackets and jerkins in the dark pool, and wrapped them around their faces, but it wasn't enough.

Nat had draped his wet armbands across Wretched's nose, but that wasn't enough either. The dog lay hunched and miserable at Gwin's feet, his head half-sunk in the pool. Every now and again he gazed up at Nat with pleading eyes, as if he thought the boy was doing the whole thing on purpose and could stop it if he really wanted to.

Gwin wished her brother *could* stop it. Smoke had been pouring in through the crevice for more than an hour, and her eyes were streaming. If it hadn't been for that precious draft, they'd be dead by now. Or surrendered.

She wondered how long it would take the pigeon to fly to the mountains. And how fast that mysterious airship could sail, coming back the other way.

If the airship even existed.

But it does exist, she thought fiercely. *It does!* And she imagined the ragged sails again, high above the Grand Monument, and Hob and Bony shimmying down a rope to attack Brother Poosk and put the fire out.

Sharkey rubbed his good eye, which was streaming as badly as Gwin's, and whispered, "We have to rush 'em. I say we do it now."

"Don't like your chances, shipmate," said Mister Smoke, who was the only one unafffected by the worsening air. "Poosk and Bartle are watchin' that crack in the rock awful close."

Sharkey's voice was muffled by the jerkin. "Then can you see another way out, Mister Smoke?"

"*The root still lives.* That says downward to me, shipmate."

Sharkey shook his head in frustration. "And how're we supposed to go downward? Dig? The ground's almost as hard as the stones. No, we rush 'em."

"We might as well slit our own throats and be done with it," said Petrel. "It's thinking that'll get us out of here, not fists."

"Aye, shipmates," said Mister Smoke. "*Clever* thinkin', that's what we need."

Except I can't think of anything except the airship, thought Gwin. *And Papa.*

It was then that Rain began to sing, quietly and with lots of suppressed coughs, about the cool sea breeze that blew across West Norn in midsummer. Her voice was very different from Gwin's, which was made for open spaces and proclamations.

But there was something about that thin, croaky song that dragged Gwin back to practicalities.

Hob won't come for a while yet, she reminded herself. *So forget about him and think about downward. How can we go downward?*

There had been times, before Mama died, when Gwin would ask a question in her head and Nat would answer it without knowing he'd done so. It hadn't happened for weeks, and Gwin had stopped expecting it.

But now Nat dipped his finger into the pool and swirled it around, as if he was listening. "It's deeper than it seems. Shallow water doesn't sound like this."

"Don't see what difference that makes," whispered Petrel. "We can't breathe water, shallow or deep."

Gwin sat up so suddenly that her rabbit-skin jacket fell from her face. Immediately the smoke seized her throat, and she bent double, trying to hold down a coughing fit.

"Downward," she croaked. "What if it's not under the ground—whatever you're looking for? What if it's—*under the water?*"

They all stared at her, their eyes red and desperate. Fin said, "But then how could we get to—" He broke off. "Sharkey, what are you doing?"

Sharkey was already struggling out of his shirt. "If there's something down there, I'll find it. Can I take the lantern?"

"Aye, take what you need," said Petrel, pushing the lamp toward him.

"But it'll go out," croaked Gwin.

"It's waterproof," said Sharkey. He tucked his eye patch into his pocket and lay flat on his back beside the pool so that the smoke drifted above him. With a look of intense concentration, he began to breathe deeply. In. Out. In. Out.

He had to stop a couple of times, when the smoke grabbed at his throat. But he always started again. And just when Gwin was beginning to think that he was going to lie there forever, he grabbed the lamp, rolled sideways into the water and disappeared with barely a splash.

Gwin, Rain, Fin and Petrel leaned over the pool and watched the spark of light spiraling away from them, deeper and deeper. Then that too vanished, as if it had dropped off the bottom of the world, and the cavern was left in utter darkness.

"I would never have guessed it was so deep," whispered Fin.

Petrel sighed and said, "We should've known the Singer'd come up with something. Maybe you're not as bad as I painted you, Fetcher girl. What's your name?"

"Gwin." Wretched's hot tongue licked her hand.

"I'm Nat," said her brother. "How long can Sharkey hold his breath?"

"Ages," whispered Rain. "Ages and ages."

They waited. The darkness was so complete that Gwin felt as if she was in a cocoon. She closed her sore eyes and let herself believe she truly was the Singer.

It took away what little breath she had left. It made her feel scrubbed and raw, with her heart right out in the open, where the wind and weather could shred it. But at the same time she felt more hopeful than she had in weeks.

"'E's been gone four and a half minutes," said Mister Smoke. "That's awfully long for one breath, shipmates."

Rain started to sing, her voice no more than a breath of air in Gwin's ear.

"Come back, Sharkey,
Come back, Sharkey . . ."

Gwin wiped her eyes and stared into the depths of the pool. She and her family had always held themselves a little separate from other people. It was what Fetchers did, how they survived. Sometimes they helped those who needed it, and at other times *they* were helped. But there was always that respectful space around them, a space that Gwin had never tried to cross.

Now, for the first time, she felt as if she was part of something else. As if she and Nat and the other four children added up to something, though she didn't yet know what it was.

She joined her voice to Rain's.

"Come back, Sharkey . . ."

Nat coughed, and smothered the sound with his arm. Fin whispered, "Perhaps whatever is down there is dangerous—"

"Come back, Sharkey,
Come back, Sharkey . . ."

They were all singing it now. Nat coughed again. So did Petrel. The smoke was growing unbearable.

"Come back, Sharkey . . ."

Suddenly Nat said, "I can hear him." At the same time, Wretched's tail thumped and Rain squeaked, "Look!"

In the depths of the pool, a light was glowing.

It surged upward like a firefly dancing, and a tiny piece of

Gwin's heart surged with it. She leaned over the pool. *"Come back, Sharkey!"*

And there he was, hauling himself out of the pool with his chest heaving and the lamp lighting up their filthy, relieved faces.

"What did you find?" demanded Fin as soon as Sharkey was back on dry ground.

"You didn't hold your breath all that time, did you?" whispered Petrel. "'Cos I couldn't hold mine for half of it. A quarter, even."

Sharkey shook his head. "No, no—it's all right. I reckon it was . . . just over a minute." He hauled in another breath, and the smoke caught at his lungs. He coughed loudly.

He slammed his hand over his mouth, but it was too late. Brother Poosk's gloating voice wound through the smoky air toward them.

"Dear me, I hope you are not sickening for something, children? It must be awfully cold in there. Here, Brother Bartle, build the fire up some more. We do not want the children to catch a chill."

Almost immediately the smoke grew thicker, which set them all to coughing, including Wretched. They no longer tried to hide it. Poosk had thought they were in there—now he had proof.

Petrel whispered, "What's down there, Sharkey? Why'd you"—*cough cough*—"take so long?"

"I got lost"—*cough*—"on the way back. There's a couple of"—*cough cough*—"different ways you can go. It was a bit confusing, even with the lantern. But I think I know the way now."

"The way to where?" asked Fin.

"The pool's like a sort of tunnel"—*cough cough*—"filled with water. It goes down, then up again, to a proper room on the other side. It doesn't look as if that part's ever been smashed. I didn't look around much"—*cough*—"just wanted to be sure there's no smoke there. And there's not. We should go, now!"

"But I cannot swim," whispered Rain. "I told you."

"Neither can I," said Fin.

"Me neither," said Petrel.

Gwin rubbed her eyes, though it made no difference. The smoke was getting so thick that the other children faded in and out of her vision. "I can. So can Nat."

Sharkey nodded. He was shivering with cold. "Then this is how we'll do it. I'll take Rain and Mister Smoke"—*cough cough*—"and lead the way with the lantern. Gwin, you come right behind me with Petrel. If you keep close, you'll be able to follow the light of the lantern. Nat, can you"—*cough*—"follow the sound of us swimming? Can you bring Fin?"

"Yes," said Nat. "But what about Wretched?"

Gwin stared at him in dismay. Wretched could swim underwater, but not for the sort of distance Sharkey was talking about. There was no way they could take him with them.

But they couldn't leave him behind, either, to die in the ever-thickening smoke. She looked helplessly around the circle.

"There's no other way," said Sharkey. "Not unless we want to surrender."

Nat buried his face in Wretched's fur and whispered something that Gwin couldn't catch. Then he raised his head and said, "I think he'll"—*cough*—"go back the way we came, once we're gone. We couldn't get past Poosk, but he might be able to, don't you think?" He stroked the dog's ears with infinite tenderness. "He's not very brave. But"—his voice broke—"but he's a good dog."

Sharkey went into another fit of coughing. "We have to go before this gets any"—*cough*—"worse. Here, wave your jackets around, see if we can thin it out a bit."

They thrashed at the air with their jackets and their arms, and the smoke *did* thin a little. Sharkey showed them how to ready themselves by taking deep breaths and letting them out slowly.

Wretched whimpered, as if he knew what was coming. The smoke returned thicker than ever, and Rain said through all the coughing and hacking, "Sharkey, I do not think I can—"

"Course you can," whispered Sharkey. "It's not far, Rain, honest. And you and I are leading the way, along with Mister Smoke. There's probably"—*cough cough*—"a song about it somewhere. *Rain and Sharkey dived into the water* . . ."

His voice was raw and tuneless, but it did the trick. Rain said, "Then can we go right now? Please? Before I . . ."

Nat was whispering to Wretched, "You go back, boy. The way we came. Go back now, go on!" He pushed the dog gently, but Wretched merely pressed closer.

Sharkey said to Rain, "Wrap your arms around my neck. No, don't strangle me. That's better. Now, deep breaths. It's going to be cold, all right? Mister Smoke, you hang on to Rain. Everyone ready?"

Petrel put her arms around Gwin's neck. *She* was trembling too, which Gwin hadn't expected.

"Don't like this"—*cough cough*—"swimming business," whispered Petrel, in Gwin's ear. "Where I come from no one even thought of it"—*cough*—"unless they were winter-mad. Turn you into a berg, a swim would. That's if the leopard seals didn't get you first."

Gwin had no idea what the other girl was talking about. And she didn't ask; Sharkey and Rain were tumbling into the pool, and it was time to go.

She took one last look at Wretched, then rolled into the water a second after Sharkey. She heard a splash behind her as Nat and Fin followed, and then she was kicking downward, her eyes fixed on the lamp.

The water was shockingly cold, but she'd been expecting it, and it wasn't the worst of her problems. Sharkey was a far stronger swimmer than she was, and that spark of yellow light was getting farther and farther away. Gwin kicked harder, afraid she'd lose sight of it. Her lungs were hurting already, from the smoke and the fear, and she was worried about Wretched and worried about Nat, too, following her in the darkness. If she failed, so would he.

But we mustn't fail. If Hob doesn't come, then Papa's depending on us, and so's Hilde. And if I'm truly the Singer, then the world's depending on us too.

Downward. Downward, with Gwin's heart beginning to struggle in her chest. *Please don't let it be much farther. Please don't let it be much—*

Ahead of her, the light disappeared.

Gwin squeezed her eyes shut, then opened them again. *Where's he gone?*

She knew that if she let panic take hold of her, she was lost. Her breath would go and so would her strength. Nat would drown. Petrel and Fin would die. Papa would be hanged, and Hilde too. The world would go on as it always had, harsh and cruel. And there'd be no one left to remember Mama.

I'm a Fetcher, she reminded herself. *I'm as strong-willed as Ariel, as stubborn as the blue ox. . . .*

Still no sign of the lamp, and now Petrel's hands were starting to clutch at Gwin's throat, as if the other girl knew they were lost and was giving in to fear.

Gwin dragged the hands away from her neck. *Where could the lamp have gone? Think, Gwin, THINK!*

And then she knew. Blindly she reached out and touched rock. With Petrel clinging to her, as helpless as a newborn kitten, she hauled herself downward, hand over hand, until she found the place that *had* to be there, the place where the rock curved under—and up again.

With a single kick, she swam beneath it. And saw the lamp exactly where she'd hoped it would be: high above her and heading upward.

She kicked harder, and the two girls shot up through the water, leaving a trail of bubbles behind them. Up and up, and Gwin's lungs were burning, and her chest was heaving, and she couldn't think of anything except air.

But just as she thought she would burst, her head broke the

surface. She sucked the air in so fast that she almost fell backward with the shock of it. Then Sharkey was hauling her out of the water, and Petrel too. Rain lay on her back next to the lamp, and Petrel fell down beside her, coughing and spluttering.

Gwin's breath sawed in and out, as hoarse as a frog. But she didn't take her eyes off that dark water.

"Nat," she whispered. "Come on, Nat."

Sharkey bent over beside her. "Should I go and look for them?"

"No, wait—"

She saw a stream of bubbles, and for a moment she thought—

"Nat!" she cried. And there was her brother, surging out of the pool with Fin on his back.

CHAPTER 27

THE DOOR

FIN'S WOUNDED ARM ACHED, AND HIS LEGS WERE STILL WEAK from the horror of that underwater journey. But there was no time to waste. He staggered to his feet and almost banged his head on the low ceiling.

The pool on the other side had looked like an accident, a place where rainwater had filled up a crack in the ground.

On this side, it was clearly manmade. What's more, although the stone walls around him were blackened with age and festooned with moss, they made up a narrow corridor that had never been destroyed.

"*The root still lives*," whispered Rain. "Someone left this place for us to find, all those years ago."

"But what"—Fin's voice cracked—"what do we do with it?"

"There's stairs, shipmates," cried Mister Smoke from some distance away. "And they go down."

Fin grabbed the lantern, and the six children followed the sound of the old rat's voice. The ceiling was so low they all had to stoop, even Petrel. As they passed, spiders the size of Fin's hand scuttled away from the light.

The stairs went down and down and down, heading first in one direction, then another. Mister Smoke led the way, issuing instructions.

"No laggin' behind, shipmates. Turn to port, that's the way. The roof's nice and 'igh, you'll notice, so you don't 'ave to worry so much about crackin' yer 'eads. Now take a sharp turn to starboard, and then down a few more steps. Keep up. 'Cos at the bottom of the steps, we 'ave a room, very like the corridor up top only not so cramped. And on the easterly side of the room, we 'ave—"

"A door!" said Petrel.

The children gathered in front of the door, staring at it in awed silence. Unlike the walls, it was made of metal. It was no taller than Petrel and completely plain.

No. Fin looked closer. Not completely. Instead of a handle, there was a small raised section with nine metal wheels set into it edgeways. Each wheel had numbers on it.

"What is that?" he asked.

"Control panel of some sort, I reckon," said Petrel. "There's one a bit like it in the *Oyster*'s engine room."

"Aye," said Sharkey. "You have to turn the wheels. And if you get the right numbers in a row, the door opens." He looked around. "Is there another way out of here? No? Then we'd better get started."

He turned the wheels. Nothing happened, so he tried again. And again.

A small claw tapped Fin's ankle. "Lift me up, shipmate."

Fin picked up Mister Smoke and brought him closer to the control panel. "Hmph, just as I thought," said the rat. "No use tryin' to guess somethin' like this. It could take you a couple of lifetimes, and we ain't got that long. We need the code."

"Code?" said Sharkey, still trying different numbers. "Where do we get that from? Could you work it out, Mister Smoke?"

"Not a chance, shipmate. Gimme a busted sea valve, and I'll have it right in two shakes of a gull's feather. But codes ain't my specialty. Maybe the cap'n could do it if 'e was 'ere. Maybe not."

"Then we must guess it," said Fin. "Otherwise we will have to turn back."

"No." Rain shook her head. "*The trunk is gone, the root still lives.* Whoever wrote that was clever. They would not have left us to guess the code. They would have pointed us toward it in some way." She turned to Gwin. "There is not a third verse to the Song, is there?"

"No," said Gwin. "Just the two."

Sharkey spun the wheels, again and again. Beside Fin, Petrel turned in a circle, inspecting the stone walls. Unlike the corridor, the ceiling here was so high as to be out of sight in the darkness.

"D'you reckon this was built by the same feller as made the *Oyster*?" said Petrel. "Serran Coc?"

Nat stiffened. "Coe? Your ship was built by *Coe*?"

"Aye," said Petrel. "He made it three hundred years ago to carry the cap'n away to the southern ice. To hide him from the ancestors of the Devouts. He made the cap'n too. Why?"

"He was a friend of Ariel, the first Fetcher," said Nat. "Papa has his timepiece. Or at least he did before Poosk took it."

Petrel let out her breath in a slow hiss. "Starting to fit together, ain't it? Let's get this door open, quick as we can."

But there was nothing quick about that metal door. Fin sat on the bottom step, twisting his fingers together and trying to contain his impatience. Every now and again one of the other children said something, but he barely heard it. Brother Poosk's voice lingered in his ears.

She thinks you do not care about her, Initiate. Saving the Fetcher cubs and leaving her behind to hang.

Fin's stomach turned over. He wished more than anything that he could have that moment by the oxcart all over again. He would tear his mama away from the Devouts by brute force. He would sacrifice himself to save her.

But it was too late for any of that. He stood up and pushed Sharkey gently aside. "Here, let me try."

And he began to spin the wheels.

GWIN WAS EXHAUSTED, SCARED AND SICK TO DEATH OF confined spaces. She wanted to feel the wind on her face. She wanted to sleep for a week. She wanted to curl up in a ball and grieve for Mama.

But more than any of those things, she wanted to save Papa.

Nat sat on one side of her with his back against the wall. Petrel half dozed on her other side. Something had shifted between the two girls since that water-filled tunnel. Petrel was as fierce and determined as ever, but the hostility was gone.

"That was just plain horrible," she'd said to Gwin as soon as they'd got their breath back. "I'm never going back in the water again. Not unless you're there to save me." Then she'd ducked her head as if she was embarrassed. "I'm sorry I treated you so bad before. Rain was right; I prob'ly would've given up the cap'n too if I didn't know him. And if it was my da's life at stake."

Despite everything, Gwin had found herself smiling—a real smile, for the first time in two months.

She wasn't smiling now. None of them were. The door was as stubborn as ever, though they'd been spinning the little wheels for hours. At first, they'd done it systematically, following Sharkey's instructions. But tiredness, frustration and a desperate fear that they were running out of time had taken their toll, and now they slumped against the door when it was their turn and let the wheels fall where they would.

At last Mister Smoke said, "Dawn's not far off, shipmates."

"Dawn?" said Petrel, sitting up and stretching. "Is it that late?"

"Aye, shipmate. I'm gunna see if I can find a way out, check on the cap'n."

"And Mama?" Fin said quickly.

"And Papa?" added Gwin. "And see if there's any sign of Hob?"

"I'll do my best, shipmates. No promises. Now give me a leg up. That bit of moss just above your 'ead looks likely. I can make my own way from there. Easy now, that's it."

"Have you got your footing?" asked Petrel, peering upward

with her hands still hovering over him. "You're not gunna fall?"

"And bust all these nice circuits? Perish the thought." And Mister Smoke began to clamber up the moss.

Within seconds he had disappeared into the gloom, and the children turned back to the door. Sharkey spun the little wheels. Fin chewed at his knuckles.

Rain yawned. Then, as if they'd been in the middle of a conversation rather than all half-asleep, she said, "What I do not understand is why the captain needed the Singer as well as the Song."

Sharkey didn't look up from the little metal wheels. "To get both verses."

"But the second verse does not tell us anything more than the first," said Rain. "There must be another reason." She nibbled her lower lip. "I wonder if you know the code, Gwin."

"No," said Gwin, startled. "I'd have said so hours ago—"

"If you *knew* you knew it, you would have said so. But if you did not know? Perhaps it is in another of your songs. Are there any with numbers in them? *Nine* numbers?"

"I don't—" began Gwin. "Wait, let me think." She closed her eyes and tried to concentrate. She knew dozens of songs, but she couldn't think of a single one that contained nine numbers.

"No," she said. "I'm sorry."

She thought that was the end of it, but Rain hadn't finished with her. "What else do you do apart from sing? When you came to our village, years ago, you folded yourself up into a little box and slowed your heartbeat down until we all thought you were dead."

"That was just a trick," said Gwin. "I haven't done it for years."

She felt Nat sigh. Sharkey spun the wheels again.

Gwin rested her back against the stone, wishing Papa was here with them. She wanted to see him so much that she could hardly bear it. She wanted him safe, that was a huge part of it. But she wanted to talk to him, too.

When Mama died, Gwin had thought *she* might die too, of a broken heart. But at least she and Nat and Papa had had each other to cling to, and they'd all agreed that they must keep going because that was what Mama would have wanted.

But as the days passed, they'd each retreated into their own world of anger, sadness or busyness. They hadn't spoken about Mama for weeks. It had hurt too much.

Gwin swallowed. She couldn't do a thing to help Papa, not until the door was open. But there was one thing she *could* change.

She leaned toward Nat and whispered, "Do you remember when—when Mama found Wretched?"

Nat's blind eyes blinked. Once. Twice. Gwin thought he wasn't going to answer, but at last he nodded and said, "She was returning from a Fetch."

"And she saw a dog," said Gwin, "lying in a ditch with his leg broken. So she picked him up and carried him all the way back to us, slung over her shoulder . . ."

"He drooled and dribbled and covered her in dog hair."

"And when Papa saw them coming up the road he laughed and said . . ."

The ghost of a smile touched Nat's lips. "He said, 'Is this the gorgeous woman I married or a wretched changeling?'"

Gwin closed her eyes. A tear rolled down her cheek, and she slid her hand into Nat's. "I'm sure Wretched got out safely," she whispered.

"Course he did," said Nat. But his voice was uncertain.

"My mama," Rain said quietly, "knew the names of the stars. We used to sit outside at night and she'd teach me."

Sharkey spun the little wheels, his fingers so quick that Gwin hardly saw them move. "My ma didn't like the stars. They made her feel queasy. But she could dive to a hundred feet or more on a single breath and come back with enough shell-fish to feed three families. And Fa was the best navigator in the fleet, even Adm'ral Deeps said so."

"I don't remember my mam and da," said Petrel. "But Squid reckons they were as brave as a couple of sea lions protecting their pups."

"Like you," said Fin. Then he flushed and added, "Perhaps we have all inherited such things from our parents. Courage, and the names of stars. The ability to dive—"

"Songs," said Nat, "and stories."

"My white hair," said Rain.

"Mine too," said Fin.

"My beads." Gwin shook her head till her plaits rattled. Now that she'd started talking about her mother she didn't want to stop. "They used to be Mama's, and before that they were—"

She froze, but in her head the sentence continued, as clear as daylight.

Before that, they were HER mama's, and right back for as long as anyone can remember. I got them when I turned ten. Mama said, "Never change the pattern, my lovely. It came from Ariel herself."

Gwin wasn't sure if she could speak. When she did, her voice seemed to come from miles away. "My beads. Nat, my *beads!*"

Sharkey, Rain, Fin and Petrel were staring at her, with no idea what she was talking about. But Gwin's brother understood; she knew it even before he spoke.

"Could it be?" he whispered.

"I think it—it must."

The others caught on quickly. Sharkey's fingers stopped moving, and an awestruck silence fell over the little group.

Rain whispered, "How many plaits do you—"

"Seven."

"Oh." There was a world of disappointment in Rain's voice.

Gwin added quickly, "But don't you see? The middle one has three sets of beads. Which makes nine sets."

Her hand rose to touch her hair. She didn't really need to count the beads in each set—she had woven them for Mama so often, and then for herself. But her heart was beating so fast, and there was such a lot resting on this that she was afraid of getting it wrong.

"Four," she whispered, touching the first plait.

Sharkey turned the first wheel.

"Seven."

The second wheel.

"Two."

The third.

"Five. Eight. One."

The fourth, fifth and sixth wheels rolled into place. Everyone was holding their breath.

"Three."

Sharkey's fingers trembled, but they didn't pause in their task.

"S-six." Gwin could hardly speak. *What if I've changed the pattern without realizing it? What if I lost some?*

It was such a terrible thought that her hand stopped, halfway to the last plait.

"What's the matter?" asked Petrel.

"I—"

Nat whispered, "You haven't changed it. I would've known."

Gwin swallowed. "F-four."

Sharkey turned the final wheel. Nine numbers lined up, numbers that had been handed down through generations of Fetchers for this very moment.

Something clicked, and they all jumped. Something else clunked.

With a rush of ancient air, the door swung open.

CHAPTER 28

INSIDE THE GRAND MONUMENT

DOLPH HAD TRIED PERSUASION. She'd tried threats. She'd tried bribery, flattery and the promise of eternal friendship, plus a lifetime's supply of ship's biscuits. But nothing would move Gant to free either the captain or Missus Slink. They lay on the floor of the oxcart with rocks dangling over their heads, just in case Dolph made the wrong move.

By the time dawn came creeping up from the east, she had backed off, to give herself room to think. The Devouts'd be here soon, crawling up the road with their hostages, and she needed to get the captain and Missus Slink to safety before then.

What would you do, Mam, if you were here?

A shout of warning from one of the bratlings caught her attention. A single Devout was hurrying down the road toward the oxcart.

He was small and unimportant looking, and he appeared to be unarmed. But Dolph jumped to her feet all the same and trotted toward the cart, afraid that Gant and his mates might give in without a fight.

She needn't have worried. The town bratlings had gained courage from their earlier foray, and now they surrounded their prisoner, with half a dozen rusty knives at the ready.

"Come any closer and we'll kill 'im," shouted Gant.

The Devout jerked to a halt, his face a picture of astonishment.

He doesn't know what's been happening at the Citadel, realized Dolph. *He doesn't know that things have changed.*

But the Devout, it seemed, was a fast learner. His surprise turned to a smile, and he took a careful step forward.

"I said no closer!" cried Gant.

"Very wise. Very wise indeed," said the man. "I can see you have a good head on your shoulders. Why, you have completely got the better of Brother Cull there, and that is not an easy thing to do."

Gant stared, as if he thought the Devout must be making fun of him. But there was total sincerity on the small man's face. "Cull is one of our finest guards, and you and your friends have beaten him. I do not mind admitting that your prowess astonishes me."

Gant preened a little. "We 'stonished 'im, too. He thought we was vermin 'n not worth worryin' about. But we're not vermin, not us."

"No, indeed!" The Devout sounded shocked. "I said Brother Cull was a fine guard, but that does not mean he was a man of sense and understanding, dear me, no." He took another small step forward and lowered his voice confidingly. "I cannot approve of some of my brothers; I really cannot. The things they say. Anyone would think they were superior beings. . . ."

"They're not," said Gant.

Dolph edged closer too. She didn't like the way this was going. The Devout hadn't introduced himself, but she'd heard all about Brother Poosk from Rain and Sharkey, and she was beginning to suspect that this might be him.

Except what was he doing here? He was supposed to be off in the northwest somewhere, hunting Fin's mam. . . .

Dolph sucked in her breath. Poosk had been gone for a while. What if he'd caught Fin's mam and was bringing her back to the Citadel for execution? What if *that was her*, kneeling in the cart with half a dozen ropes around her?

Dolph stared at the woman, trying to see past the grime and the bruises. Trying to see some resemblance to the white-haired boy who had become part of the *Oyster*'s crew.

Aye, it's her, I reckon. Which means I need to get her away too.

She raised her voice, just a little. "Gant!"

The boy glanced over his shoulder at her.

Dolph nodded toward the Devout. "Don't trust him. He's famous for his clever tongue. Poosk's his name, and he can talk folk into tying themselves in knots—"

"He won't talk me into nothin', Witch. You keep your nose out of this, if you don't want your friends gettin' squished." And with that, Gant turned back to the small man and said, "You Brother Poosk?"

The man shook his head ruefully. "Did I not say that you had a good head on your shoulders? And now I see that you are even sharper than I thought. I am Poosk, and I will make a confession, young sir."

Gant's chest swelled, and he glanced at his friends to make sure they had heard that respectful address. Dolph rolled her eyes. If she didn't do something smart quick, Poosk'd have the town bratlings lying on their backs to have their tummies tickled and still thinking they'd got the better of him.

"When I first approached," said Poosk, "I was going to order you to hand over your prisoners. But that will not do, will it? If I want Brother Cull back, I will have to negotiate with you. And I am not at all sure that I will get the better part of it."

"You won't," cried one of the other bratlings. "We'll make sure o' that."

Gant scowled at his mates. "I'm doin' the talkin', not you."

"We can talk if we want," said yet another bratling. "You ain't boss of us, Gant."

"I am too."

While this exchange was going on, Poosk stared at his boots, as if momentarily lost in his own thoughts. "It is just as well," he murmured, "that we are here rather than back up the road apiece. . . ."

Gant spun around, all sharp eyes and ears. "Why? Why's it just as well?"

"What?" Poosk's head jerked up. "Oh. I—I would rather not say, young sir."

"You've got to," said Gant. "We got your man 'ere. If you don't tell us, we'll kill 'im."

"But I *cannot* tell you. It is a matter of pride."

Gant's eyes shone. "I don't care. You tell me, or else."

Brother Poosk sighed as if the boy had got the better of him and pointed back the way he had come. "The Grand Monument is just around that corner. It was the scene of our first great triumph, three hundred years ago. I would truly hate it to be the scene of my humiliation."

Dolph murmured, "He's playing with you, Gant. He's got a reason for wanting you to go further up the road."

"Maybe he 'as," said Gant, over his shoulder. "But 'e's right, all the same. Grand Monument? Ha! We'll go up there, and when the rest o' the Masters come up the road, they'll see us perched on their stupid monument, laughin' at them."

He waved generously at his friends. "We'll get all your little brothers 'n sisters back. And maybe we'll have the Masters kiss our backsides while we're at it."

His friends snickered their approval. There was no persuading them out of it, though Dolph tried. They hoisted their human prisoners off the broken oxcart and marched them up the road, with Missus Slink and the captain dragged along behind.

Brother Poosk scampered before them with his hands raised in protest. "No, please!" he cried. "Will you not turn around? I would much rather stay where we were. Please, young sir, think of my wounded pride."

Oh, you are so clever, thought Dolph. *But I'm no town bratling, Brother Poosk. I'm Orca's daughter, and you won't fool me.*

She almost missed the quiet *Psst!* from the roadside. But she glanced down just in time to see a tiny paw beckoning her from under a bush.

She stopped in her tracks. "Missus Slink? But I thought—"

"Nah, it's me, shipmate."

"*Mister Smoke?*" Now Dolph was even more astonished. She bent over, pretending she had a stone in her boot. "Is Petrel here with you? Or Fin? Or Sharkey and Rain?"

"They're inside the monument, shipmate, along with the Singer and 'er brother. Poosk's got 'em trapped, but that's not so bad as it sounds, 'cos they're lookin' for somethin' that might 'elp us, and with a bit of luck they'll find it. I came out to check on the cap'n. And Fin's mam and the Fetcher."

"She *is* Fin's mam. I thought so." Dolph explained what was happening. "They've got the cap'n all tied up. Missus Slink too. They think they'll be able to use 'em for bargaining."

She glanced south and shaded her eyes. Then she groaned out loud. "And here come the rest of 'em."

Up the road from the Citadel came the Devouts, with Brother Thrawn still at the forefront in his wheeled chair, and the bratling hostages still keeping them safe.

Even from this distance, Dolph could see that some of the Devouts had an air of bewilderment about them, as if they couldn't understand why they were no longer in the Citadel, living off other folk's labor. But most of them stumped up the road with fury and contempt in every inch of their bodies.

"They might be out of the Citadel, but they're not beaten yet," said Dolph. "Not while they've got those hostages. Mister Smoke, are you going back to the others?"

"Aye, when I've checked on the cap'n," said the rat.

"Then whatever they're doing, whatever they're looking for, you tell 'em to hurry up, you hear me? Because if the Devouts get hold of the cap'n and Missus Slink, they'll be dead within minutes. And so will Fin's mam and the Fetcher."

PETREL HADN'T MOVED SINCE THE DOOR SWUNG OPEN. None of them had. They stood there, shocked into stillness. All the urgency, all that desperate need to hurry, was forgotten. Even Nat, who could see nothing, was frozen to the spot, as if the echoes of a world three hundred years old were ringing in his ears.

After weeks of mud and squalor, after the hate-filled crevices of the Grand Monument, *this* was almost impossible to believe.

Petrel closed her mouth, which had fallen open, and took a single step forward, holding the lantern high. Metal gleamed at her, as bright as a sunstruck glacier. She saw rows of dials, banked up to the ceiling, with so many colored wires running between them that she felt dizzy. There were steel ladders to the uppermost levels, and an enormous stack of what might have been batteries, only there were more of them than she could count. Above the batteries, huge black pipes ran in one direction, while small white pipes crossed them. The far wall was curtained from top to bottom with heavy cloth, and a red lever was set in the middle of the floor.

There was not a speck of dust anywhere.

Petrel was in the habit of measuring everything she saw against the *Oyster*. That was the world she knew best, and so far West Norn had come a very poor second. But this place— even her beloved ship couldn't match it, mainly because the *Oyster* was rusty and tired, whereas this hidden room looked as if it had just been built five minutes ago.

In a daze, she tiptoed forward. A white coat hung on the back of a chair, as if whoever owned it would be back at any moment. Petrel wondered if it had once belonged to Serran Coe. Maybe he had drawn the arrows and numbers on that big blackboard. Maybe it was his china cup resting on the edge of one of the control panels.

This is the world the cap'n came from, thought Petrel. *This is the world that made him.*

Gwin was the first to break the silence, whispering an awed description to her brother. She had names for hardly any of the things she saw, so it was the oddest description Petrel had ever heard, but at least it got things moving.

Sharkey said, "It's like a giant engine room, only I can't see any engines."

"Whatever it is," said Fin, in a voice that was very close to breaking, "what are we going to do with it?"

That brought the urgency back again. Only now it was worse than ever because they had found something important and must use it—if they could only work out how.

Sharkey ran across the floor, saying, "Bring the lantern, Petrel."

She hurried to the curtain, which the Sunker boy was already pulling back. Behind it was a thick glass wall, and on the other side of the wall, something moved.

"What is it?" asked Rain, standing back a little.

"Can't quite see." Petrel shaded her eyes. "But it's alive. It's—"

Something rushed at the glass and she leapt backward, half expecting the wall to shatter. But the glass was so thick that it didn't even shake.

"It's water," said Sharkey. "It's the sea. There must be a tunnel from the coast."

The wave fell away, white-edged, then surged again. Sharkey ran back to the center of the room and grasped the red lever.

"Wait," cried Petrel. "We don't know what it is."

Sharkey pointed to the lettering. OFF. ON. "This is where your cap'n was supposed to come. And this was left here for him. It's off right now, but I swear we're meant to turn it on."

"But what will it do?" asked Rain.

Sharkey nodded toward the glass wall. "My guess is it'll set something moving, a turbine or something like that. But there's only one way to find out." He looked at Petrel, as if asking permission.

Petrel chewed her thumbnail. Sharkey was right; it seemed very much like an engine room of some sort. Maybe the water moving back and forth fed the batteries, the same way the wind did on the *Oyster*. But what if they pulled the lever and it made a lot of noise starting up? Would the folk above hear it, and if they did, would it make things worse for the captain or better? Would it save Fin's mam and the Fetcher? Or would it bring their deaths closer?

And even if it was quiet, what could she and her friends *do* with it? They needed a lot more than an engine room if the prisoners were to be saved.

It was then that Mister Smoke returned, scuttling into the lantern light so quick and quiet that he was peering up at Fin before Petrel realized he was there. "Your mam's still alive, shipmate, and so's the Fetcher, though it's a bunch of town bratlings holding 'em prisoner now instead of Poosk. The bratlings've got the cap'n too, and Slink, but that won't last, because the rest of the Devouts are comin' up the road. 'Undreds of em, with 'ostages, so no one can attack 'em Dolph says—"

"Dolph's *here*?" said Petrel.

"Aye, and tryin' 'er best to fix things. But she's 'ad no luck so far, and she says to get a move on with whatever you're doin', before it's too late."

"But we don't know—" began Petrel.

"You seen a workshop anywhere?" continued the rat. "Place like this should 'ave one. Over yonder, maybe." And he dashed off again, disappearing through a doorway in the far corner.

Sharkey touched the lever again. Petrel caught Fin's eye.

They both gulped, knowing what was at stake. Fin nodded, meaning he was prepared to take the risk. Petrel looked at Gwin. She nodded too, though her eyes were so astonished they looked as if they might pop out of her head.

Petrel turned back to Sharkey and said, "Do it. Now."

Sharkey's hands tightened on the red lever. And with one swift motion, he shifted it from OFF to ON.

CHAPTER 29

BARGAINS

By the time Dolph reached the foot of the Grand Monument, the town bratlings and their prisoners were perched a quarter of the way up it, looking down on Brother Poosk. They had all seen the approaching horde, and Gant was puffing out his chest, saying, "I'll bargain with the number one Master, I will. And I'll get the better of 'im. You wait 'n see."

His mates snickered and tried to look as if they believed his boasts. But they were all terrified, even Gant—Dolph could see it in their faces.

She thought she heard a faint rumble of thunder and wondered if there was a storm approaching. But the sound came once only, and she soon forgot about it.

She didn't try to climb the immense pile of squared stones that loomed in front of her. She thought she could race up it fast enough, but Gant and his mates were so jumpy that she was afraid they might kill one of their prisoners by mistake, so she stopped just a little way past Brother Poosk, and waited to see what would happen next.

Poosk was waiting too, his pale eyes fixed on the prisoners. He ignored the approaching Devouts, even when the combined scuff of their feet slurred to a halt, and their leaders were close enough for a shouted message.

Dolph, however, watched them warily. She saw the moment when they recognized Poosk, and their confusion, and the heated arguments that took place over Brother Thrawn's head. She saw Thrawn raise one hand an inch or two above the arm of his wheeled chair and say something that silenced those around him.

She saw the army of shipfolk and Sunkers too, keeping pace with the Devouts. There was no room for them on the road, so they strode on either side of it, trampling bushes and clumps of grass, and forcing their way through thickets of trees, until the whole countryside looked like storm-tossed seaweed.

Behind that determined army came townsfolk and villagers, twittering and crying like a flock of birds whose fledglings have been snatched by kelp gulls.

Thrawn gestured, and one of his companions broke away to speak to Poosk. Dolph couldn't hear what they said, but after a brief exchange the man shook his head contemptuously, glared up at Gant and cried, "If you know what is good for you, you will hand over the prisoners *right now*. And if *one hair* on Brother Cull's head has been harmed, you will pay for it."

Gant managed a defiant smirk. His voice trembled a little, but there was no hint of submission. "And if you know what's good for *you*, you'll 'and over our little brothers 'n sisters." He paused dramatically. "Or all these prisoners'll die, includin' your Brother Cull. Right 'ere in front o' your eyes."

The Devout spluttered a bit, then trotted back to report this outrage to Brother Thrawn. Poosk followed, all smiles and humility. Thrawn loathed him, that was clear even from a distance, and so did his hangers-on. But Poosk bowed and nodded and murmured, and before long they seemed to be listening to him.

Dolph would've given a month's supply of toothyfish to know what he was saying.

By this time, First Officer Hump, Admiral Deeps and Chief Engineer Albie were closing in on Dolph. When Gant saw them, he crossed his arms to make himself look a bit bigger and shouted at them, "Don't you come no closer. I'll talk to the witch and Brother Poosk, no one else."

Dolph had to hand it to him; it was exactly what she would've done. The boy was smarter than she'd thought.

Admiral Deeps scowled and beckoned Dolph. She took no notice. She'd seen something from the corner of her eye—a flicker of movement that started near the top of the monument and headed downward. She watched it without seeming to and thought she saw Mister Smoke slip from one stone to another until he was right next to the captain.

And then Brother Poosk was back, as humble and worried as ever. "Dear me, dear me, young sir, they will not listen to me. I told them they must hand over the little brothers and sisters, but they would not. They do not take you seriously, I fear."

"Don't take me serious?" cried Gant, jumping to his feet. "Then I'll make them." He put his knife to Brother Cull's throat. Cull's eyes bulged above the gag, and he gazed desperately down at Brother Poosk.

But Poosk merely shook his head in a helpless sort of way and said, "You are right; perhaps that will convince them. Although . . ." He paused and looked embarrassed.

"Although what?" demanded Gant.

"I should not say it. After all, every life counts for something."

Dolph narrowed her eyes. She knew manipulation when she heard it. Brother Poosk might as well have had an invisible hook in Gant's mouth and been hauling him up the side of the ship.

Gant, however, didn't even know he'd been caught. "You say it, or else."

Poosk sighed mightily. "I told you before that Brother Cull was one of our finest guards. And so he is. But he is not popular, young sir. Even I do not like him, and I get along with most people—"

Gant interrupted him. "So no one'll care if I slit 'is throat, is that what you're sayin'? It won't make no difference?" His face reddened, and he swung around to Fin's mam. "How about if I cut 'er throat?"

"No!" cried Poosk. "No no no no no! Please, you must not harm her, or any of your other prisoners. None of them, I beg you." He was almost weeping with sincerity, his hands clasped so tight that the knuckles showed white.

Gant grinned, and the knife touched Fin's mam's neck. She jammed her eyes closed, as if that might stop what was coming.

"No!" cried Poosk again.

And there's the hook, showing itself at last, thought Dolph. She took a step forward. "Gant!" she shouted. "He wants you to do it; he wants you to kill her. Can't you see?"

The knife hesitated. Gant said, "No 'e don't."

Poosk shot Dolph a poisonous look.

"He does," she said. "I told you he could talk anyone into anything, didn't I? Well, that's what he's doing now. Only he's going about it backward because he knows you'll do the opposite of whatever he says. He wants you to kill all of 'em except Brother Cull."

Gant consulted his mates, but they were as confused as he was. They mumbled to each other, then Gant's eyes flicked back to Brother Poosk. A slow smile spread over his face.

"How about . . . ," he said. "How about I let them go, instead? All of them except your mate Cull. How about I let them loose if you don't 'and over my friends' little brothers 'n sisters?"

Poosk blanched—and this time it was an honest reaction, Dolph was sure of it. "Aye," she said. "They won't like that."

"No." Poosk set his shoulders. "We would *not* like that, young sir. But I should point out that once you have released them, you will have nothing left to bargain with."

"I'll still 'ave Cull."

"So you will. And we would be sorry to see him die. But we would not give up our hostages just for him. If we did . . ." He gestured at the grim ranks of shipfolk and Sunkers. His meaning was clear. The Devouts couldn't give up the bratlings, not if they wanted to survive.

It was a deadlock.

But Poosk hadn't finished. There was something in the pocket of his robe, something that he pulled out and glanced at, then quickly put away again. "Perhaps," he began.

Gant hadn't learned his lesson. "Perhaps *what*?"

"Perhaps there is a way around this that will suit all of us," said Brother Poosk. "But it might take some time to persuade my colleagues. Will you give me till noon, young sir?"

What's he up to now? thought Dolph. *That's a couple of hours he's asking for. Why does he need a couple of hours?*

Gant consulted his mates again, then nodded. "But don't you try nothin'. If you do . . ."

"We will not approach you or your prisoners in any way," said Brother Poosk. The wheedling was gone, and he sounded as straightforward and honest as First Officer Hump.

Which made Dolph trust him less than ever.

She wished she could get word to Petrel and Fin about what was happening.

But I can, she thought. *I CAN get word to 'em.*

And she backed away from the monument and ran toward Krill and his barrels.

THE MESSAGE CAME THROUGH LIKE A WHISPER FROM ANOTHER world. It was the Fetcher boy who heard it first, and he held up his hand to stop their explorations.

"Listen," he said.

Petrel listened and heard a faint and distant clanging. Her thoughts were so entangled in dials, switches, wires and turbines that she almost didn't recognize it. But then her old life caught up with her, and she said, "Officer code."

The others gathered around her, all except Mister Smoke. He had dashed off again ten minutes ago, trailing all manner of spare parts and muttering in satisfied tones about something called a Baniski coil. Which left the six bratlings standing in a circle around the red lever with the lantern flickering at their feet.

There had been one dreadful rumble when Sharkey pulled the lever from OFF to ON. But now it was so quiet that even Nat could hardly hear it.

All that lectricity going to the batteries, thought Petrel. *If we could only work out what to do with it.*

She didn't speak till she'd heard the whole message and knew she hadn't missed anything. Then she said, "It's Dolph. She says Poosk's trying to delay till noon—that's two hours away—and she doesn't know why. But she thinks he's got something up his sleeve, something that'll tip the balance."

"Why would he delay?" asked Fin. "What would make a difference in two hours that would not work now?"

"Don't know, but it's good for us, ain't it? It means Mister Smoke's got a bit more time to get the cap'n back to his senses. And maybe we can figure out what we're gunna do with this place."

"It seems to me," said Rain, "that we must work out why Uncle Poosk wants a delay. He does nothing without purpose. What is so special about noon?"

The dials flickered around them, and the water behind the glass wall surged in and out. Petrel couldn't concentrate; her mind kept turning to the captain and Missus Slink. She couldn't bear the thought of losing them, not after everything that had happened.

Sharkey rubbed the back of his neck. "Maybe something to do with tides? That's all I can think of."

"Midday meal," said Petrel.

"The shadows are shortest." That was Fin.

Nat frowned. "I'd say the sun, or—"

"Sun," said Gwin under her breath. Then, "Sun!" She turned to her brother. "Hob said an eclipse was coming, remember? And Papa said—he said tomorrow at midday. Which is today."

"Eclipse?" said Petrel. "What's that?"

Gwin was talking so fast she stumbled over the words. "We'd never heard of it, but Hob told us about it. It's when the sun and the moon come together—"

"—and the middle of day goes dark as night," said Nat.

"Hob said there hasn't been one in West Norn for two hundred and seventy years, but according to the old stories the day'll get colder—"

"—and the birds'll go to bed—"

"—and the villagers'll be terrified."

That last word seemed to echo around the walls. Rain's

eyes widened. "But if Uncle Poosk knows it is coming, *he* will not be terrified, and neither will the other Devouts because he will tell them about it. He will use it somehow to get the prisoners back."

"Then we've gotta stop him," said Petrel. "One way or another, we've gotta stop him."

CHAPTER 30

MOSS AND DIRT

THE TWO HOURS PASSED SLOWLY, AND POOSK WAS VISIBLY ON edge for all of it. Dolph watched him so closely that she could almost see the dirt around his ears, and the way his upper lip twitched when he spoke. At first, he was engrossed in conversation with Brother Thrawn. He took that *thing* from his pocket again, whatever it was, and the other Devouts drew away from him in horror, then slowly came back, as if they could see the sense in what he had suggested, even if they didn't like it.

That was the end of any sort of negotiation, as far as Dolph could see. Poosk was marking time, and whatever he had in his pocket was part of it.

And so she, too, waited, and so did the impatient ranks of shipfolk and Sunkers, and the townsfolk, who pressed forward among the broken trees, watching the Devouts and their captive bratlings with hungry eyes.

As noon approached, a dog started to howl. It was some

distance away, back down the road, but Dolph was so on edge that she jumped. Poosk, however, took it as some sort of signal. He nodded at Brother Thrawn and strode toward the base of the monument, with half a dozen hefty Devouts following along behind him.

Dolph braced herself for whatever was coming.

The last thing she expected was that Poosk would drop both false humility *and* false honesty. But that was exactly what he did. He glared up at Gant and cried, "Release the prisoners, or I will bring doom upon you."

At first, Gant and his mates just gaped. Then Gant jumped to his feet and said, "Is this your persuasion? Things ain't changed, not that I can see. You said you was goin' to bring somethin' new. So where is it?"

The dog was still howling, and now another one joined it. And another. For no reason that she could understand, Dolph shivered.

"*That* is the beginning of it," cried Poosk, pointing in the direction of the dogs. "They know what is coming. They know what I am bringing down upon your heads."

Gant laughed nervously. "There's nothin' above my 'ead but sky. You got your balloony things back, 'ave you? Goin' to start droppin' stuff on us? If you try it, we'll just let the prisoners go. All except Cull. He can stand 'ere and get 'is 'ead bashed in."

"Not sky," said Poosk, lowering his voice so that Gant had to lean forward to hear it. "Not sky, but *sun*."

Dolph couldn't help herself; she glanced upward. She wasn't

foolish enough to look straight at the sun, but she looked close to it and thought she saw some sort of shadow.

She narrowed her eyes. The day felt . . . odd. It wasn't just the howling dogs; the air was too still, the way it sometimes was before a storm.

"You think the Devouts are finished?" hissed Poosk. He turned in a circle and raised his voice so that the nearest ship-folk and Sunkers could hear him. "You think our day is done? You know *nothing*. We still have strength beyond anything you can imagine. Surrender now, or feel our wrath!"

It should have been ridiculous. After all, the Devouts had been starved out of their Citadel; they were on the run, and the only thing saving them from immediate defeat was their hostages. Their time was clearly over.

And yet—

Poosk was such a fine actor that the day seemed to grow colder as he spoke.

Dolph blinked and shook herself. *If Mam could see me believing such nonsense, she'd laugh herself silly.*

The town bratlings, however, were eyeing their prisoners and arguing in heated whispers.

"Don't take any notice of him," shouted Dolph. "It's talk, that's all. Devouts haven't got the strength to crack an albatross egg, not anymore. They're finished."

Gant shook himself. "I know that, Witch. I don't believe 'im, course I don't."

But Dolph could see the telltale whiteness around his eyes.

Poosk raised his voice again, and the uncannily still air

carried it all the way across the ranks of shipfolk and Sunkers to the whispering townsfolk and villagers.

"You will believe me soon," he cried. "Surrender now or I will bring about the end of the world. Surrender—or I will send a demon to eat the sun!"

GWIN WAS HALFWAY UP THE STONE WALL OUTSIDE THE engine room door. Her fingers and toes dug into each minuscule crevice; her heart beat so wildly that she was afraid it might flip upside down in her chest.

She and Nat had climbed many a cliff together in the years before Mama died. It was one of the few areas where their skills were equal, and they used to race to the top, both of them laughing all the way.

But none of those cliffs had been as sheer and terrible as this wall.

Mister Smoke went up here twice, Gwin reminded herself. *And I can feel a breath of air on my face, which means there's an opening somewhere above me.*

But still she had to force herself to keep going, scrabbling at the stone with torn fingers, while the ground tried to drag her back.

She stopped for a moment, her head swimming, her hands aching. "As strong-willed as Ariel," she whispered to the stone. "As stubborn as the blue ox."

She thought about the astonishing revelation that she truly *was* the Singer, and about the code she had carried all her life without knowing it.

She thought of Papa and the way he had shouted "Run! *Run!*" as if he didn't care what happened to him, as long as his children were safe.

She thought of Mama murmuring, "We Fetchers help keep the heart of the world beating. The Devouts have tried to stop it so many times, but as long as there are songs, that old heart will just keep going."

With a great effort, Gwin unclenched her fingers and wriggled them higher.

Far below, Petrel's anxious voice whispered, "You still got the ropes and the cable, Nat?"

"Yes," came the reply. "They're round my ankle."

Gwin couldn't turn her head to check on her brother, couldn't turn any part of her body. Moss and dirt trickled down all around her. She swallowed it; she breathed it in. Her fingers clutched at the stones, and so did her bare toes, and she dragged herself upward inch by inch.

They had tried to get out the way they'd come in, of course. But when Sharkey had dived through that horrible water tunnel and out the other side, he'd found the cave still full of smoke, with Brother Bartle on guard outside. Poosk might think them all dead, but he wasn't taking any chances.

There'd been no sign of Wretched.

"He must have escaped," said Rain, and they'd all agreed. No one had said that he might equally well have crawled behind a rock to die.

Gwin coughed. The dust was getting into her lungs and

into her hair and down her back, and she wanted to scratch, but couldn't.

For the briefest of moments she allowed herself to think about Hob and Bony. Maybe their airship was sailing across West Norn right now, getting closer and closer to the Grand Monument!

And maybe it wasn't. Maybe it only existed in her imagination.

"Nat?" she whispered.

"I'm here."

At last Gwin reached the place where wall met ceiling, and the only way to keep going was to crawl into a narrow shaft and squeeze between stones that didn't want to be squeezed between. She clawed her way upward through spaces so small that they hadn't been discovered in three hundred years. She scraped the skin from her arms and ankles. At one point she had to bend almost double to get between two of the stones, then curl sideways and wriggle, with one hand in front and the other trapped at her waist, and her plaits falling across her eyes so she couldn't see where she was going.

"Bad . . . bit," she gasped when she was through. Nat grunted, but was too busy squirming between the stones to answer.

And still the monument rose above them. Gwin had lost track of time by then, and she began to worry that they were too late, that the eclipse had come and gone and that Papa had been given up to the Devouts and dragged away to his death.

That thought almost drove her to a frenzy. She forgot how

hard it was and climbed faster. She squeezed and wriggled and scraped—

And suddenly that tiny breath of fresh air became a lungful, and above her was a patch of sky. "Nearly there," she gasped.

She dragged herself upward, closer and closer to that wonderful blue patch, until it was just a few inches above her. With one final heave she was outside, almost at the top of the monument, but round the back, where no one could see her, just like Mister Smoke had said.

The first thing she did was look up at the sky, hoping to see tattered sails and a ship full of ferocious mountain folk.

But the sky was empty, apart from the sun and a few clouds, and Nat was scrambling out after her, right on the edge of a treacherous drop.

She grabbed his hand. "We in time?" he whispered.

"I think so. Sun's still shining." Gwin unfastened the ropes from her brother's ankle and looped one of them around a good solid stone. When she'd tested it to make sure it wouldn't give way, she picked up the other and began to pull on it.

This bit was almost as nerve-racking as the climb. Far below, the other end of the rope was tied to a sack, and Petrel was set to help it along, making sure it didn't bang against anything as it rose up the wall, then easing it gently through the stones while Gwin pulled just as gently from above.

It was more than likely, thought Gwin, that the precious contents of the sack wouldn't arrive in one piece. Or that Petrel would miss her footing and crack her head, or be unable to wriggle through one of the tight bits. And they'd never get the sack around all those corners without her.

"We should've brought it with us," she whispered to Nat. "Tied it to *my* ankle, maybe."

"We'd have broken something," he replied.

"Can you hear her? Is she still coming?"

"Yes. She's about halfway. I can hear Poosk too. He says—he says he's going to send a demon to eat the sun. If they don't hand over the prisoners, he's going to darken the world forever."

Gwin groaned. *Hob, where are you? Hurry!*

The waiting was almost unbearable, and so was trying to keep that cautious pressure on the rope. Gwin wanted to haul on it, to jerk it upward. She wasn't sure what the lead-up to an eclipse was supposed to feel like, but the air around her was thick and sullen. Somewhere to the south a dog was howling like a brokenhearted child.

"What if they believe Poosk?" she whispered to Nat. "What if they hand Papa over *before* the eclipse?"

Nat shook his head. "They haven't yet. Poosk's still threatening them."

At last the rope slackened, and Gwin heard an urgent hiss. And there was Petrel, her face scraped and speckled with dirt, peering up at them from between the stones with the sack in her hands.

They pulled it out, and Petrel climbed after it with such a fiercely determined expression on her face that Gwin was suddenly glad to have the other girl on their side.

She opened the sack—and heaved a sigh of relief. Nothing

was broken, nothing was spilled. Everything was exactly as it should be.

"Once Sharkey's got things connected up, he's gunna try and climb the rope," whispered Petrel. "And so're Fin and Rain."

"They won't fit through that last bit," said Nat. "They'll get stuck."

Petrel grinned unexpectedly. "That's what I told 'em. But Sharkey said he wouldn't be left behind, not for anything, and that he'd get out somehow, even if he had to pull the whole stinking monument down around his ears." She picked up the end of the cable and pointed upward. "Let's get into position."

And the three children began to climb toward the top of the monument.

CHAPTER 31

THE END OF THE WORLD . . .

GANT AND HIS FRIENDS WERE HOLDING FIRM, BUT ONLY JUST. Dolph could see them trembling, even from where she stood.

"Don't believe him," she shouted. "There's no such thing as demons. And nothing can eat the sun. He's lying."

"You will see," cried Poosk. "The darkness is coming. Can you not feel it in the air?"

The trouble was, Dolph *could* feel it. Or at least, she could feel *something*. And she didn't like it one bit.

"If you give up your prisoners to the Devouts," she shouted to Gant, "you're as good as dead. Bring 'em down here; shipfolk'll take care of you."

Gant looked from Dolph to Poosk and back to Dolph. From the expression on his face, he was wishing he'd never seen the prisoners, much less snatched them. Behind his back, his mates were whispering nonstop and nodding toward Brother Poosk.

Dolph edged closer to the base of the monument. *If I could get up there beside them, I reckon I could persuade Gant to hold out.*

And I'd best get up there anyway because Poosk'll have to make his move soon, before folk realize all this stuff about a demon is just empty threats. If I was in his shoes, I'd—

She never finished the thought. Because the impossible was happening. The air was growing colder. The birds stopped singing, as if it was dusk. The dogs howled one more time, then they too fell silent.

It was noon, and the sun was going out.

It was the most terrifying thing Dolph had ever experienced. As she stood there, shivering, the watching townsfolk fell to their knees, crying for mercy, and so did most of the Devouts, all the way back down the road. Dolph wanted to fall to her knees with them and beg Poosk for forgiveness. It was only the thought of her mam that stopped her. First Officer Orca had never begged for anything. The world could've splintered into a million pieces, and she would've stood there, sharp as a knife, trying to see a way through it for her and her folk.

So that's what Dolph did. With her breath hissing in and out, she reminded herself that *her* beliefs were built around ice and saltwater. She didn't give a toss for demons. She believed in a world that made sense, however strange that sense might sometimes be.

Which meant that Brother Poosk had nothing to do with what was happening.

She wasn't the only one standing firm. There were a good number of shipfolk and Sunkers on their knees, but Admiral Deeps and First Officer Hump were lighting lanterns with shaky hands, and Albie and Krill and a few others were striding through the ranks, clapping folk on the shoulder and trying unsuccessfully to haul them to their feet.

As for the important Devouts—the ones who'd spoken with Poosk—they held burning torches, and although the torches shook even more violently than the lanterns, the faces above them were grim with expectation and hope.

They knew this was coming, thought Dolph. *They're relying on it to get hold of the cap'n and save themselves in the bargain.*

Up on the monument, in the rapidly failing light, Gant and his mates crouched in terror with their hands over their heads.

"Give up your prisoners," cried Brother Poosk, but the town bratlings merely wrapped their hands more tightly, as if that might hide them from both the Devouts and the sun-eating demon.

Poosk smirked and began to climb the monument, with his half-dozen fellows close behind.

No! thought Dolph. And she leapt up the dark stones with reckless abandon.

Poosk and his fellows saw her and tried to beat her. But Dolph had spent her life climbing the *Oyster*'s nets and jumping from one whalebone deck to another. She was as nimble as a swimming seal, and before the Devouts were even halfway up the stones, she was standing in front of the prisoners with her knife in her hand.

Gant and his friends scrambled out of her way with a muffled whimper. But Poosk paused. Below him, the great throng was still crouched in darkness, with the townsfolk screaming,

"Bring it back, Master!" "Bring back the sun!" "Please, gracious sir, forgive us!"

Two of the Devouts on the monument had also lit torches, and now they raised them so that Poosk looked like a man of flames and shadows. He held up his hands for silence and cried, "The sun will not come back until the invaders are beaten. Kill them!"

Dolph could see little of what happened next—it was getting too dark—but she could hear it. Scrambling feet, howls of desperation. The clash of blindly wielded weapons.

Somewhere Krill was bellowing, "Don't let 'em catch you on the ground. Up and fight!"

Poosk swung back to Dolph with the torchlight roiling around him. "Out of my way," he snarled.

Dolph laughed in his face. "You think I'm one of your village folk, too scared to breathe without permission?" She jabbed at the air with her knife. "Come on. Who's going to die first? You, or one of your men?"

From somewhere near her feet there was a rough cry. "I'm with you, shipmate."

"And I," said a more precise voice.

And there was Mister Smoke, with a tiny knife in his paw. And beside him, freed from her bonds and brandishing an equally tiny but very sharp screwdriver, was Missus Slink.

At the sight of the rats, Poosk and his men reeled back, but only for a moment. Dolph could see the anticipation of victory in their eyes, reflected along with the torchlight and the cudgels. Nothing would stop them now.

She swallowed. Even with the rats on her side she couldn't fight half a dozen grown men, not all at once. But she'd do her best, right up to the end.

She leapt at them.

They weren't expecting that, and for the first minute or so they got in each other's way, and cursed, and burnt themselves with their torches. Dolph screamed in their faces as she attacked them, and Mister Smoke and Missus Slink darted in and out like fireflies, stabbing at their ankles and slicing through their bootlaces.

Before long, one of them had tripped over his own feet and fallen right down the monument, cracking his head as he went. Another two lay groaning on the ground, and for a brief moment, Dolph let herself hope that she might get out of this alive, that she might even be able to save the captain and Fin's mam.

But there were three men left, not counting Poosk, each of them warier than their fellows, and quicker too. One of them threw his torch at Dolph, and its flames scorched her as she jumped aside. Another tore off his robe and threw it over Mister Smoke and Missus Slink. Then he and his fellows rushed Dolph, all three of them at once, swinging their cudgels like ice axes.

They were hopeless odds, and Dolph knew it. But . . . *right up to the end*, she thought, and she kept fighting, ducking under those terrible cudgels, dodging the torches and wielding her knife with such speed and ferocity that she managed to put another man out of the fight.

Somewhere beneath her feet the two rats were struggling

to escape from the robe. Dolph wished she had time to bend down and rip it off them, but she didn't have a spare quarter second, couldn't even brush the hair out of her eyes or listen for what was happening below.

And then, somehow, Poosk was behind her. Dolph was so focused on the fight that she'd almost forgotten him; a mistake her mam would never have made. Dolph realized it just in time. She managed to duck the vicious blow aimed at her head, but it caught her wrist.

Her fingers opened; her knife tumbled from her grasp. She dived after it, so desperate to retrieve it that she didn't see Missus Slink—who had wriggled out from under the robe—until the very last minute.

Dolph twisted to miss the old rat, and lost her balance. As she fell, Poosk loomed over her, smiling gently even as his cudgel descended. . . .

Somewhere high above them a monstrous voice cracked open the darkness.

"I. Am. Coe!"

Dolph was braced so hard against the coming blow that she thought for a moment it had fallen.

But it hadn't. Poosk's cudgel trembled in midair.

It's another of his tricks, thought Dolph.

Except Poosk looked as stunned as she felt. He and his men were staring upward so fixedly that Dolph took the risk of looking up too.

At the very top of the monument, flames were leaping toward the sky. Directly behind them stood a giant, at least twice the height of a man. He wore a long cloak and a hood, and he raised his arms and roared again. "I am Coe!"

Gwin couldn't see much of the eclipse. The curtain fell across her face, and the brightness of the flames made her feel as if she were in a world of her own. She wasn't, of course, because Nat's shoulders were steady under her bare feet, and Petrel was behind her somewhere, keeping out of sight. But if she fell, neither of them would be able to help her. If she fell, she'd tumble right into the fire.

I've done this before, she reminded herself. *I've stood on Nat's shoulders and on Papa's too. I was always better at balancing than I was at leaping.*

Except she'd never had to balance like this, with half a curtain draped over her and the other half burning at Nat's feet. She'd never had to balance while her brother bellowed through a speaking trumpet that they'd made out of a sheet of tin. She'd never had to balance when there were so many lives at stake.

Hob'd better hurry up and get here, she thought. But in her heart she knew he wasn't coming. Perhaps the pigeon had fallen prey to a hawk or an arrow and had never reached the mountains. Perhaps Hob didn't believe her note. Perhaps the airship had only ever existed in her imagination.

Whatever the reason, she understood now that no one was going to save them. It was up to her and Nat and Petrel. And Sharkey, working away inside the Grand Monument.

She heard a muffled whisper from Nat. "Should I shout again, do you think? I can't hear much under here. What are they doing?"

"I can't see," replied Gwin. "Petrel, can you see?"

"No, but it sounds as if they've stopped fighting. I think they're all looking up at you. Ain't it dark! Spookiest thing I ever saw. Glad you told us about it beforehand."

Gwin swallowed. "If they're looking up here, then we should do the next bit."

"It's not ready," said Petrel, "Sharkey said the cable'd hum when he got it all connected, but it's not humming, not yet."

Nat's shoulders shifted slightly, as if he was trying to control his impatience. "We can't just stand here. We have to say something more. Or *do* something. Otherwise that first shock'll be wasted."

"'Twasn't wasted," said Petrel. "We had to stop 'em killing each other. And it worked—"

"For the moment," said Nat. "But they'll soon start again if nothing else happens. Maybe they'll come after us as well. I think I should say something more."

Gwin shifted her balance to compensate for her brother's movements. "There's nothing more to say. There's just the bit about the light."

"Then I'll say that."

"No!" Gwin was just about jumping out of her skin with worry, but she knew they had to get the timing right. "Don't you dare, Nat. *We wait!*"

FIN WAS PACING. He wanted so badly to help, but when it came to wires and switches and suchlike he was useless, so he strode up and down the underground room, wondering what was happening outside and trying very hard not to shout at Sharkey to hurry up.

Rain nibbled the nail of her little finger. She was useless too, but at least she could make up a song to go with whatever it was that Sharkey was doing.

"Deep in the heart—of the first to fall," she sang, her voice trembling,

"A boy worked hard to save them all . . ."

Sharkey knelt on the floor with a bundle of wires in his hands, mumbling to himself. "I should've paid more attention when Adm'ral Deeps taught me this stuff. Red goes to red; aye, of course it does. And white to white. But is white the earth? Or is it black?"

He had not put his eye patch back on, and every now and again he rubbed at his bad eye as if he could make it see. Beads of sweat glistened on his forehead.

Rain sang,

"Wire to wire and switch to switch,

His fingers m-move without a hitch."

"I wish they did, Rain," murmured Sharkey, without looking up. "I truly wish they did. This one *has* to be the earth. So I should connect it like . . . this." He twisted two of the wires together. "And then like . . . this. Except that's the way Sunkers do it—at least I think it is." He scrubbed at his bad eye again. "What if they did it different three hundred years ago? What if the colors mean different things? Then I'm done for."

"He trusts himself to d-do it right,

Red to red and white to white."

Sharkey heaved a sigh. "Suppose I have to trust myself, don't I." His hands sped up. He twisted more wires together in a pattern that Fin could not follow. One of his hands scrabbled for the switch he had found in the workshop. Sweat rolled down his face, and he wiped it away with a damp sleeve.

Fin was almost screaming with impatience, and it must have showed, because Rain broke off from her singing and said, "You have to trust Petrel."

"I do," said Fin, standing still for the first time in what felt like hours. "I would trust her with my life. It is just taking so long." And he went back to his pacing.

At last Sharkey took a deep, shuddering breath and stood up. "I think—I think that should do it."

He did not sound at all sure of himself, but by then Fin did not care. He ran across the room to the other boy and said, "Turn it on, then. Turn it on!"

Sharkey looked at him, then looked down at the switch. His finger moved. "There," he said quietly. "If that doesn't work, nothing will."

Dolph was inching away from the Devouts, as slow as a sea snail so as not to draw their attention.

She didn't know who or what the monstrous figure at the top of the monument was, but it had come just in time, and she was going to take full advantage of it. If she could get to her knife and then to the prisoners . . .

She eased her elbows a little farther along the stone. There was the robe, with Mister Smoke still struggling to get out from underneath it. Dolph raised the edge of the cloth and put her finger to her lips. Down below the monument all was silent, as if the whole world was in shock.

Mister Smoke crept out from under the robe, nodded at Dolph and made a beeline for the captain. Dolph picked up her knife, wondering where Missus Slink had got to and whether the giant figure had anything else up its sleeve.

It hadn't said a word since its second "I am Coe." It just stood there, arms akimbo, while the flames leapt around it. It was impressive and a little frightening, even to Dolph, who'd been raised by the toughest, sharpest officer on the *Oyster*. She couldn't imagine how it must seem to the townsfolk.

The three Devouts who were still on their feet were staring up at it, mouths agape. No. Wait. Poosk's mouth had closed and one of his hands was twitching—

Not yet, thought Dolph. *Don't get your wits back yet. I'm not close enough to the prisoners.*

She wriggled a little faster and at the same time silently begged the giant, *Do something more. Keep 'em off balance.*

But the giant just stood there.

There were noises from below now, as if folk were beginning to get over that first shock. Soon the fighting would start again.

As for Poosk, he shook himself like a seal coming out of water and said, "It is a trick. It cannot hurt us." And he spun back to Dolph.

She was on her feet in an instant, knife at the ready. But her wrist wasn't working properly, and now the other two Devouts were shaking off their awe too and advancing on her.

Dolph shifted her knife to her left hand and tried to look as if it made no difference. But it did. She could hardly even fillet a toothyfish with that hand; her mam had been the same. With her right hand, Dolph was the best fighter on the *Oyster*. With her left, she wasn't much better than an unweaned bratling.

Right up to the end, she reminded herself. *If I can just delay 'em a bit, Mister Smoke and Missus Slink might be able to get the cap'n away. And Fin's mam and the Fetcher too.*

Poosk had that gentle, evil smile on his face. "It is time we finished this once and for all," he murmured to his men. "Kill her. Then fetch me the prisoners."

Dolph braced herself. "Mam," she whispered, "I'm sorry we argued so much. I was too much like you to be an obedient daughter. But I *am* your daughter and proud of it. They won't take me down easily."

Then she stepped forward to meet those hulking men, knowing it was the last thing she would ever do.

THE HALF-CURTAIN WAS ALMOST COMPLETELY BURNT, AND there was nothing more to throw on it. The fire was dying down.

Gwin could hear Nat talking in a rapid undertone. "First principle of Fetcher performance: Keep your audience's attention. Because if you let it slip, it's twice as hard to get it back. And the shock only comes once." He paused. "What's happening, Gwin? Can you see Papa?"

"I—I'm not sure." Gwin swayed a little, trying to see past her improvised hood. "No. I can see Poosk though. He's turning away from us, Nat. And so're his men!"

"I knew it," said Nat. "I knew that'd happen. What's taking Sharkey so long?" His voice rose. "What's he *doing*?"

Gwin had no answers. She was strung so tight with wishing and hoping that she was afraid she'd snap in half. *Come on, Sharkey*, she thought. *Come ON!*

The noises from below grew louder. Someone screamed. The fighting was starting up again.

"The cable," hissed Petrel. "It's humming! We're ready. Go, Nat. Go!"

Gwin saw Poosk raise his cudgel. But before it could descend, Nat spoke again. The flames had died, so his amplified voice came out of complete darkness.

"I am Coe," he cried. "The Devouts take the light away. *I give it back!*"

And suddenly, shining from the topmost stone of the monument, there was the sun. . . .

CHAPTER 32

I AM NOT MADE FOR FIGHTING

PETREL'S BLOOD WAS HUMMING AS LOUD AS THE CABLE, BUT she held the powerful spotlight nice and steady, so it lit up the monument and the villagers and the combined army of ship-folk and Sunkers. It lit the Devouts too, and their hostages, trailing back down the road.

The villagers had fallen on their faces in awe. More important, so had the Devouts. A few of them might've known about the eclipse, but they had no idea what *this* was. West Norn hadn't seen lectricity for three hundred years. The brightest thing they knew, apart from the sun, was a brace of candles or a flaming torch.

Brother Thrawn was cowering in his chair with his hands over his eyes. Poosk and his fellows seemed to be trying to bury themselves in the stones of the monument, frightened out of their senses.

The Sunkers and shipfolk, however, were rallying. *They* recognized lectric light when they saw it. This might be brighter than they were used to, but they didn't fear it. After that first shock, hundreds of them dashed toward the column of Devouts, seized the hostages and carried them to safety. Others snatched cudgels and knives from their owners, or found ropes and began to tie up anyone who looked important.

There was little resistance.

We've got 'em, thought Petrel, with amazement. *We've done it!* And she eased the spotlight down onto the stones so her hands were free.

Beside her, the lower half of Coe whispered, "Do you think I should shout again?"

"Don't reckon it's needed," murmured Petrel. "But stay where you are a bit longer just in case. I'll leave the light turned on too. And I'll free your da, don't worry."

She set off down the monument, skipping from stone to stone with her bones feeling as light as a gull's. *We've done it. We've DONE it!*

Dolph was already cutting the prisoners loose. She looked up when she heard Petrel and grinned widely. "Thought it might be you. Where'd you find a great big light like that?"

The woman whose ropes she was loosening—*Fin's mam*, thought Petrel—whispered, "I've never seen such a thing."

"It's just lectricity." Petrel smiled and grabbed the discarded ropes. "It's nothing to be scared of."

She was determined to be pleased about Fin's mam. *No*, she told herself firmly. *I AM pleased. Soon as we've tied Poosk up, I'll say something to her about Fin, about how brave he is and how he'll be here as soon as he can. And maybe I'll tell her that he's my best friend because she should know that if she's gunna take him away—*

Her thoughts were interrupted by a familiar and very dear voice—one she'd feared she might never hear again. "Hello, Petrel."

It was the captain. His eyes were open, and although half his face was battered almost beyond recognition, he was gazing up at Petrel with all his old joy and wonder.

"Cap'n! You're back!"

"There's nothin' like a Baniski coil for settin' things to rights," said Mister Smoke, his paws working busily at the captain's ropes. "But Slink and I could do with a hand on these knots."

Petrel dropped down beside the two rats, her fingers pulling at the knots even as the words poured out of her. "We found the Singer, Cap'n. She's the one who gave you up to Poosk, but she had good reason for it, and I don't blame her anymore. And we found the root of the tree—I mean, we found what the root *meant*, the one in the Song, remember? That's it underneath us, did you hear the rumble when it started up? I reckon it was your Serran Coe who left it for us—at least he really left it for you, but you were in no condition to do anything about it. I hope you don't mind us jumping in and pulling that lever, but we didn't know what else to do. There, that's the last knot, I think."

She stopped to take a breath, and heard a whisper of sound behind her. Dolph shouted, "Watch out!"

But before Petrel could react, an arm went round her throat

and jerked her upright, and a violent kick sent Mister Smoke and Missus Slink flying.

Dolph flung herself at Poosk, but pulled up short when he tightened his grip on Petrel's neck. "Any closer," he snarled, "and your friend dies."

Petrel struggled, but it was no use. Poosk dragged her across the stones to his two remaining men, and booted one of them in the ribs. "Get up, fool."

The man didn't move, but Petrel heard his muffled voice say, "But, Brother, they brought back the sun—"

"It is not the sun," hissed Brother Poosk. "It is something from the old times, that is all. Are *they* afraid of it? No. So we should not be, either. Now get up, both of you, if you want to live. Quickly, or I shall have you hanged."

The men scrambled to their feet, averting their eyes from the bright spotlight. Poosk turned back to Dolph. "Hand over my prisoners. And your weapons."

Dolph didn't move.

Poosk nudged Petrel forward until her feet teetered on the edge of a stone. "It is some distance to the bottom of the monument," he said, in a conversational tone. "Especially headfirst. I doubt if your friend here would survive it."

Before Dolph could respond, one way or the other, the captain stood up. "Here I am. There is no need to hurt anyone."

"No, Cap'n," croaked Petrel. "You've gotta fight 'em."

"I am not made for fighting," came the quiet reply.

"You hear that, Brothers?" cried Poosk. "It seems we are not beaten after all. Take hold of the creature."

His men didn't want to touch the captain, that was clear, even though there were two of them and only one of him. But after a bit of whispering back and forth, they slung one of the ropes around his arms and knotted it tight.

Above their heads, the sky was just beginning to lighten, like a new dawn. But Petrel's heart had seldom felt darker. *Idiot!* she raged at herself. *Sharkey and Rain told you how tricky Poosk was. You should've run a rope around him straight off, before you said a single word to the cap'n.*

It was too late for that now. One of the Devouts picked up a chunk of stone and weighed it in his hand. "Can we smash the demon, Brother Poosk? Then burn it? We will not be safe till we do."

"Very soon, Brother," replied Poosk. "Very soon." He swung back to Dolph. "My other prisoners, if you please. Or the girl dies."

Fin's mam had been untying the Fetcher when Poosk seized Petrel. Now, after a quick glance at each other, they stepped forward too.

Poosk nodded approvingly. "Woman, untie Brother Cull. Quickly! Now relieve *her*"—he jerked his chin toward Dolph— "of her weapon."

With a sigh, Dolph handed her knife to Fin's mam, who passed it to the newly freed Cull. Behind them, Mister Smoke and Missus Slink were limping back up the stones.

Poosk raised his voice. "Come no closer, imps. And you"— he pointed at Dolph again—"go and join them . . . farther away than that . . . farther still. Ah, that will do. Brother Cull, watch them, if you please. Make sure they do not move."

Down below, shipfolk and Sunkers were beginning to realize that things weren't going quite the way they'd thought. As the sky grew lighter, they squinted up at the monument, trying to work out what was happening.

"Bring the demon over here," Poosk said to his men, "so they can see we have it. Hold it up, and prepare to throw it onto the stones below." He grabbed Petrel under the arms and picked her up so that her feet dangled in midair.

Petrel could hardly believe that everything had changed so suddenly and disastrously. *We came all this way for nothing*, she thought. *Fin'll never get to hug his mam. Gwin and Nat'll never get their da back. And the cap'n and I—*

"Invaders!" shouted Poosk. "Where are your leaders?"

There was a bit of shouting back and forth below, then Admiral Deeps, First Officer Hump, Krill and Albie shoved their way through the crowd and strode to the base of the monument, murmuring to each other as they came. Behind them, the villagers could see the way things were heading and were beginning to slink away, with their freed bratlings clutched to their sides.

"Stop there and throw down your weapons," shouted Poosk, "or my prisoners will die."

Krill and Hump exchanged a glance; then all four of them stopped. But they kept hold of their knives and wrenches.

Out of the corner of her eye, Petrel saw five figures jumping from stone to stone down the monument. Gwin and Nat were at the front, hand in hand, and behind them came Sharkey, Fin and Rain, their faces bleeding and their clothes in shreds from that awful climb.

Cull tapped Brother Poosk's shoulder. "The rest of the cubs have turned up, Brother. Including the Initiate."

Poosk's chest creaked like an unoiled hatch, and Petrel realized he was chuckling. "Initiate!" he cried, beaming at Fin, while at the same time keeping half an eye on those below. "How kind of you to grace us with your presence. As you can see, your mama has changed sides yet again. She is now *my* friend. What do you think of that, eh?"

Fin didn't answer. His face was like ice, and he didn't even look at his mam. But Petrel knew him well enough to see the pain behind that blank expression.

There she is, so close, and he can't do a thing, she thought. *And Gwin smiling so wide and bright at her da, though there's nothing to smile about, not that I can see. And Sharkey waving to the adm'ral, who hates him. . . .*

"Make sure they stay at a good distance, Cull," said Poosk, with another of those horrible chuckles. "We do not want any little accidents, do we?"

He turned back to the four leaders below, and the chuckle vanished. "Down weapons. I will not warn you again."

Admiral Deeps gazed up at him for a long, long time. Then, "Your first mistake," she said loudly and clearly, "was thinking that we care about the girl."

To Petrel's horror, Krill nodded as if he agreed with the

admiral. She felt a sharp pain in her chest, which had nothing to do with the danger she was in.

"Your second mistake," continued Deeps, "was thinking that we care about the mechanical boy."

This time it was First Officer Hump who nodded.

No! thought Petrel.

"Perhaps there is some residual fondness for the two of them, among our crews," Deeps said blandly. "But nothing more than that. You will not get what you want by holding their deaths over our heads."

It's a trick, Petrel thought desperately. *It's got to be.*

She could understand folk not caring about *her*, but the captain was special. He carried all sorts of important knowledge inside him, ready to rebuild things when the Devouts were beaten. What's more, he was kind and honorable. And he was Petrel's friend. *He* wouldn't turn away from her, like Krill had just done.

I can't let the cap'n die, she told herself. *I WON'T let him die!*

Poosk glared down at Deeps. "You'll change your tune when we burn the demon."

"Burn away," said Deeps. "You won't get a thing out of us." She paused. "But we *are* willing to consider a truce."

She took another step forward and lowered her voice a little so that Poosk and his men had to strain to hear her. "Personally I don't like the idea. As far as I'm concerned, you're all scum."

"But . . ." prompted Albie, from beside her.

"But I cannot deny your strength. You've held this country

for three hundred years—we were mad to believe we could destroy you in a few weeks." She threw up her hands in disgust, paced a few steps one way, then back again, as if she was thinking aloud. "Besides, I don't like the mood of the peasants. We can't feed them as much as they want to be fed, and they're growing angry because of it. If they turn against us, we'll be in trouble. And if we throw down your lot, the peasants will be leaderless. The land will fall into chaos, and who knows what will happen then? Perhaps an even worse regime will arise. . . ."

Poosk couldn't take his eyes off the admiral. Petrel could tell from the way his hands tightened on her arms that he was imagining the future, imagining the Devouts returned to their lives of power and luxury. With Poosk the one who had negotiated it.

He hadn't forgotten about Dolph and the others, and neither had his men. But Petrel's friends had no weapons, and besides, they were too far away to take the Devouts by surprise.

Which meant that Petrel was the only one of them who saw what happened next.

Gwin and Nat had taken a step away from their companions and were wiping their hands surreptitiously on their knee pants. Gwin, her face pale, climbed onto a higher stone as if she wanted to see better. Her brother cupped his hands and braced his legs.

Petrel thought she heard someone whisper, "One, two, three." Then Gwin jumped down toward her brother.

No sooner was her foot in his cupped hands than he heaved upward with all his might. And Gwin flew! She somersaulted across that uncrossable gap, as quick and clever as anything Petrel had ever seen. And when she came out of the somersault, one of her feet was aimed straight at Brother Poosk's head.

Petrel was ready for her, but the Devouts weren't. At the last moment, they saw something flying toward them and ducked. Their grip on their prisoners loosened. Gwin's foot clipped Poosk's ear and knocked him sideways. Gwin's da threw up his arms—and caught his daughter.

Petrel was away from Poosk and grabbing hold of the captain before the Devouts had time to draw breath. "Come on, Cap'n!" she cried.

A mechanical boy couldn't move quickly, not on those treacherous stones. But three seconds later Dolph was there and so were Sharkey and Fin, helping Petrel with the captain, helping Fin's mam and the Fetchers, while Mister Smoke and Missus Slink skipped along behind them, stabbing at the Devouts' ankles with knife and screwdriver. Rain stood higher up, shouting, "Sharkey, behind you. Dolph, on your left!"

And then Admiral Deeps, Albie, Krill and Hump were surging up the monument and into battle, with fish knives and pipe wrenches in their hands. Albie winked at Petrel as he passed, as if they were old friends.

"We fooled you, lass, with our talk of negotiation," he cried. "I could see it on your face."

And then he was gone, slipping in and out of the fight with his usual vicious cunning, leaving Petrel dumbfounded and not sure what to believe.

The Devouts fought with desperate intent, but they were

outnumbered. Within a couple of minutes they were lying on the stones, bruised, bleeding and begging for mercy.

Only Poosk still resisted. He had tucked himself in behind the fighters, looking so pathetic that no one had bothered with him. But now, with his fellow Devouts overpowered, he dashed toward Petrel and the captain.

Petrel didn't know if he was trying to escape or intending to grab them again. But she wasn't taking any chances, not at this stage. She tried to drag the captain out of the way, trusting that someone else would stop Poosk.

But the captain wouldn't budge. Instead, as Poosk ran past, he stuck out his mechanical foot.

Brother Poosk tripped and fell, headlong down the monument. He landed on the very spot where he would have thrown Petrel, and did not move again.

Petrel stared at that still body. "I—I thought you weren't made for fighting, Cap'n."

"That was not fighting," said the captain, in his sweetest voice. "That was science. If a body is moving at a certain speed, and you stop one part of it, the rest of it will keep going. For a little while, at least."

And with that, he left Petrel where she was, saying, "There is a lot to do. We must get started immediately."

CHAPTER 33

OUR ZEPPALEEN

Gwin hadn't moved since Papa caught her. She didn't *want* to move—she wanted to stay safe and warm in his arms, the way she used to when she was small.

But she couldn't stop the world from moving on, no matter how strong-willed she might be. And besides, they had to go and look for Spindle. And Wretched.

She slid to the ground.

Below her, the collapse of Brother Poook and his men had ripped the heart out of the Devouts. Their hostages were gone and so were their weapons. Their fine brown robes were filthy. Up and down the road, for as far as Gwin could see, they sat with their heads in their hands and their world in pieces around them.

"Nat! Here!" shouted Papa.

Gwin looked up in time to see Nat making his way across the stones with his hand on Rain's shoulder.

Papa hugged both his children tightly. "Thank you," he said to Rain, over their heads, then he hugged them again. "I am Coe," he muttered into their hair. "That was clever, my dears. That was so clever."

"Mama would've liked it," said Gwin. "Don't you think so, Papa?"

Her father kissed the top of her head and said, "She would indeed."

Gwin's battered heart felt warmer than it had in weeks. The three of them were a proper family again, and between them they'd keep Mama's memory alive. They'd sing when the sun was shining, and they'd sing in the middle of the storm. . . .

"Watch where you're treadin', shipmate," said a voice at Gwin's feet.

She took a hasty step backward and saw Mister Smoke peering up at her, with another rat, green-ribboned, by his side.

Papa squatted down. "Sir rat, you are even more amazing than I realized. I never thought to hear you speak. Or see you fight."

"Well, now you 'ave, shipmate," said Mister Smoke.

"I don't suppose," said Papa, "that you and your friend would consider joining us? Such a performance it would be—"

The other rat, the one with the green ribbon, interrupted him. "Too much to do," she said. "Crops to be sown, laws to be made and unmade, lessons to be taught. Smoke? We'd best get started."

And the rats skipped away.

Gwin was just turning back to Papa when she heard a yelp of delight. And there was Wretched, barreling up the monument toward them, barking all the way. His ragged coat was even filthier than usual.

"Wretched!" cried Nat, with an enormous smile on his face. "You got out!" He squatted down and opened his arms. "Here, boy!"

The dog raced around him, wagging his tail so hard that it looked as if it might fall off. But then he stopped and looked toward the northwest.

Nat stood up, saying, "There's something coming. I don't know what."

A moment later, Gwin heard it too: a clattering sound, like a hundred oxcarts jolting over stone. It bounced off the Grand Monument and rolled up and down the road, so that all the people who were milling around, with no idea what to do now that the Devouts were beaten, stopped in their tracks and stared.

Something came over the horizon.

Gwin couldn't put a name to it. It floated through the air like a monstrous, oval-shaped bubble, wobbling this way and that, but somehow heading all the while toward the Grand Monument.

Most of the villagers fell to their knees, shrieking with fright. A few glanced suspiciously up at the Grand Monument, as if Gwin and her friends were responsible for the approaching monstrosity, just as they had been responsible for Coe, and for the sun coming back.

The noise grew worse. It rumbled and buzzed and rattled and whined and roared, until Wretched began to howl in sympathy. Gwin could see ropes crisscrossing the bubble, and a huge cradle hanging below it, and puffs of smoke issuing from the back of the cradle in time with the clatters.

"'Ware below!" bellowed a loud voice, and the monstrous vessel began to descend.

People screamed and scattered. Parents covered their children's eyes, as if to protect them from something evil.

But as the whole contraption sank slowly toward the base of the Grand Monument, Gwin gasped. Because in a way she *was* responsible for it.

"Nat," she shouted, trying to make herself heard above the racket. "It's them! It's Hob and Bony! They've come to save us!"

Then she realized what she'd said, and she began to laugh. "Except we don't need them anymore. We saved ourselves!"

Nat and Papa laughed too. Wretched yipped with delight. Below them, Hob swung his leg over the edge of the cradle, leapt to the ground and beamed up at them.

"Afternoon, Fetchers," he cried. "What d'you think of our zeppaleen?"

PETREL COULDN'T FIND FIN; THERE WERE JUST TOO MANY people. Shipfolk and Sunkers were tending wounds, consulting with their leaders and inspecting the zeppaleen with professional curiosity. The villagers tiptoed around them, or climbed onto the monument to peer down at the Devouts with stunned expressions on their faces.

They can't believe it's over, thought Petrel as she scrambled down to ground level. *And neither can I.*

But it *was* over, and Fin's mam was safe, which made Petrel both happy and sad. *I'm pleased for 'em, I really am. But I hope Fin doesn't forget me. I hope he doesn't go without saying good-bye.*

She passed Sharkey and Rain, who were talking to Admiral Deeps. "We'll let bygones be bygones, then," said Deeps, smiling in a severe sort of way. "You and your friends did a fine job, Sharkey."

Farther along, Krill and his daughter, Squid, were hugging each other and laughing. "Never seen you move so fast, Da," said Squid. "Don't reckon the Devouts knew what hit 'em."

Petrel would have asked Krill if he'd seen Fin. Except she couldn't help remembering how he had agreed with Admiral Deeps.

Your first mistake was thinking that we care about the girl.

One part of Petrel knew that the whole thing had been a trick. But the bit of her that would never forget the loneliness of being Nothing Girl couldn't help believing it.

Your first mistake . . .

Sadly, she turned away from Krill and Squid. Then she stopped. "No," she told herself. "You ain't been Nothing Girl for a long time. You've gotta speak up."

And instead of creeping away, she marched up to the Head

Cook and jabbed him in the ribs with her finger. "Are you my friend or not, Krill?"

"What?" The big man spun around. "Course I am, bratling. Why?"

"'Cos you . . ." Now that she was standing right in front of him, it was surprisingly hard to say. "Um—you nodded. When Deeps said that stuff about no one caring for me."

Krill laughed. "Aye, I did. It was part of—" He looked at her more closely, then reared back, astonished and appalled. "You didn't *believe* it, lass? What, when you're as dear to me as a second daughter?"

"I—I am?"

"He's always talking about you," said Squid. "He was just saying the other day—" She nudged Krill. "No, you tell her. Go on."

"I wondered if—if maybe you'd like to call me Da." Krill hesitated, suddenly shy. "That's only if you want to, of course, and no disrespect to your real da; he was a fine man. But he's not here, and I am." He looked sideways at Petrel. "What d'you say?"

Petrel's heart swelled up, so big and warm that she could hardly speak. But she managed to whisper, "Aye."

Krill threw back his head and whooped. Then he picked Petrel up, danced a few steps and put her down again. "Squid, you've got a sister at last!"

"Couldn't ask for a better one." And Squid hugged Petrel too.

Petrel felt muddled and happy. At least, she *would* be

happy, once she got over her best friend leaving. "Have you seen Fin?" she asked.

"Nope." Krill shaded his eyes. "But if you come with me, I'll find him for you."

As the Head Cook strode through the crowd, Petrel trotted alongside him, listening to the conversations that were springing up in all directions. Some of the bolder villagers had gathered around the captain and were bombarding him with questions.

"Who's going to rule us now? You?"

"What do we do with the Masters? Can we set them to work for us?"

"What do you mean, a water pump? What's that?"

"Are you going to stay and teach us stuff?"

"Can you take that mask off, Witch?"

"It is not a mask," said the captain calmly. "It is my face. I am not a witch, nor am I going to rule you, or tell you what to do with the Devouts. You must learn to govern yourselves. But I will stay and teach you whatever you want to know. That is what I am for."

"Does this mean we ain't got a cap'n anymore?" Petrel asked Krill when they'd passed out of earshot. "Is he gunna leave us? Is he gunna leave the ship?"

"Don't know, daughter." Krill beamed on the word "daughter," then grew serious again. "Don't know much about anything right now, including whether or not *we* go back to the ship. I don't think we can leave these folk straightaway, not even with the cap'n to advise 'em. Their whole world's been about the strong trampling on the weak, and it'll take 'em a while to get used to something different. Those mountain folk are stopping around to help, and I reckon we could too, if we cared to. Then there's the places beyond West Norn. No one knows what things are like there. Maybe we'll help out here for a while, then go and see." His beard swiveled one way and then the other. "Isn't that Fin over there? Talking to a woman? Who would that be?"

"His mam?" Petrel craned her neck. "I can't *see*, Krill."

"We're nearly there. What's his mam's name, d'you know?"

"Hilde."

Krill surged through the crowd like a ship through spring ice, and Petrel bobbed in his wake, trying not to fall too far behind. By the time she caught up with him, he was shaking Hilde's hand.

"I'm Head Cook Krill," he said. "And this—where is she now? Ah, this is my daughter Petrel, heroine of the *Oyster* and loved by all. Well, except for Chief Engineer Albie, of course, but he doesn't love anyone except himself."

Hilde smiled. "My son"—she looked at Fin as if she couldn't believe he was truly there—"my son has been telling me about the *Oyster*. And about Petrel."

Fin blushed and stared at his boots. His mam continued, "I'm indebted to you all for taking such good care of him. I never thought I'd see him again. But here he is. My own boy. My Hew."

"Hew?" Krill wrinkled his great brow. "His name's Fin."

"No, his real name is Hew. I gave it to him myself, the day he was born."

It doesn't suit him at all, thought Petrel. *But I don't spose I've got any say in it. Just as I've got no say in what happens next. They'll go off together, and I'll never see Fin—I mean Hew—no, I mean Fin, again.*

Except that wasn't right. *You've gotta speak up.*

"So what're you going to do now?" asked Krill.

Hilde shook her head. "I don't know. I was thinking about going to my cousins . . ."

"You could stay here with us," Petrel said quickly. "Both of you. Sounds as if shipfolk might be here for a while, and you'd be very welcome. Fin's part of the crew, and we don't want to lose him."

Fin looked up at her, and she met his eyes. This was the boy whose life she'd saved twice over, the boy who had saved *her* from loneliness. This was her best friend.

"I mean, *I* don't want to lose him. I don't, Fin. I don't want you to go."

"Hew, not Fin," said Hilde.

"Mama—I am Fin."

"No," said his mam. "That's not—"

"I have been Fin for months; it is how I think of myself. When you say 'Hew,' I do not know who you are talking about."

Hilde swallowed. "But what would we do? If we did stay here?"

"There's a whole country to be rebuilt," said Petrel. "There'll be lots to do."

"I don't know." Hilde shook her head uncertainly. "This is all very hard to get used to."

"What you need," said Krill, leaning over her, "is a bowl of soup. There's no problem that can't be made better by soup."

CHAPTER 34

THE END OF THE BEGINNING

An hour or so later, Fin, Petrel, Krill and Hilde stood by one of many cooking fires with bowls of soup warming their hands.

"I do like the sound of doing something useful," said Hilde. "And besides, I'm not sure my cousins'd take us in, not really. Hew? I mean—Fin? Would you like to stay here?"

"Yes," said Fin. "I would."

Krill leaned toward him and said, in what he obviously thought was a whisper, "Fine woman, your mam."

Petrel grinned into her soup. Somewhere nearby a voice rose above the crowd, a voice used to making itself heard. "This is a day that will go down in the history of West Norn!"

It was the Fetcher, standing on a nest of barrels with a fiddle in his hand and Gwin and Nat on either side of him. Wretched was there too, tucked in behind Nat's legs, and the Fetchers' ox stood patiently beside the barrels, chewing its cud, with the remains of its harness dangling on the ground.

"I'm not denying there's grief aplenty to go round," Gwin's da said loudly. "There'll be nights yet when we weep for those we've lost. But the Devouts are beaten and the Citadel's empty. There'll be no more tithe, no more stealing of children."

A few folk cheered, but most of them were too stunned to recognize the truth of what the Fetcher was saying.

Nevertheless, he kept going. "So what comes next, people of West Norn? What are we going to do with this brand-new world of ours? Any ideas?"

No one answered him. They just gaped, too used to being told what to do to take him seriously.

The Fetcher laughed. "No? Me neither. But we'll have plenty of help from those who know what it is to be free. Including mountain folk, who came too late for the fighting, but just in time to help us with whatever comes next. They're talking of village councils and of machines too, if we want them, to make our lives easier."

A buzz ran through his audience, half-afraid, half-excited. The Fetcher raised his hand for silence. "But you know what I think? This isn't about machines; it never has been. It's about how we treat each other. It's about kindness and respect. That's what we've lacked. But we've got a chance at them now, and I think we should celebrate!"

With that, he raised his bow and began to play. A few notes in, Nat joined him on a musical pipe. Gwin started to sing, her voice as big as her da's.

"There once was a girl, a blue-eyed girl,
A girl with a song

And a bold, bold heart . . ."

Petrel had never heard music like it. It made the hairs on her arms stand up and her blood fizzle. All around her, ship-folk and Sunkers were tapping their feet. Villagers were shaking off their shock and beginning to smile. The folk who'd come in the zeppaleen, some of them even bigger and hairier than Krill, sang along with gusto.

"Come sing with us of her hidden world
As she traveled the land
With her ox and cart."

By the end of the second verse, the villagers were joining in the last two lines. By the third, they were grabbing each other's hands and dancing in circles. They were clumsy and unpracticed, but no one seemed to care. And as they moved, they grew more graceful, as though the memory of dancing had been tucked away inside their poor wintry bones, waiting for spring.

"'No songs?' cried she, and her blue eyes blazed,
'No tunes for the ear?
No joy for the heart?
Then I will sing loudly for all of my days,
As I travel the land
With my ox and cart.'"

A voice said in Petrel's ear, "I know many things, but I do not know how to dance. Will you teach me?"

"I'm not sure I know myself, Cap'n," said Petrel. But the tune was irresistible, so she took his hand and joined one of the circles. Fin came in next to her, with his mam on his other side, and Krill one step farther along, dancing so vigorously that his beard looked as if it might fly off.

And then Squid was there too, and Rain and Sharkey, and Dolph, dancing the same way she fought, with a fierce intensity that had everyone around her watching out for their toes.

But when she saw Petrel, Dolph laughed and shouted, "We beat 'em, cousin! Huzzah for us! Huzzah for the *Oyster*! Huzzah for the Sunkers!"

Her cheers, copied by everyone in the circle, got caught up in the song and the dance, and before long they were being echoed on every side.

"They chased her east and they chased her west,"

"Huzzah for the west!"

"They placed a price
On her head and heart."

"Huzzah for her heart!"

"A hundred crowns in a wooden chest
As she traveled the land
In her ox and cart."

"Huzzah for her ox! Huzzah for her cart! Huzzah huzzah huzzah!"

Petrel danced and cheered with the rest of them and thought about the folk who had started all this, so long ago. Serran Coe. Admiral Cray and Lin Lin. And the very first Fetcher, Ariel. *What would they think if they could see us now?* she wondered.

She thought of her parents too and wished they were here to witness such an amazing day.

Except if they WERE here, I'd never have been Nothing Girl.

Which means I might never have met Mister Smoke and Missus Slink or saved Fin from the ice or woken the sleeping Cap'n. Everything would've turned out differently.

Something grabbed at her ankle as she skipped past, and there were her two beloved rats, jumping backward and forward to avoid being stepped on. Petrel scooped them up and sat them on her shoulder.

"Crops to be sown," said Missus Slink in a querulous voice. "Boxes to be dragged up from the bottom of the ocean, books to be written. And what do they do? They dance." But one of her paws was tapping out the rhythm on Petrel's ear, and she joined in the "Huzzah!" at the end of the next verse.

"Full speed ahead, shipmate," cried Mister Smoke. "There'll be time later for boxes and crops. Full speed ahead!"

And Petrel leapt back into the dance.

"I am the spark that will not go out,
I am the life,
I am the song."
"Huzzah for the song!"
"Loud is my voice and my heart is stout
And I'll travel the land
My whole life long."
"Huzzah for life! Huzzah for the land! Huzzah huzzah huzzah!"

All across the fields, up and down the Grand Monument, folk cheered. The ground shook with their dancing; the sky rang with their singing. The sun shone.

The long darkness was over at last.

ACKNOWLEDGMENTS

This has been such a great series to work on, and as usual I've been helped by many people. My heartfelt gratitude to my US publisher Feiwel and Friends, particularly editor in chief Liz Szabla and senior creative director Rich Deas for giving the books such care and attention. And extra thanks to Liz for the wonderful title, *Battlesong*.

Thanks also to my Australian publishers, Allen & Unwin, especially publishing director Eva Mills and editor Kate Whitfield, who helped me make the book a lot better than it would otherwise have been.

Thanks to the very insightful Peter Matheson, for being such a critical (in a good way) first reader, and to my excellent agents Jill Grinberg and Margaret Connolly, who continue to look after my interests so well. And last but not least, thanks to my niece Gwyn for kindly letting me use a slightly different version of her name for the heroine of this story.

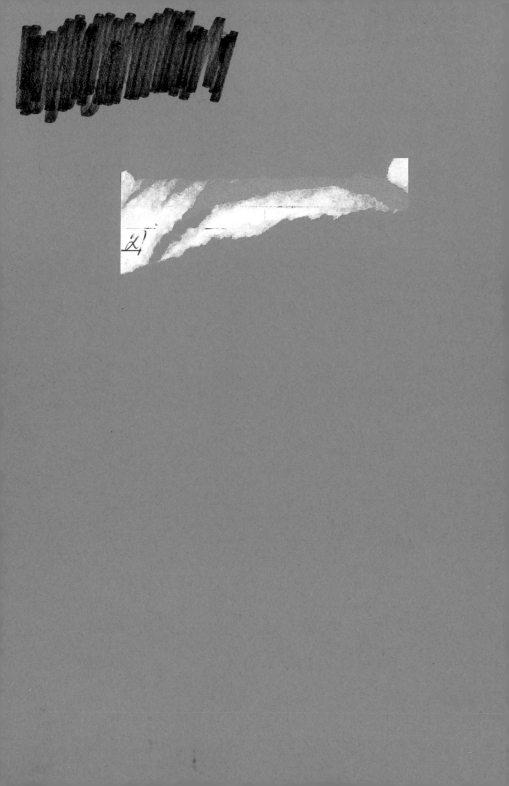